PRAISE FOR LUANNE G. SMITH

The Vine Witch

A *Washington Post* and Amazon Charts Bestseller

"Cleverly crafted . . . *The Vine Witch* is a grown-up fairy tale with a twisty-turn-y storyline of magic, love, and betrayal that holds your attention . . . Pure escapism."

—*Forbes*

"An ambitious debut from a promising author."

—*Publishers Weekly*

The Raven Spell

An Amazon Best Book of the Month: Science Fiction & Fantasy

"This fun, atmospheric outing is ideal for fans of C. L. Polk's Kingston Cycle."

—*Publishers Weekly*

"Smith wraps up the plot neatly while leaving a clear hook to entice delighted readers back for the next book."

—*Booklist*

The Witch's Lens

"A delicious foray into a new series that melds history with the supernatural . . . Smith's fans, as well as new readers, will delight in the heady mixture of historical fiction, fantasy, and horror."
—*Library Journal*

"Smith's thorough descriptions make this first novel in the Order of the Seven Stars series an immersive experience for readers."
—*Booklist*

"Smith puts the historical horrors of the 'war to end all wars' through a prism that both amplifies and elucidates the degree of evil that war unleashes on the world, all while telling a spellbinding, captivating story. As antidote to this dark theme, Smith portrays the redeeming idea of loyalty and sacrifice that transcends evil."
—*Historical Novels Review*

THE GOLDEN AGE OF MAGIC

ALSO BY LUANNE G. SMITH

The Vine Witch Series

The Vine Witch

The Glamourist

The Conjurer

A Conspiracy of Magic Series

The Raven Spell

The Raven Song

The Order of the Seven Stars Series

The Witch's Lens

The Wolf's Eye

THE GOLDEN AGE OF MAGIC

A NOVEL

LUANNE G. SMITH

47N♁RTH

This is a work of fiction. Names, characters, organizations, places, events, and incidents are either products of the author's imagination or are used fictitiously. Otherwise, any resemblance to actual persons, living or dead, is purely coincidental.

Text copyright © 2025 by Luanne G. Smith
All rights reserved.

No part of this book may be reproduced, or stored in a retrieval system, or transmitted in any form or by any means, electronic, mechanical, photocopying, recording, or otherwise, without express written permission of the publisher.

Published by 47North, Seattle

www.apub.com

Amazon, the Amazon logo, and 47North are trademarks of Amazon.com, Inc., or its affiliates.

EU product safety contact:
Amazon Media EU S. à r.l.
38, avenue John F. Kennedy, L-1855 Luxembourg
amazonpublishing-gpsr@amazon.com

ISBN-13: 9781662525018 (paperback)
ISBN-13: 9781662525025 (digital)

Cover design by Kimberly Glyder Design
Cover images: © Sybille Sterk / ArcAngel; © Wirestock, © Surasak Suwanmake, ©Jose A. Bernat Bacete / Getty

Printed in the United States of America

THE
GOLDEN
AGE OF
MAGIC

CHAPTER ONE

Danse Sauvage

More than a century had passed and still the air in Paris carried the stench of revolution. Celeste sometimes wondered if all the blood and mayhem of those times had been mixed in with the paint and mortar of the city's buildings as a warning against allies of the *ancien régime*. She pressed a perfumed handkerchief to her nose and checked the instructions Dorée had sent her. She'd been summoned here to meet her superior after "the incident," but she was having trouble getting her bearings in the bustling City of Light, where the clop of horses had long since given way to the rumble of fast automobiles. One thing she didn't have trouble spotting was the glossy rook watching her from the top of the nearest lamppost. His daggerlike beak pointed straight at her, underscoring the unsettled business behind her visit.

Celeste was one of the thirteen Fées Gardiennes, or at least she would be soon. She was still an initiate in training, but all she had to do was find her first protégé and usher them onto their star path, and then she'd be granted her full status. Walking along the city streets, she couldn't help comparing herself to those who'd come before her. She belonged to the same magical sisterhood portrayed in children's stories as fairy godmothers, but those women of old had all been bound by royal protocols. In those days, they'd been restrained in their duty by the expectations of kings and queens. But once the bloodshed of revolution had begun and the wigged heads had been lopped off, the alliance between the sisterhood of the Fées Gardiennes and the House of Bourbon had been severed as neatly as if the guillotine blade had sliced through the last remaining thread holding their agreement together. There hadn't been a royal wedding arranged between an arrogant prince and a lowborn woman in France since before those bloody days of revolution, which meant the thirteen Fées Gardiennes had to reinvent their purpose in the grand scheme of life.

Most of the Gardiennes had left the city, scattering themselves and their talent around the continent. Some chose to serve foreign kings for a time until another, more recent war took down those royal houses too. Others were drawn to the burgeoning art scene and expression of freedom in the written word, opting to take on talented new protégés who tickled their fancy. Celeste hoped very soon to take on one of her own, but first she had to answer for "the incident."

Celeste knew perfectly well why she was being forced to navigate the city at night rather than receiving her first assignment in the usual manner, via special courier. She'd followed the wrong instinct with Anaïs, her fellow Fée Gardienne, and now she faced some unknown punishment. Only she hadn't followed the wrong instinct. She'd followed her heart, which was all anyone could have asked of her. But she'd been warned before that Anaïs wasn't one to cross. The woman had a ruthless streak in her that ran as wide as the Champs-Élysées.

At last, Celeste spotted the bright lights of the Folies Bergère flashing at the far end of the street. "Ah, it's that way! You see, Sebastian, we managed it after all." The stoat, who'd been nestled deep inside her beaded handbag, peeked out, sniffed the air, then curled back up as if the correct direction had always been plain to his trained eyes and ears. Sebastian had been her constant companion ever since he was presented to her on her twelfth birthday ten years earlier. The gift of an animal familiar was a significant milestone on the journey to becoming a Gardienne, each assigned a companion they could depend on for the rest of their life.

Inside the lush cabaret, a dazzling crowd of the city's privileged mingled: men in tuxedos with satin trim and women in shimmering sleeveless gowns with fringe that slinked against their bodies as they walked. Dorée waited for Celeste at the top of the carpeted staircase, dressed in a floor-length silver gown that sparkled from the rhinestones that had been sewn in a starburst pattern down the front. Around her neck hung a diamond pendant the size of a quail egg. The old woman twinkled like a heavenly body fallen from the night sky. On her head she wore a sequined headband with a white feather tucked in at the side. The feather cleverly hid the cornucopia-like curl in the woman's updo where Benoit, the woman's mouse companion, would be curled up with his tail over his nose.

At eighty-two years old, Dorée had begun using a cane to steady herself, but Celeste knew better than to assume the walking aid implied any frailty. As the oldest of the Gardiennes, Dorée had more skill and knowledge in her possession than the rest of the women in the magical sisterhood combined.

Dorée beckoned with her free hand as she cast her eye on Celeste's choice of apparel for the evening. The deep-green silk, accented with a sheer overlay of organza and matching wrap, appeared to meet her approval. "Come, my dear, we don't wish to be late for the show."

Celeste made a quick apology and hurried up the last three steps. After exchanging a welcoming kiss on each cheek, the pair strolled to their balcony seats in a private space directly in front of the stage on the mezzanine level. The static of enchantment that skittered across Celeste's skin as she entered through the curtain suggested the prime seats had been ensconced in protective magic to shield them from prying eyes and curious ears. Below, the orchestra members prepared their instruments to begin playing. The stand-up bass was balanced on the floor, the mouthpieces of clarinets and trumpets held beneath wetted lips. The drummer twirled a pair of sticks in his fingers above the snare drum, as though releasing a burst of last-minute nerves. He counted to four and hit the beat.

"Thank you for agreeing to meet here," Dorée said, splaying open a black silk fan as the music started. The scent of gardenias rose in the stirred air. "I simply couldn't miss her return."

If Celeste remembered correctly, Dorée's latest protégé was an American, something that had shocked her fellow elders at the time. The old woman held her breath as the house lights dimmed and the spotlights came on. The music kicked into a jazzy rhythm, and a slim woman dressed in a skirt made of bananas, a pearl necklace, and not much more danced across the stage, gyrating her hips, crossing her eyes, and swinging her arms at a frenzied pace. The silly faces she made seemed to poke fun at the audience's appetite for the so-called exotic, but the crowd loved it, erupting in applause.

Dorée nodded her head to the beat. "Isn't she amazing?"

Celeste agreed. The performer's energy was palpable. Sparks of light trailed off her lithe body as she moved, with some of that invisible shine landing on the faces of those nearest the stage. "How much have you enhanced her talent?" she asked. Figuring out the right balance between helping and interfering was something she was told could take years to perfect.

Dorée scoffed. "I didn't do a thing in that regard. The talent was always bottled up inside her. It's the essence of what we sense about them, is it not? What attracts us to them? The talent and the desire to do something with it. All I did was give her the nudge she needed to leave America so she could set all that energy free." She waved her fan as though in a trance. "They didn't deserve her if they couldn't see how bright she shines."

The subject of protégés made Celeste's posture shrink some in the velvet seat. She'd made only one attempt so far at applying her magic in the real world, and she'd failed. The entire experience had devolved into chaos, pitting her against Anaïs in the end. The fiasco that became "the incident" was the reason she'd been summoned, and now she feared she'd be demoted, if there was anything lower than being a failed initiate.

A sense of fate hung over Celeste's head while the skinny woman shimmied onstage, filling the old woman's eyes with glittering pride. "I'm not entirely sure what Anaïs is capable of," Dorée said at last, not taking her eyes off the performer.

"I've written her a letter of apology." Celeste's words held little conviction.

"You don't know her the way I do. She won't be satisfied until she has retribution."

Celeste knew better than to speak against the fellow Gardienne in front of Dorée, but hadn't her reputation and pride been wounded too? "I did what anyone would have done in that situation."

"You gave her former fiancé's mistress your favor at a christening."

"I meant the other part," Celeste said, flinching slightly from the accusation.

"You mean the part where you were taken in by a man who knew how to manipulate a young, naive Fée Gardienne into getting what he wanted?" Dorée let out an exasperated breath. "You humiliated Anaïs when you counter-crossed her curse."

"She wished death on the child for her twelfth birthday!"

Dorée snapped her fan shut. "She would have rescinded the curse once she calmed down. Eventually."

Celeste wasn't so sure. It was why she'd stepped in after Anaïs had cursed the child and stormed out of the christening hall in a fury. Yes, perhaps she deserved to be reprimanded. She'd made a terrible mistake in judgment accepting the invitation, but in her heart of hearts she didn't think it compared to the harm Anaïs had unleashed on an innocent child. "I wasn't aware of the history between Monsieur Fontaine and Anaïs. I was just flattered to be invited to offer a blessing."

"Your first?"

Celeste nodded.

"You're still very green, Celeste. Fontaine knowingly took advantage of your eagerness to please. He knew Anaïs would show up and make a scene and wanted you there to temper the blow. Those types of family affairs are far too emotional. I rarely say yes to intimate celebrations anymore for that very reason. And you would do well to dig a little deeper into people's relationships next time."

Next time? So, she wasn't being cast out. Not yet anyway. If she didn't think Dorée would scold her for the unprofessional display of emotion, she would have thrown her arms around the old woman in gratitude.

"Have you encountered Anaïs since?"

Celeste patted the side of her beaded bag, feeling the steady heartbeat of her small companion inside. "No, but she has her rook following me. I saw him just before I stepped inside the theater tonight, and twice before that outside my house. He ate all the fruit off the mulberry tree in the garden."

Dorée pursed her lips. "She has Gideon spying for her. She's become quite adept at scrying through his vision." The crowd erupted in applause again as the young woman blew kisses to the crowd and exited the stage. Dorée leaned closer to Celeste to be heard over the ovation. "She knows you're meeting with me, then. Normally, after an incident like this, the injured party would be expecting me to convene a meeting of the eldest sisters to discuss a worthy punishment."

Celeste closed her eyes briefly in shame. She'd only just emerged into the world as an initiate, and already she was facing a reprimand. Being one of the Fées Gardiennes was an ancient honor, bound by a nine-hundred-year-old covenant. In that long-ago age of kings, alliances were made, wars were waged, and advantageous weddings were arranged under *their* direction. Naturally, in those days the Gardiennes' magical talents resembled devil's work to the mundane eye as they set out to recharge their gemstones under the midsummer sun or pay tribute to the feminine energy of the full moon while gathering flowers to wear as a crown. Some were incarcerated or hanged, but once the Wisewomen of the woods proved their value to those in power, they were allowed to continue their "unnatural" forest rituals in exchange for continued blessings upon the newly crowned royals.

The agreement had been upheld for hundreds of years without issue. The reputation of the Fées Gardiennes grew in prominence and distinction until they'd achieved near mythical status as fairy godmothers worthy of their own stories. In those days, every young maiden and field hand spent their idle moments dreaming they could be chosen for an enchanted life, until the Great War came down like a felled tree to crush the royal houses. Now, hardly anyone recognized the old alliances or the role of the Gardiennes, an honor Celeste refused to take for granted. To have brought disgrace on her position was something she regretted with all her heart, even if she'd been right.

"Punishment? I was protecting the poor babe, and I'd do it again." Celeste might have crossed her superior by countering her curse, but she wouldn't be made to feel guilty for saving a child from an untimely death.

"Yes, well, as a result of your do-gooding, the main thrust of the curse was disrupted, but not all of it. The girl may very well suffer from narcolepsy for the rest of her life."

At least she'll live past her twelfth birthday!

The theater applause died down as the audience waited for the next act to appear. Dorée produced her fan again and waved it slowly in front of her face. "I'll grant you weren't altogether wrong," she said. "Your heart is true in that matter. But you weren't right either. Anaïs's approach might be a touch medieval, but she was within her rights to issue her curse. We can't have people manipulating our magic for their own ends. Not when there are forces constantly at work to disrupt the equilibrium."

The Infortunii.

If the Fées Gardiennes were tasked with elevating talent and beauty, the Infortunii—or Skulks, as several of the women called them behind their backs—acted as a counterweight that pulled against the rise of celebrity and success. It was explained to Celeste while she was growing up that without the pull of misfortune, the world of fate and fortune would become too lopsided, too grandiose and bloated, and tumble over on itself. Celeste hadn't crossed paths with a Skulk yet, though sometimes she half suspected Anaïs was one of them, the way she operated in the shadows without fear of causing mischief wherever she went.

"What would you have me do to make amends?" Celeste knew a punishment was coming, but how severe?

Dorée set her chin at a prim, self-deprecating angle. "In that regard there might be a small hiccup. We seem to have lost track of Anaïs."

"Lost track?"

"She's gone missing," the old woman said, modifying the information with a tilt of her hand as though it rested atop a scale, tilting one way and then the other. "At least, none of the sisters have been able to find her in any of her usual haunts. Typically, when there's a dispute between sisters, there's a protocol for mediation. Both sides sit down and work out an equitable solution that satisfies the injured party with a heartfelt apology or, occasionally, monetary damages paid. Realize, however, that's a very modern approach that Gertrude and I have worked hard to implement. The fundamental decrees that formed our sisterhood are still very much steeped in medieval practices, including a trial by ordeal. Anaïs is within her rights to ask for a resolution by fire, water, or combat. And the problem with Anaïs is she's rarely satisfied with anything less than blood."

Combat? Celeste's lips opened to reply, but the words stalled in her mouth. She'd already witnessed Anaïs's wrath firsthand, and that was against a child. What would she do to an adult?

"As of right now, Anaïs isn't responding to our calls or telegrams," Dorée said. "She's being stubborn and self-righteous. But if she has Gideon following you, she can't be too far away. I'm afraid that puts you in a very dangerous predicament, my dear. She may simply be waiting for the perfect opportunity to strike."

Celeste shivered, rustling inside her silk gown as she thought about how she'd walked alone to the theater. "Can't someone do something? Force her to see reason?"

"What is there to do?" Dorée said with a slight lift of her shoulders. "Anaïs is Anaïs. There's always been a tempest swirling inside her, ever since she was a child. Again, she would be well within her rights to engage you in combat. However . . ."

"Yes?"

"It's a bit extreme, but the other sisters and I have come up with a temporary solution we think might be effective in saving your life." The old woman tapped her closed fan against her elaborately fashioned hair. "Wake up, Benoit. We're ready for your part now."

A white mouse poked his nose out of Dorée's cornucopia curl and twitched his whiskers at the feathered headband as though he were La Petite Souris himself. He disappeared inside her hair again briefly before dragging out a folded-up envelope by his teeth.

Dorée stretched out her hand beneath her ear, and the mouse promptly dropped the envelope into her palm. "These are your travel documents," she said, checking the papers briefly before extending them toward Celeste.

"Travel documents? For what?"

"It's been decided that the best course of action is for you to get as far away from Anaïs as physically possible until the situation has calmed down. Gertrude and I are not getting any younger, and the sisterhood cannot afford to have its numbers diminished by seeing our latest initiate reduced to a pile of ash before she's even had a chance to fulfill the most basic duty of her position as a Fée Gardienne." Dorée secured the papers in Celeste's hands. "You are expected at the port in Le Havre tomorrow. Your ship sails for New York City on the evening tide. From there, you will be instructed on how and where to board a train."

"New York? But I can't just leave on a moment's notice." Celeste's heart drummed in syncopation with the frantic beats played in the pit below until the blood throbbed in her ears. "What about my things? My obligations?"

Dorée leaned on her cane and stood. "Benoit has seen to it that everything you need for a comfortable journey has been packed. Your trunk has already been delivered to Gertrude's apartment in the sixth arrondissement, where you are expected for the night. As for your obligations, they are owed entirely to this sisterhood and what is best for its survival."

Celeste knew she'd spoken out of turn. Of course the sisterhood came first. That had been ingrained in her since she was plucked up as a babe out of the crib and taken to live in a cottage in the woods, where her sister Fées Gardiennes had raised her to be one of their own. But all the way to America?

"Oh, I should warn you." Dorée tucked her fan away in her retinue. "Gertrude has opened her salon to several up-and-coming writers and artist types. Her latest protégés. You aren't likely to find it a restful retreat before a long day of travel, but perhaps you can get some good reading recommendations. I dare say, she's juggling more than a few raw prospects currently. Don't know how she does it at her age, but then she's got Basket, that great leaping poodle of hers, to help."

"But how am I to live in New York City? What am I to do?" Celeste asked. There was no use in protesting a decision once Dorée made up her mind, but it was such an awfully long way to travel. America was still so young, its edges too rough. The nation hadn't yet benefited from the sanding of time to mature as Europe had. The way a red wine needs to age for years before it's mellow enough to drink with pleasure. Though she'd never been there, she envisioned America as being more like a bubbly beaujolais. Ambitious and new but somewhat forgettable in the end, though she supposed there was something wild and exciting about certain elements.

"You're not going to live in New York." Dorée mocked the idea. "Who said anything about living in New York? That's merely where the ship lands. Where you go from there is entirely up to you."

"Truly?" Celeste pursed her lips, wondering about fate's crooked path. She clicked her tongue at Sebastian. The little stoat poked his head out of her bag and nudged a colored postcard, slightly bent at the corners, out of the opening with his nose.

"What's this?" Dorée asked.

"There *is* a place I've been desperately curious about lately." Celeste retrieved the colorized card from the stoat and smiled wistfully at the blossoming orange trees that framed the rolling hills in the background. Small white letters that looked like they'd been impaled in the hillside read HOLLYWOODLAND. And below that was a caption almost too good to be true.

"Land of Enchantment? That's what they're calling it?" Dorée perused the card with a skeptical glance. "I'm old enough to remember when *these* lands were enchanted. But the Great War seems to have scraped the last flake of gilt off the place." The old woman's eyes misted slightly. "Where did you get this?"

Celeste tried not to smile as she flipped the postcard over in Dorée's hand. "I'm not sure where it came from. Someone named Edward mailed it from America to his brother William in Strasbourg." She pointed to the signature. "But it went to the wrong address and somehow ended up in my mail delivery. I can't make out the address where it was meant to go to or else I would have forwarded it."

"Yes, our magic often attracts lost items with a whimsical feel," Dorée said. "I once received a string of pearls intended for Sarah Bernhardt because her admirer was a foreign businessman who confused the name of the theater she worked at with a left-bank museum. I still have them in my closet at home."

It was the first Celeste had heard of the phenomenon, but she didn't doubt the words of the eldest Gardienne. Magic was always in flux, sometimes swelling with power and awe, sometimes shy and playful, surprising even the most astute practitioner with the odd "coincidence."

The band struck up a bouncy tune as Dorée's protégé strutted across the stage in a new costume, a beaded silver gown with a matching feathered headpiece. "What if I went here?" Celeste asked, pointing to the card.

"Where? This Hollywoodland in California, where they make the movies? Not sure how likely your prospects would be there, but if there's a protégé to be found in the West, you'd have the place to yourself. None of the other sisters have shown much interest in that part of the world. They were scandalized when I tapped an American for my latest."

"Have you been to the western part of the country?"

Dorée demurred. "Oh, no, not me. New York has attained a certain level of sophistication that I enjoy, but the rest of America presents itself as too uncouth for my taste. But my intuition tells me this place might just be the change you need right now. With our European kingdoms firmly diminished, there may soon be too few opportunities left for all of us to pursue here. Unfortunately, expansion to places like this Hollywoodland may be inevitable for your generation." Dorée flipped the postcard over and back again, seemingly amused by the depiction. "Go. Find a protégé that suits your talents without any worry about interference. A simple advantageous marriage for a young woman will suffice for your first protégé. Perhaps with one of these new princes of Hollywood all the women devour with their eyes at the movies."

"An advantageous marriage?" Celeste tried to hide her disappointment. Such a thing was obviously a large part of their magical heritage, but weren't there more exciting prospects for women in this new age of freedom?

"They are the least complicated arrangements to master. Just tell a man he can't have something or someone, and that's all he'll want. Simple as could be."

"And I can't do that here?"

"You need time to step into your power, Celeste. And I fear you will not get the chance if you stay on this continent. In fact, I doubt very much you'd survive the week so long as Anaïs's ire is inflamed. Don't fret. You've been given all the training you require to succeed. Now it's time to leap."

Dorée returned the postcard to Celeste's hand beside the steamship ticket with a final pat, as if to say the matter was settled. "Good luck and good tidings," she said, as was their way. The oldest and wisest of the Gardiennes exited the balcony and passed through the red velvet curtains, leaving Celeste to ponder the muddle she'd made of her young life.

CHAPTER TWO

Bon Voyage

The New York–bound ship proved an elegant, modern vessel. The interiors were done in the decorative art deco style with frosted lamps held up by silver nymphs, geometric wallpaper tucked into secret alcoves, and framed art with a surprising emphasis on dragonflies. The attention to every beautiful detail made the passenger feel as if they were part of a grand undertaking. Celeste supposed she was doing just that, embarking on the biggest journey of her twenty-two years.

But while the ship's elegant salons drew most passengers indoors to pass the five-day voyage by swapping bits of gossip, sampling small tea cakes, and playing endless games of mah-jongg, Celeste preferred to spend her time on the foredeck. Being a creature who subsisted on sunlight and warmth, she leaned against the railing and watched the sea as the salty air blew against her face. The deep Atlantic water was never the same from one day to the next. The colors shifted from greens to blues to blacks, sometimes with frothy white waves that broke across the surface as though pushed by an invisible underwater hand. The motion of the sea didn't bother her. Her kind was born to ride on the wind and the waves in teacups, or so the old fairy tales claimed. She half believed it herself, standing on the bow of the ship with the wind in her hair as the breeze did its best to wear away her shame and embarrassment at having been banished from the only home she'd ever known.

When Dorée had proclaimed she was to set sail for America, Celeste was confused, afraid, hurt, and perhaps a little curious too. But the longer she was on the water, the more she felt a sort of yearning. Something called to her from the far shore. Something her intuition recognized as important but hadn't yet decrypted, waiting for her, tugging, luring her in. An invitation to wander a land still filled with untamed open spaces.

A small group of children interrupted Celeste's thoughts just as she'd begun to wonder if Dorée hadn't cast some spell over her to ease her transition. The half dozen boys and girls came galloping along the deck pretending to be whales and leaping dolphins, and then a girl of about eight years old stated definitively she was a mermaid, making Celeste smile.

When the children turned their attention to the side of the ship to gape at the waves, one boy stood out from the others. Unlike the boisterous children who pointed and roared at the power of the ocean they sailed upon, he remained sullen as he squinted at the view as though he wanted to punch it in the face. Such a cloud of melancholy enveloped him that she couldn't help but forget her own anxieties for a moment to study him. After all, it was in her nature to seek out those who needed a nudge to get them moving in the right direction.

"Shall I engage?" Celeste asked Sebastian. The little stoat poked his head out from beneath her fur collar, where he'd been napping on her shoulder. He sniffed the air and made one of his small squealing sounds that Celeste took for a yes. She nonchalantly adjusted her position along the railing until she and the boy, who was perhaps going on twelve years old, were near enough it was only natural for them to speak to each other.

"Are you excited to land in New York?" Celeste asked, hiding her own trepidation behind a smile, keen to know what had made him so withdrawn.

The boy looked over his shoulder as though searching for someone. His eye caught on the deck above and he straightened. "Not really," he said. "My father is making us move."

"I was rather forced to travel against my will as well," she said, eyeing the man on the upper deck in his long black coat and bushy mustache.

"Did you have to leave all your friends too?" the boy asked.

Celeste nodded, gazing out at the sea. "I don't know a soul in America."

"Me either." The boy dropped his chin against his folded arms again, leaning on the railing while the other children threw chunks of bread at the seagulls that had found the ship now that it was making for the harbor. Uncertainty oozed out of the boy's heart. Celeste held her breath and listened to his energy, trying to determine his deepest wishes. His innermost dreams were still small and boyish and not yet ripe enough to take him on as a protégé. But it didn't mean she couldn't give him a small gift before they parted, a fragment of true wonder that he could pin to his memories. Something to make him lift his head and remember to keep his eyes open on his journey, to search for hope in the unknown instead of dread.

"Well, at least now we know each other," Celeste said. She closed her eyes as though taking in the warmth of the sun and smell of the sea. Instead, she sank deep within her third-eye vision to ask the sea for a small favor. As their ship headed into the Lower Bay, she held the pear-shaped sapphire pendant that always hung around her neck. The Gardiennes had outgrown the use of wands in the last century, preferring the understated elegance of gemstone necklaces to serve as instruments for wielding their power.

When she opened her eyes again, a humpback whale had breached the surface of the dark water, rising silently like a leviathan ghost just in front of the boy. The animal was so large, so magnificent, so unexpected, it left its audience awestruck and silent. The boy froze with his mouth open and his hands gripping the railing as he watched the creature sink beneath the waves again. When he'd recovered, he pointed in excitement and called to the other children. And then the whale rose again, only this time he brought a friend. The pair breached nearly in alignment, their fins raised high in the air. The show delighted the passengers on deck, who rushed to the boy's side to see the whale surface for a third and final time before returning to the deep. And just in time. Celeste's magic had worn thin at the end as the tail disintegrated into mist prematurely above the water's surface. Still, a good omen, they all said, and the boy, who couldn't stop smiling, took their words and folded them into his heart.

While he stood in the glow of his miracle sighting, Celeste closed her eyes one more time. Using her third-eye vision she sought the boy's pulse, the heartbeat that connected him to his star path and the rightful journey his life was meant to take. There'd been a slight correction. The interaction with the whales would influence the boy so profoundly she believed he'd make a lifelong study of the creatures.

Before she opened her eyes, Celeste noted the boy's mother was somewhere nearby, though not in physical form. Dead for some months now, but still close. The woman's spirit ignited with gratitude to see her son excited again. A wish Celeste had been happy to grant. She let the shudder of spent magic reverberate through her as the children crowded around the boy—Hasan, as she perceived his name to be. A good exchange of energy, just as the sisterhood had taught her to feel when magic struck its mark.

Celeste reminded herself that such progress was the thing to focus on, despite the small mishap at the end. She'd been sent abroad to get as far away from Anaïs's thirst for revenge as possible, but she wasn't just running away from possible danger. She was also sailing *toward* something. A place where she could fulfill her sole obligation, one that had been entwined with her purpose in life since she was first taken to live at the cottage in the woods as a baby. She'd long been taught that to set a protégé on their star path was the entire point of her magic. Her responsibility, her contract with the source of that power, was to see it done when she came of age. And here she was, feeling the first tingles of a small difference in a human's life. She couldn't imagine how good it would feel to find her very own protégé.

Celeste hadn't noticed the boy's father had left the upper deck to come stand beside her. She was startled when he held his hand out to her and spoke.

"For you," he said.

"What for?" she asked, genuinely puzzled.

"For whatever you did for my son to take away his sadness."

"Oh, I didn't. I couldn't."

"I insist." He put a small coin of some kind in her hand, bronze with a palm tree stamped on one side. "For luck on your journey," he said and walked away. "I no longer need it."

Celeste turned the amulet over in her palm. It was a small thing of little monetary value, though she suspected it was imbued with the energy of a thousand unrealized dreams.

CHAPTER THREE

Raison d'être

After five days of traveling by sea and another four days by train to reach her destination in Los Angeles, Celeste stood road weary on the station platform clutching her valise to her chest. Sebastian, too, appeared to have had enough of subsisting on soft-boiled eggs and scraps of fish from her breakfast plate. Starving for something with the pulse of life still thrumming inside, the stoat shimmied out of her handbag to hunt the local fauna while she took note of the odd scents on the crosswind—orange blossoms drifting in from the north and black oil seeping up from the ground to the west.

A porter in a blue uniform, with a speck of cinder dust on his shoulder, hefted her trunk off the baggage cart. "Your baggage, miss."

"Oh, thank you, I'd be lost without that," she said. She dug in her purse for a coin when her hand touched the palm tree amulet. Not willing to part with the coin just yet, she reached for a large bill instead as a token of appreciation. "Will this do?" By the stunned look on his face, she surmised she'd managed the interaction of tipping passably well.

"Miss, for that price I'll carry the trunk clear across town for you on my back."

"Oh, that won't be necessary," she said, fastening the clasp on her purse. "But could you tell me which direction I might find the castles of the new Hollywood princes?"

"Princes?" The porter lifted his hat and scratched his head. "You talking about those actor folks from the movies? I reckon there's a lot of them that keep to the hills yonder west of here." He laughed like an accomplice to her depiction. "Some of their houses are as big as castles, I expect."

Celeste squinted against the sinking sun, where the cross scents of oranges and crude oil met. "West?" She didn't know why, but the direction resonated inside her as vital. "West it is."

The porter flagged down a cab, then gave her a handful of hotel brochures to consider before he crossed the platform to attend to other passengers. Celeste snapped her fingers twice and opened her handbag. "Time to go," she called. Sebastian scurried out from behind a wooden crate and jumped into her purse, his mouth stained pink from whatever poor vermin he'd just devoured. He seemed to be on his way to happily adjusting to his new environment. She was quite certain she could do the same once she got settled and sank her teeth into a little metaphorical prey of her own.

Having little more information to go on than that she wished to travel west, Celeste perused the hotel brochures while the driver loaded her trunk into the back of his yellow cab. She sat in the back seat, still considering her options, when the driver got in and gave her the once-over in the rearview mirror as though wondering which side of town he'd be taking her to. "Where to, miss?"

A picture of one of the hotels made her look twice. The building was surrounded by palm trees and had a red Mediterranean-style tile roof. Just like the coin the man on the ship had given her. She knew better than to believe in coincidences, so she passed the brochure to the driver.

"What do you know about this place?" she asked, pointing to a picture of the hotel and lush gardens.

"That's the Beverly Hills Hotel. Swanky place, plenty of rooms. They've also got these little bungalows in the back you can stay in. I shouldn't share this, but I drove John Barrymore up there the other day."

"Who?"

The driver made a face in the rearview. "The actor? Don't tell me you never heard of John Barrymore!"

"Ah, of course, the actor," she said with a nod. Celeste had no idea who this Barrymore fellow was, but if he was one of the new princes of Hollywood, she was headed to the right place. Feeling no objection within her core, Celeste said, "The Beverly Hills Hotel sounds lovely."

Thirty minutes later the cab pulled up a long curving driveway lined with palm trees, just like the photo. A bell tower with flags flying above and a covered portico awaited at the top of the small rise in elevation. A pleasant shiver tickled the back of Celeste's neck as she stepped out of the cab, letting her know she'd chosen correctly. The grounds were immense, full of cover for whatever illusions or glamour she may need to employ while visiting.

After her trunk was loaded onto a golden bell-shaped trolley, Celeste approached the front desk, where a young man in a black suit greeted her with a genuine smile.

"Welcome, madam. Checking in?"

"Mademoiselle, actually." Celeste patted her handbag to warn Sebastian to behave himself. They were there to work, not create mischief. Of course, there might be a need for a little intervention of the property's layout, if the room didn't suit. "I may need to stay long term," she said. "For a little while anyway. Could I get one of those charming bungalows in the back I've heard about?"

The clerk opened a ledger book and ran his finger down the page. "I'm afraid all twenty-one bungalows are currently spoken for. There's a big polo match this weekend. A charity event for the children's hospital. Absolutely everyone has replied that they're coming. We could put you in one of our main rooms. They're quite suitable for . . . single residents? Maid service provided every morning."

"Oh, no. That won't do. I've spent several days on a ship and then a train. I could use a little more space than a single room." Celeste leaned in against the front desk to read the clerk's name tag while Sebastian slipped out of her bag and ran down the carpeted hallway, his fur coat bristling with the spark of magic. "Are you certain *all* the bungalows are occupied, Rodney? What about number twenty-two?" She held her sapphire pendant and pointed to the bottom of the ledger, where a new entry scribbled itself onto the page before the clerk looked back down.

"But we don't have a bungalow twenty-two," Rodney said before taking a second look at the addition in the ledger. The writing wavered for a faint second, worrying Celeste, before it settled in strong black ink. The poor man looked up, confused, as a key appeared on a hook near his desk. "I don't understand."

"Is it by chance available?" Celeste tried to sound hopeful and not overly confident, the way she'd been taught to do when using her glamour for gain. She had to leave room in his imagination for him to believe he was still in charge of the decision. She smiled and waited for him to come around to the idea there had always been twenty-two original bungalows and that the small one at the edge of the property was available, being too far of a walk for most guests wishing to be nearer to the main lobby.

"Um, yes, I believe it is," the clerk said, tentatively reaching for the key with the number twenty-two stamped on the brass. "I'll have a bellhop escort you there with your luggage." Rodney pounded the bell on the counter a little more sharply than was necessary, but Celeste supposed he was still in the adjustment phase of his revised reality.

She felt slightly guilty over the abrupt way she'd manipulated the situation, so Celeste opened up her intuition just an inch to listen to his heart's desire. Rodney was no candidate for a protégé. His dreams were on the small but satisfied side, his talents already on full display. He'd be the manager someday, but he didn't require her help to achieve that goal. She was quite pleased to find him content with most aspects of his existence, save for his love life. He yearned to speak to a pretty brunette who ate lunch at the same delicatessen counter every Friday. All he lacked in that area was a little confidence and an excuse to start a conversation. "Thank you," she said, accepting the key, then stirred the air with a little favor. "Such a charming young man you are. I'll bet the ladies are drawn to you like bees to honey." He stood a little straighter and smiled as the bellhop arrived to escort her to her bungalow.

The bellhop didn't even question his instructions to accompany the hotel's newest guest to a bungalow that hadn't existed five minutes earlier, which meant the glamour had already melded into the property and the minds of those who worked and lived there. Once the energy manifested into physical form—in this case with a little help from Sebastian—it was as though bungalow twenty-two had always been tucked away at the back of the tree-lined acreage.

The quaint cottage was even lovelier than Celeste had imagined. She could hardly tip the bellhop fast enough so he would leave and she could jump on the velvet sofa and sink into the plush cushions. "Oh, Sebastian, you've outdone yourself! You've delivered my vision perfectly." The tingle of spent magic brushed against her skin as she admired the lush silk bedding in the single bedroom, the glittering crystal chandelier hung over the dining room table, and the marble floor in the very modern bathroom. She plopped down on the sofa and absorbed the last remnants of the floating magic before it settled into the wood and plaster, turning the artifice of a dream into solid reality. And while the furnishings, roof, and walls were fabricated purely from filaments of her imagination, they were as real as in any of the other bungalows. Well, so long as her magic held out.

Celeste rested her head on the pillow and gazed up at the ceiling. A stray cobweb swung between beams. "Whatever did you use for the base of the transformation?" Celeste asked. As with all Gardienne magic, nothing was created out of thin air. There had to be something solid at the core for the magic to adhere to.

The stoat pointed his nose toward the chandelier over the table. Celeste squinted at the light, and soon the outline of a wire trash bin came into focus within the design. She gave him a scratch behind the ear for his ingenuity.

"Now, where should we store the trunk?" she asked. The stoat stood on his hind legs at the end of the sofa and pointed his nose toward the far wall in the bedroom. "Very well. We'll unpack everything later tonight." The stoat tossed his head, admonishing her for procrastinating. "I know, I know, but some of us haven't eaten and I'm famished. Let's hope room service is as quick as that bellhop."

Sebastian wrinkled his whiskers and gave up before curling into a ball atop a velvet pillow. While her companion snored, Celeste ate a room service dinner of oysters Rockefeller, duchesse potatoes, and something called a cheeseburger. While she sipped from a glass of champagne, she took a moment to appreciate the journey she'd taken to arrive at this enchanted place. To imagine a single postcard could have inspired a trip clear across the ocean, all the way to America, landing her in a place so brimming with possibility.

The thought would have been unfathomable two weeks earlier, when Anaïs was out for blood. She didn't know if a Gardienne had ever murdered another in the long history of their sisterhood, but she'd come as close to finding out as she dared. She was almost certain that if she'd protested with enough righteousness, the elders would have let her hide out in one of the many chalets they owned deep in the old-growth forests of Europe until things blew over, but leaning back against the hotel's velvet sofa, she wasn't that sorry about the way things had turned out in the end.

Celeste, like all the Fées Gardiennes through history who'd presumably come before her, had been raised in a small cottage, not unlike the bungalow she occupied now. But the one from her childhood had been trimmed in rough wood and flaking plaster. The windows had been covered in scratchy linen, the food served on plain-as-mud crockery. Her bed had been a simple tick mattress filled with straw, her dresses woven out of ordinary gray wool, and her shoes carved from willow wood for trekking through muck. Though life had sometimes been difficult, she understood why the elder sisters had insisted on such a humble beginning. All the while they'd been teaching her to read the alphabet, bake bread in a woodstove, and mend a worn sock for the third time, she'd also absorbed the ache of deprivation. She understood deep in her marrow how a tiny spark of hope could start a forest fire of dreams in one's heart. And that was the most useful lesson of all, because as she learned when she got a little bit older, the entire raison d'être for the Fées Gardiennes' existence was to bring that spark of life into the world, to keep the dream-fires burning in the hearts of humankind.

And now here she was freshly landed in California, the new epicenter of unborn dreams. All she had to do was find her protégé, strike the match of inspiration, and send up that flare of hope bright enough for others to see. The thought was mesmerizing as she sank deeper into the cushions, letting her own wild dreams serve as a coverlet until morning.

CHAPTER FOUR

ONE IN A MILLION

It took a little manipulation of the space and energy inside the bungalow, but Celeste and Sebastian managed to get the trunk moved into the bedroom the next morning. The thing had been double padlocked, secured with a leather strap, and bound with an enchantment to protect it for the long journey. Now it was time to take inventory and make sure their belongings had arrived safe and sound.

Sebastian unbuckled the leather strap with his teeth while Celeste put the key in the lock, and together they convinced the protective energy surrounding the trunk that they were the rightful owners by placing their cheeks against the lid and visualizing their release words: "lemon cake" for her, "raw salmon" for him. The clasp sprang open, the lid lifted, and a series of drawers, large to small, slid out into shelves that were filled with an enviable display of bottles, ointments, books, and odd bits of feathers and colorful stones the pair had been collecting since the day they'd been introduced. There were also three flattering dresses and two suits neatly folded in paper at the bottom among her various personal sundries, along with a small stack of ancient reference books with gilded spines that she'd been gifted upon graduating from the cottage at age eighteen.

"Everything appears to have made it," Celeste said. She uncapped a purple atomizer and took a sniff of the alluring perfume, then shook out the contents of a small envelope. Three baby teeth scattered onto the wooden shelving. They were an odd childhood souvenir, yet she carried them everywhere she went. And she'd moved a lot since becoming an initiate, training with each Fée Gardienne sister for a few months at a time until she'd landed in the soup with Anaïs. She supposed she kept the baby teeth out of some longing to remember who she was and where she'd come from before being snatched up at a year old to live in the cottage deep in the woods. They were a reminder that she'd been born someone else, holding open the possibility there was a world she could go back to someday should she fail at her current life. The thought dropped a stone in her stomach, so she put the envelope away.

Sebastian nudged his nose toward the apothecary bottles on the top shelf.

"Yes, they're all good." Celeste uncorked the small jar of gemstones as proof, showing off the marquise-cut diamonds, rubies, sapphires, and emeralds. He backed away and sat on his haunches, seemingly satisfied, but he'd been right to be concerned. The gemstones worked like a battery for her power while she was still an initiate unable to sustain her glamour on her own, like the others. But they also served as the conduit for the magical energy that passed between Sebastian and herself, working somewhat like an invisible telephone wire to keep their thoughts connected. Without the jewels she'd be no different from any other woman on her own, something she didn't wish to imagine. "We'll recharge soon, but I think we're still good on energy." The little stoat wiggled his body in agreement before he trotted out the door to go catch his breakfast.

An hour later it was time to get to work. Celeste, dressed in the sapphire-blue dress with the drop waist and blue velvet bow, walked up the garden path to the hotel's front desk. Sebastian caught up at the last moment and climbed into her handbag just as she entered the lobby. His belly still bulged from whatever rodent he'd ambushed under the hedge.

"Good morning, madam. How may I help you today?"

Celeste detected a woman's perfume on Rodney's jacket and the faint trace of lipstick on his cheek where he'd missed a spot with his handkerchief. She was reasonably confident, after sprinkling the desk clerk with favor the day before, the lipstick was from the brunette at the lunch counter and not some out-of-town aunt who'd recently shown up for a visit. She smiled at his improved luck. "It's 'mademoiselle,'" she corrected again, understanding why he might be distracted.

Rodney showed the proper humility to make up for his mistake by shaking his head in apology, then asked how he could be of help.

"What kind of vehicle are the fashionable people driving in the city these days?" she asked in all sincerity.

The clerk was momentarily stumped by her question, or rather, she thought, by her asking the question in the first place, but after a moment he snapped his fingers. "I've been seeing a few Pierce-Arrows lately," he said. "A real beauty. Leather seats, fender headlights, convertible top, and beautiful white-rimmed tires with a spare on the back."

"A Pierce-Arrow?" Celeste crossed her heart before tugging on her sapphire pendant. "Thank you, Rodney. You've been very helpful," she said and headed for the door.

"Going anywhere exciting today?" he called as he came around the desk to hand her a complimentary map of the area. "Since you didn't arrive by car, may I call you a cab?"

"Oh, no, that won't be necessary. My automobile should be out front by now." Celeste gave a quick wave as she approached the powder-blue Pierce-Arrow that had rolled to a stop on the driveway out front. A young valet stepped out and held the door open for her. Bewilderment floated off him as he made eye contact with the similarly perplexed front desk clerk. "Oh, there is one thing," she called as she got behind the wheel. "Which way to Hollywood?"

The pair pointed northeast in unison, then closed their mouths and went back to work.

"Sebastian, you doll, you've matched the car to my dress." Celeste tossed the map on the seat and put the car in gear.

The stoat hopped out of the bag and jumped up on the dashboard to better see the road ahead. Together they headed northeast on Sunset Boulevard as the men had indicated, where every quarter mile there seemed to be some new building under construction. The town was experiencing a major growth spurt it could barely keep up with, but the array of roadside flowers were lovely as they drove along the boulevard with the wind in their hair.

"I have a good feeling about this," Celeste said to her seatmate as they passed under a colonnade of palm trees lining the road. "Just think, Sebastian, I'm going to find my very first protégé. I can change someone's life. Maybe even make them a star. A shooting star for all to see." A rash of goose bumps broke out on her arms as she thought about the woman whom she'd seen performing at the Folies Bergère and the artists and writers who'd gathered in Gertrude's Paris salon, each unaware of the influence the Fées Gardiennes had over their collected fates. Celeste considered then, too, the young man Anaïs had once been attached to who'd been destined for a brilliant career in the law under her patronage. She wondered if that future would still play out after the way things fell apart. Monsieur Fontaine might soon find his life in a perpetual downward spiral after his unfortunate pairing with Anaïs. There was always that fickle side to what they did, and no two ways about it.

Sebastian eyed her from the dashboard.

"I know." Celeste pretended to be concerned with traffic rather than meet her companion's eye whenever he got that intense stare on his face like some wise old prophet. "You think I'm being simpleminded. Naive. Life is more complicated than simply finding a suitable candidate and granting their wishes or enchanting the pathway for them. Well, I know all about the other side of things. The price for having one's dreams come true. The right candidate must have the stamina and maturity to withstand the demand that will be made of them when the balance comes due on the other side. And that no one's life, no matter how successful, is ever without tragedy or hard times. And yet we both know the fall can prove all the harder for those who rise the highest. I have little control over that side of the bargain, even if I'm the one who'll bring it to bear on their life."

Celeste pulled over onto the dirt and shut off the engine. She rested her chin on the steering wheel as she gazed up at the scruffy hills overlooking the valley. The task of finding the right individual suddenly seemed too daunting. The enthusiasm she'd carried out of the hotel lobby fizzled as the magnitude of her venture weighed on her shoulders. Because even though she could change the trajectory of a life and make it magnificent, she had to live with the fact that whoever she chose would someday find wolves waiting on the other side of success, and there was nothing she could do to protect them from it.

And yet the bargain must be made.

Celeste almost turned the car around, but then she felt the tickle of a whisker against her arm. A gentle reminder from Sebastian, letting her know she had the time and the talent to find the right protégé. There was someone out there in the city of nearly a million people. Someone ready and waiting for the life-changing opportunity that only she could deliver to them.

She'd needed that small reassurance from her companion. Because despite the downfall effect she would inevitably set in motion for whoever she chose as her protégé, their rise would at first be glorious and hopefully worth all the later tumbles into hardship they were bound to go through when the Skulks came to collect their recompense. Now she just had to find that special someone whose head was filled to the brim with lofty dreams and enough talent to keep them suspended in the air.

CHAPTER FIVE

A Chorus of Wishes

Celeste drummed her fingers against the steering wheel. It was day two of their quest for a protégé in this "land of enchantment," but her enthusiasm had noticeably dipped. She'd been advised to make a love match to secure her first protégé. She understood why Dorée had suggested it. Arranging an advantageous marriage between a poor woman and a powerful man was the quickest and easiest way for Celeste to earn her full status as a Fée Gardienne. But the notion was so old-fashioned. A leftover from the days when castles stood in the center of daily life and her kind were still revered as the court's Wisewomen. On the other hand, it was an arrow-fast route to becoming the one thing she was meant to be. The sooner she earned her status, the sooner she could claim her full powers and perhaps return home. Besides, arranging an advantageous marriage for a young woman in a city of newly molded princes ought to be manipulated easily enough. After all, everyone was looking for love, just not always with the people they ended up marrying. Another disadvantage of the downfall effect.

Celeste sighed and pulled over in front of a mansion set on a hillside surrounded by majestic palm trees. The house reminded her of the Mediterranean villas she'd visited on the southern coast of France, giving her a twinge of homesickness. A man in a tan suit stepped out the front door and lit a cigar while speaking to a gardener clipping roses. The man was handsome enough, and apparently rich enough to make a good match. But something about manipulating two strangers into colliding and falling in love still bothered her. "Happily ever afters are no guarantee," she said to Sebastian, who once again stretched out on the dashboard. "And what's to be gained by arranging a marriage between a member of this so-called Hollywood royalty and, say, a pretty gal who works as a telephone operator? There's no truce between nations at stake, no ailing king in need of an heir to keep his monarchy intact. Just the random collision of two people who wouldn't have even looked for each other without a big magical push to throw them together." She shook her head. "Let's keep looking," she said and put the car in gear. "Everyone says I'll know when I know."

Sebastian gave no objection, curling up on the dashboard just in front of the steering wheel. With a new mindset, the pair cruised the boulevard in the blue convertible with the top down. They passed gift shops, gas stations, hotels, and a food market, slowing down each time to see if they felt anything from the people coming and going, but ultimately they drove on. Half past noon they passed a sidewalk café, where Celeste noticed a man sipping a coffee. He looked up at her in the dark sunglasses she'd slipped on to combat the glare of the sun and missed his mouth with his cup, spilling the coffee in his lap. She smiled at him, then pressed the accelerator. Two blocks later, as they headed slightly east, a magnetic pull hit her full in her chest, as sure and strong as a divining rod pointing toward water.

"Here," she said to Sebastian. "I felt something. Wow, what a wallop!" Her heartbeat sped up in anticipation as she pulled to a stop in front of a white stone building lined with matching white columns and a balustrade. Two dozen Model Ts were parked in front, and a line of men and women wound around the corner to the other side of the massive building. A sign in gold lettering above the entrance read WEST COAST STUDIOS. "What is this place?" The stoat leaped onto the seat and kicked the tourist map toward her. After perusing the highlights on the street, she looked up at the impressive building again. "It says it's a movie studio. They make moving pictures here."

Celeste parked in the last spot on the street and jumped out of the car, while Sebastian slipped inside her purse to stay close. She couldn't be sure, but she thought the little stoat sighed and shook his head before disappearing among her lipstick, sunglasses, and hotel key. But she was right about this. That pull in her chest couldn't be wrong. She was meant to come to this place.

"Excuse me." Celeste waved at the nearest woman in line. "What's everyone waiting for?"

"New picture," the woman said. "Central casting put the call out this morning for three parts, but they ain't looking for a brunette." The woman's hair was bleached platinum under her cloche hat with a white ribbon. She wore heavy eyeliner and chewed gum like a rabbit trying to gnaw its way out of a cage.

"A movie? How wonderful." Celeste gazed at the more than fifty men and women standing in line. They were a scruffy lot. Some of the men looked as though they'd been living rough, with unwashed hair and wrinkled suits, and others looked like they could be ranch hands in their fringed leather and cowboy boots. The women all wore summer dresses that hit at the knee, but despite the flowy fabric, hard angles still poked through on a few of them. "So, you're all actors?" she asked.

"Yeah, of course. Everybody here's an actor." The blond woman chewed hard on her gum. "Been my dream to be in the pictures ever since my family came out from Ohio last month. I'm not gonna be a background actor forever, though. I'm gonna get the part, and then I'm gonna be a star."

"Not if I get the part first." The woman behind her smirked when met with a scowl from the blond woman.

Since dreams and wishes were what Celeste was seeking, she thanked the women and walked a little farther up the sidewalk, ignoring the warnings shouted behind her about cutting in line. Finding a refreshing spot in the shade near the front steps, Celeste turned her back to the line of actors, gripped her sapphire pendant, and closed her eyes. She had to open herself up to listen for the kind of hope and ambition that sprouted sturdy-enough wings to fly through the inevitable storm. Surely there was someone in the crowd aching to share their talent with the world.

Celeste relaxed her shoulders as she hugged her handbag to her middle. She'd need Sebastian's help, too, if this were going to work. The protections around her fell away, letting in the random hopes of all the strangers lined up along the road. The first whispers of their desires circled around her head. There were so many she couldn't have named them all. The stronger aspirations thumped like dozens of heartbeats pounding against her eardrum. And then the voices behind the wishes became fully formed: *I want to be famous! Make me rich! I want to be adored by millions! I'd trade my right kidney for a night with John Gilbert!*

The chorus of wishes turned into a cacophony of demands, each one shallower than the last. The voices came at her from every direction, expanding beyond the line of actors to the people in the shops and offices, until her ears filled with the slush of hopeless pipe dreams and flimsy fantasies. Waves of self-delusional and empty desires sloshed against her equilibrium. Her vision filled with white lights that flashed behind her closed lids, and then her legs gave out beneath her.

Celeste awoke moments later to a man lightly slapping her cheeks.

"Isn't she the one driving that blue breezer over there?" The man who'd spilled coffee on himself at the sidewalk café was holding her on his lap on the ground. He patted her cheek again. "That's it, doll. Time to wake up."

"Yeah, that's her," the blond woman said, smacking her gum at an even more frenzied pace as she leaned over to reveal her ample cleavage in front of the man's face. "She pulled up in that beast and started asking questions about what everyone was doing here. Hey, aren't you Nick West? Well, ain't that swell. So happens I'm here to audition for your next picture." She stuck her hand out while still bent forward. "Lila

Thompson. Pleased to meet you, I'm sure," she said with a shimmy of her torso.

The man ignored the extended hand. "Help me get her inside."

"Oh, sure. Anything you say, boss. I'm great at following direction."

Celeste had to object at that point. "No, really, I'm fine." She managed to sit up, though she was anything but fine. Her knees still wobbled, and her head throbbed with the echo of a thousand voices. She'd never experienced anything like that before. It felt like she'd been hit by a freight train carrying every heart's desire within the city. Everyone wishing for some version of the same thing all at once: fame and riches.

"No, I think you'd better come inside with me," the man said as he lifted Celeste in his arms in one swoop and carried her up the stairs and through the front doors of the studio's main entrance. A guard held the door open for them, then closed it again before the blond woman could follow.

The man carried her through a grand foyer with vaulted ceilings, down a long marble hallway, and past a glass-enclosed office with a secretary who gawked at them before leaning over her desk to call out, "Mr. West? Is everything all right? You're due in casting in fifteen minutes."

"I'll be in wardrobe," he yelled out, then smiled at Celeste. "You are feeling better, aren't you?"

"Well enough to walk on my own," she said, though she decided she was in no hurry to have him release her.

"This part is your doing, by the way." He grunted and adjusted her weight in his arms as he turned a corner.

"You mean the part where you kidnap me and haul me off to some stuffy old closet full of costumes?"

"Actually, I was perfectly happy minding my own business, eating my sandwich and sipping my coffee, when you drove by in that breezer gleaming bright as a summer day." He tried to rein in a smile, but his eyes still gave him away. He kept sneaking glances at her every few steps—at her eyes, her cheeks, her lips. She accepted the attention as a compliment, considering the clientele he must have worked with daily at a movie studio. "Imagine my surprise when I came back to work to find that very same driver passed out on my steps," he said. "I should thank you. You've saved me the trouble of having to look you up."

"Glad I could oblige," Celeste said, feeling less muddled in her head than she had moments earlier. Getting some distance from the source of all that desperate wishing seemed to help. "Now, would you please put me down." She didn't mean it—the scent of his aftershave was intoxicating—but she thought she ought to at least put up some fuss about being carried away by a strange man.

"Almost there," he said, ignoring her demand. He turned them around and backed his way in through a set of double doors that swung inward. There he set her down on a chaise lounge covered in red velvet and skirted in gold fringe. They'd walked into a high-ceilinged room filled with racks of clothes. The space appeared organized, like a library for costumes instead of books. It was warm inside, and a stuffy odor reminded her of the old attic at the cottage in the woods, where woolens had been stored in chests before the Great War. The sound of sewing machines buzzed in the background.

"What's this? A new fitting for the Diaz movie?"

"Good morning, Gladys." Nick straightened to greet the woman. She was perhaps fifty years old, wore a pair of wire-rimmed glasses with a chain around the back of her neck, and had tied a gray work smock over her day dress. Her shoes were scuffed black leather with low heels, a telltale sign of a woman who worked on her feet all day. He introduced her as the assistant to the head costume designer. "This is . . . I'm sorry, I didn't actually get your name yet."

"It's Celeste."

"Celeste." The left side of his mouth curled in a smile after feeling the shape of her name on his lips. "Celeste has taken a spill." Then he looked down at his suit. "Actually, we both seem to have taken a spill. Could you be a doll and get her a glass of water. Or perhaps we could offer you something stronger?" He swung around to test if she was interested, but she declined. "Right, a glass of water for our guest while I duck over in that direction for a minute to find some dry clothes to put on."

"The trousers you like are on rack five," Gladys said.

"Promise you'll stay put until I get back," he said to Celeste. "I'll only be a minute or two."

Celeste was so swept up in the whirlwind of her first Hollywood studio encounter she could hardly lift her head, let alone say no. Besides, he was shockingly handsome with his wavy brown hair, blue eyes, and a smile so bright it could stop traffic.

Gladys said she'd be back as soon as she could find a clean glass, so Celeste took the opportunity while she was left alone to open her handbag and check on Sebastian. "All right in there?" The little stoat climbed out and nestled against her shoulder, sniffing for signs of trouble. "I'm fine," she said. "But wasn't that the strangest thing? My intuition insisted I stop and talk to those people, but there were so many paper-thin wishes they all flew at me at once, like they'd been shot out of a cannon to clog up my brain."

Celeste got little sympathy from Sebastian. He'd been skeptical from the start about her scheme to pluck some unknown actor off the sidewalk. Seemed the city was full of people all wanting the same thing, and wanting it so badly they'd created a logjam in her perception. The messages had come at her so fast and thick, the entire city might as well have been calling out to her with its dreams. She cradled her stoat companion in her arms as she sat up to test her dizziness. The buzzing in her head had subsided, but doubt and fear remained. Maybe she really wasn't cut out for this kind of work if she couldn't sort the shooting stars from the starry-eyed dreamers. What if she'd come all this way to be in exile for nothing? What if she was just a dud, and the Fées Gardiennes who'd stolen her away as a babe had made a mistake?

The thought set Celeste's emotions on edge until Sebastian reminded her by way of one of his sly looks that the Fées Gardiennes didn't make such mistakes. "Then how did things get so mixed up?" she asked. "With all these people sharing the same dreams, how will I ever hear any one of them properly?" His solemn eyes implored her to try again now that things were quieter. Doubt dug its claws in deep, but the stoat was insistent. Celeste knew better than to ignore the eyes that shone back at her like black pearls.

Sitting with her knees together and her feet flat on the floor, Celeste closed her eyes. The hum of the sewing machines in the next room distracted her from her doubt long enough to focus on her breathing. She tentatively reconnected, listening for the heartbeat of dreams. She'd expected to be drowned out again, but there was only one small voice that spoke to her this time. The wish rode on the rhythm of the machines in the other room. Stitching and striving. Revving and whirring. A dream trimmed in silk and satin, ink and paper, and lace, and feathers, but built on a framework of ambition and vision.

Celeste opened her eyes, astonished at the clarity of what she'd felt and seen. She rose and crossed the hall. On the other side of a wooden door with a glass window, she spied a dozen women at work at their sewing machines. A slender young woman stood on a raised platform, her nose in the air, while an older woman with pins in her mouth marked the hem on a rich magenta gown straight from the Victorian era. Celeste's eyes roamed the room for the person whose dream she'd caught, but it was her heart that did the true searching.

And then she found her, a young woman with her hair tied up in a scarf on top of her head. She wore the same smock as the other women, but hers had taken more of a beating. It was covered in mud and coffee and something that could have passed for blood. The woman was working on a pair of old-fashioned men's trousers, rubbing them against a rough stone. She held them up to gauge her progress, though what her goal was, Celeste had no idea, as the woman seemed to be destroying the clothing while everyone else was busy creating.

"There you are. Thought I'd lost you." Nick extended a glass of water to Celeste. He'd changed into a pair of brown plus fours with a matching vest, which he'd slipped on over his white button-up. "Feeling better, then?"

Celeste didn't want to take her eyes off the young woman for fear of losing her. "Uh, yes, thank you. I just needed to get some air." She accepted the glass of water but didn't drink from it. Her mind was too occupied with thoughts of what she ought to do next. Her heart hadn't been wrong when she'd stopped the car. It had just met with more interference than she'd anticipated. With a little luck and intuition, she believed she'd found her potential protégé. Now she just had to figure out exactly what the young woman's dream was, since all her ambitions were wrapped up in gauze, glitz, and soft lighting. Ball gowns and headpieces. Almost like she was picturing a bridal gown. Was this meant to be a love match after all?

"Who is that interesting young woman in the corner?" she asked.

Nick narrowed his eyes and frowned. "I'm embarrassed to say I can't recall for certain. She's one of our newer seamstresses, but the name Rose seems to ring a bell. Why do you ask?"

"Oh, I was just curious," Celeste answered. "She seems a very hard worker."

"I suppose they all are."

Yes, he'd gotten the name right or she would have felt a shudder of discord. His eye lingered on the young seamstress in mild curiosity but only briefly. She supposed the woman wasn't much to look at currently when scrutinized through the lens of conventional attractiveness. Oh, but this Rose, in her unadorned and dirty workaday clothes and unkempt hair, was a flower that simply hadn't emerged from the soil yet. First appearances had never been obstacles for the Fées Gardiennes' work before, and they wouldn't be now.

"What is it they're working on?" Celeste asked.

"Costumes for a new movie." Nick stepped away from the door's window. "We're making a follow-up to *London After Dark*."

She didn't recognize the title, but she didn't wish to appear rude and say so. Instead, she asked, "And what is it that you do in the picture business?"

"Me?" He made no effort to hide his amusement at the question. "The clue is in the name of the studio," he said.

West Coast Studios! Celeste felt the zing of mortification. "You own this place?"

"My brother and I started the studio about eight years ago. He writes some. I direct some. And we both produce. We've been fortunate with a few of our releases."

"Mr. West, you're needed on Stage One," his secretary called from down the hall. "*Now*, if you please."

"Coming," he answered, then gently maneuvered Celeste away from the sewing room by hooking his arm with hers at the elbow. "I have to get back to work, but is there some way we can meet again?"

He held her close, as though he didn't want to let her go, but it was nothing to complain about. She enjoyed the warmth radiating off his aura. "You're in luck, Mr. West. I happen to be free tomorrow. If nothing else comes up, I'll make every effort to drop by. Maybe you can give me a tour of the rest of the place."

"You're on."

The look of delight in Nick's eyes sent a jolt through Celeste that repaired whatever damage had been done by her earlier embarrassment. She was tempted to listen in on his wishes just to see if he was headed for bigger things, but she got the impression he'd already achieved whatever it was he'd been after. Well, perhaps with one exception, she thought, eavesdropping slightly on his emotions. There was a distinct void in his personal life. The hope of meeting the right someone glowed all around him. When she had first opened her eyes and seen his dazzling face looking down at her, she had wondered if she'd finally stumbled on one of the new princes of Hollywood. Now she wondered if she'd actually found a new royal in need of a wife.

She glanced back at Rose through the window in the door, a poor thing if ever there was one, who purposely ripped a bigger hole in a dirty rag of a shirt only to carefully arrange it on a hanger with a handwritten note pinned to the front. Could this be the makings of an arranged marriage after all? She still wasn't convinced, but perhaps there was a solution to both subjects' desires. One that only a Gardienne could fix.

CHAPTER SIX

Gemstones and Day-Old Coffee

Back at the hotel bungalow, Celeste opened her travel trunk and removed the jar of precious gems. She unscrewed the lid and poured one ruby, one diamond, one sapphire, one amethyst, and one emerald into her palm. The cut stones caught the sunlight, reflecting the rays in spangles that danced on the ceiling and walls when she opened her hand flat.

"Ready," she said to Sebastian.

The stoat swallowed the last of his latest meal as a gray tail disappeared behind his lips. They needed a boost in energy to forge ahead. After what had happened with Anaïs and her last attempt at Fée Gardienne work, Celeste planned to thoroughly scrutinize the seamstress before she invested the full focus of her magic into her. To do that she needed to know where the young woman lived, who her parents were, how she spent her days, and most importantly: Did she have any skeletons in her closet, like an old fiancé intent on sabotage? Celeste and Sebastian would have to split up to get everything done. She had the ability to use her glamour to go unnoticed in a room full of people, but the stoat would have to be her eyes and ears in other situations. And that meant they'd have to recharge their bond to be confident it was functioning at its highest level after so much travel.

Sebastian gave his whiskers a quick wipe with his paws, then climbed on top of the trunk. Celeste held her palm out, tilting it from side to side until she found the perfect angle of sunlight coming through the window. The spangles reflecting off the gems encircled them until they were surrounded by sparkly, golden light that made the fur on Sebastian's back ruffle. Celeste felt it, too, as static lifted the stray hairs around her face. She cleared her throat, then held her sapphire pendant above the other jewels. "Source of light, burning bright, infuse your glow, let energy flow. Channel the force, steady the course, feminine divine, power be mine."

The magic, carried in the shape of the words, coalesced in the sequined light until filaments of energy formed. Thin strands of light encircled Celeste and the stoat in a figure eight, binding the pair together. The beat of his tiny heart echoed within her own, her heart a locket holding his precious life force. Their vision linked and their thoughts conjoined as the bonding spell took effect. After the light dissipated, Celeste saw remnants gleaming in the stoat's eyes. They'd reconnected, and now their bond would allow her to see and hear and feel whatever her companion wished to share.

Sebastian shook out his fur, then found his place on a soft pillow. The pair had been through the bonding process dozens of times, beginning soon after they'd first been introduced when Celeste was twelve years old. She'd taken to the little fellow immediately, drawn by his curiosity and playful nature. He'd been a gift from Dorée and the other Gardiennes. A confidant for Celeste to depend on as she fulfilled her obligations to the sisterhood. She'd known, of course, from the start that he was a born killer, but one couldn't hold another's innate nature against them. The two were a pair and would be for life. However, she couldn't deny there were days when being bonded to an animal, mind and soul, struck her as sorrowful, reminding her she had no human blood relative she could put a name to.

The next morning, Celeste and Sebastian rose before dawn. "Hurry," she said, holding her purse open. "We need to observe her at work. I want to see how she walks, who she talks to, what she wears. Everything." So soon after renewing their bonding spell, it was easy to trace the smile on the little stoat's face as he jumped into the comfy corner of her handbag. He was as anxious as she was to see if this Rose was the one.

Celeste parked the Pierce-Arrow around the corner from the studio, where a few scraggly trees grew close together. She remembered there'd been a guard at the front, where she'd gone in before, but she didn't want to waste time and energy trying to avoid him, so they planned to sneak in a back way. With a little nudge, Sebastian cloaked the car in the illusion of a Model T so it would blend in with the dozen other cars parked along the avenue. She'd told Nick she would swing by the studio if she had time, but she didn't need him spotting her too soon, not when there was so much preliminary work to be done with Rose.

"This place is enormous," Celeste said after realizing the studio was more than just the main building. The lot in the back seemed to take up at least three city blocks. Big enough that a pair of castle turrets rose above the wall surrounding the property. A torn mainsail poked up to the left, suggesting a ship, and the pointed top of a giant pyramid floated like a mirage on the far side of the property. "There has to be a way in besides the front door."

The sound of a saw biting through wood alerted Celeste that people were already at work on the other side of the wall. If she and Sebastian were going to sneak in, they'd have to be stealthy, but she didn't want to use her glamour just yet. Instead, she walked along the wall's perimeter until she came to a double-wide metal gate, secured with a padlock, where she assumed delivery trucks drove in and out. Looking through the bars, she got her first full view of the massive back lot. Some of the sets, like the ship and an old burned-out building, appeared to be in a state of neglect. Others, like the castle and an Old West saloon, were still actively being built, with huge spotlights and folding chairs surrounding them. Nick had mentioned a movie he was working on, but it was impossible to figure out where it was being filmed on the lot.

She'd have to be stealthy indeed if she wanted to avoid running into him too soon.

Celeste tested the gate. The lock was fastened tight, but it was nothing a little ingenuity couldn't fix. She reached into her purse, where Sebastian had already configured a skeleton key out of her lipstick tube to fit the lock. "Thank you," she said, feeling the magic passing between them sharp as glass. She inserted the key and heard a satisfying click. "Now we just have to find our way back to the wardrobe department."

After slipping inside the gate, Celeste walked along the rough makings of a log cabin, but one that had been built on a seesaw sort of contraption that would allow the house's foundation to be tilted. She wasn't a big moviegoer, but she'd seen enough comedies to imagine the wonky house was built for an actor whose gimmick was to slide across the floor out of his lover's arms and into the grip of a storm of trouble on the other side of the room, usually in the shape of a jealous ex or a landlord demanding the overdue rent. By the end, of course, he'd slide back to the other side, reunited with his lover for the happy ending.

Celeste and Sebastian crept along the perimeter of the lot until they were in sight of the main building. They were close enough that she could use her glamour to make herself unseen if she wanted to, but then a janitor exited a back door to dump a pile of trash in the large outdoor garbage bin not ten feet from where they stood. The door was in a dingy, shadowy vestibule she hadn't noticed until the bald man had pushed his cart outside. It was the perfect place to sneak inside unnoticed.

Once the janitor finished emptying the bins and headed back in, Celeste made a run for it, ducking inside the shadowy area just as a trio of men walked past with heavy tripods on their shoulders. She clapped a hand over her mouth to stifle a gasp when she spotted Nick among them. The sight of his wavy hair and wide shoulders had her biting her lip behind her hand. She'd met a few princes as a child in Europe before the Great War had sucked the power from their blue-blooded veins. Those princes had walked with the same confidence as Nick, as though the world were made solely for their pursuits. She wondered what elixir had been poured into men's mouths when they were babes to make them so cocksure as adults, when she was shaped by so much self-doubt despite all the power at her fingertips.

Seeing Nick pass by gave Celeste an idea. "Perhaps you ought to follow him," she said to Sebastian as he poked his nose out of her bag and sniffed the air. "Let's find out just what kind of modern-day prince he really is, hmm?"

The little stoat bounded out of her purse and down the steps to chase after the men. No doubt he'd get distracted by a mouse or two, but she was confident he'd get the goods on Nick West.

Inside, electric light bulbs buzzed behind frosted glass domes as Celeste tiptoed down the hallway, trying to remember which direction she'd gone the day before. A single sewing machine whirred in the distance, so she followed the sound back to the wing where the wardrobe department and sewing room were housed. When she reached the costume department—where she'd been so gallantly carried over the threshold the day before—she paused and peeked through the glass door leading to the sewing room. Alone at the back, Rose sat in front of her machine, snipping off a length of thread with a pair of scissors in the shape of a bird. Unlike the day before, when the young woman had been working on rough rags and men's trousers, this morning she concentrated on a delicate satin gown under the needle. The material was a creamy beige the color of freshly churned butter slathered over bread. Rose was attempting to attach a string of crystal beads to the neckline when Celeste walked in.

"Hello, I hope I'm in the right place." Celeste hesitated by the door as she came up with an idea of using her glamour to blend in as just another seamstress. She'd deliberately worn a simple day dress to avoid causing any unnecessary suspicion, and now she was doubly grateful for the prescient decision. "I'm supposed to start work as a seamstress this morning," she said, grabbing an apron off the wall and slipping it over her head as she'd seen the other women do the day before. "Gladys said to be here sharp at seven."

"That's odd." Rose looked up at the clock. "Gladys and the rest of the girls aren't due in for another hour." She'd swiped the satin garment she was working on off the table and stuffed it in her lap when Celeste had walked in, but now she brought it back out. She delicately straightened the material, eyeing the shape with a tilt of her head. "I generally come in early to catch up on a few odds and ends that need doing. My name's Rose. You can take that machine there," she said, pointing to the one in the corner beside her own at the back of the room.

Celeste took a seat in front of the sewing machine. "I like to get an early start too," she lied. She'd much rather be snuggled up in bed, dreaming of warm croissants delivered by room service, but she couldn't deny the shiver of excitement she felt at being alone in the room with her first possible protégé. Sparks of energy snapped in the ether all around them, Rose none the wiser.

"We must have fallen behind again," she said. "They have so many extras in the new horror picture they're working on, none of them allowed to wear their own clothes. Here, you can work on these beggars costumes with me."

Celeste eyed the buttery dress on the young woman's table. "Since when do beggars wear satin?"

"Oh, this?" Rose's face blushed a pale pink. "I'm just finishing up a little side project I've been working on." She did a quick fold-up job and packed the garment in her carryall bag, where the corner of a sketchbook stuck out of the opening.

Celeste let it go and picked up a pair of trousers from the pile. The cuffs had been deliberately cut to make them look tattered, but the rest of the material was clean and new looking. She lifted her brows in question about the task she was expected to do.

"We scrub the knees against rocks and pull the threading loose to make the hems ragged," Rose said with little enthusiasm, plucking out a second pair of trousers to show her how it was done. "With the shirts, we dip them in cold coffee to make them appear old and stained. Looks more authentic on the film."

Celeste gave it a try and was delighted with how satisfying it felt to put holes in the knees of the trousers and rip out the seams. Rose approved of her efforts, but instead of joining Celeste to finish working on the pile of costumes, she grabbed a pair of green leather lace-up boots, biting her lip as she examined them.

"Are those for the same project?" Celeste asked.

"Yes, but these are for the star, Dolores Diaz. She plays Teresa Escalante, a Spanish songstress who's touring the royal opera house in Madrid in all her finery when she's kidnapped by the villain." Rose held the boots up, eyeing them from different angles. "She's not as standoffish as some of the other actors we work with. She's very genuine. Anyway, if you're all right doing the beggars clothes on your own, I'm going to work on these to give them a little more charm. They're needed for the shoot this afternoon, but I'm not quite happy with the way they look yet. They just require a little more detail," she said and reached for some gold paint.

For the better part of an hour, Celeste followed Rose's instructions, stomping on the clothes, scraping the elbows of shirts against the rough plaster finish on the walls, and strategically spilling cold, stale coffee in the armpits before hanging the garments up to dry. She was beginning to enjoy coming up with new ways to destroy the fabric when she was interrupted by the pandemonium of eight chatty seamstresses arriving for work, followed by their supervisor. Rose quickly tucked her bag holding the satin dress out of view.

"Who's this?" asked a young woman whose long, dark braid hung halfway down her back.

Rose opened her mouth to introduce their newest seamstress when she realized she couldn't answer the question.

"I'm Cel . . . *ine*," Celeste said, offering her hand along with her new alias.

Gladys, the supervisor she'd met the day before, looked over in her direction. Celeste gripped her sapphire pendant and amped up her full glamour to ensure her true appearance remained disguised. Or, more accurately, to smudge out the image of what she'd looked like the day before in the woman's memory. She also had to plant the notion in the woman's mind that she'd been legitimately hired as an extra seamstress. She saw the embedded idea hit Gladys square between the eyes just as she squinted suspiciously at the new face in the room. The woman's expression relaxed once the glamour took effect, and she turned her attention to handing out assignments instead.

"We have much to get done today, ladies," Gladys said with a clap of her hands. "They begin filming some very pivotal scenes for *The Madman of Madrid* this afternoon. We also have an important fitting tomorrow morning." She pointed to the woman with the braid. "Graciela, I need the primary character's waistcoat and jacket before we break for lunch. Top hats too." She lifted her chin and scanned the back of the room. "Rose, I need Ms. Diaz's boots pronto. No need to keep perfecting them. They just need to be finished."

"Stop wasting so much time on a pair of boots that no one is even going to see on camera," whispered a red-haired woman with freckles who sat in front of them.

"Worry about your own projects, Zelda." Rose sighed and looked down at her work as though she'd heard the same sort of comment before. Celeste made a quick map in her head of the connections in the room. Most of the women were friendly with each other, sharing thread, cloth, and needles freely between them, but none of them, other than the redhead, paid much attention to Rose and her beggars costumes. And yet there was an acknowledgment, however small, in each of their hearts that she was the better seamstress.

"Everyone else, continue working on those evening gowns," Gladys said with a clap of her hands to cheer them on. "Every detail must be affixed according to the specifications. Let's make Jacobi proud." Pleased to see the women in the front of the room go straight to work,

Gladys turned her eye to Celeste in the back. "And you. Keep scrubbing those rags for the beggar scene. Margarite will have more trousers ready for you by the end of the day."

Celeste leaned toward Rose. "Who's Jacobi?"

"Who's Jacobi?" Rose nearly spilled her gold paint. "Isaac Jacobi is one of the greatest costume designers working in Hollywood. He's even got Paris couture nervous. Some of his choices are outshining their best designs."

Celeste took the boast with a grain of salt, but she understood intuitively from her training that she'd have to evaluate this Mr. Isaac Jacobi for his effect on her protégé. Everything Celeste did going forward had to be viewed through the lens of Rose's future. It was now her responsibility to mold Rose's destiny by favorably influencing the events around her, even the physical space at times. First and foremost, she had to shape the young woman's forward momentum so that her star could ascend and she could climb out of the back of this dreary workshop.

The prospect gave Celeste a secret thrill as she picked up another ragged garment and soaked it in yesterday's coffee.

CHAPTER SEVEN

Brocades and Besoms

The clock on the workshop wall made a half-hearted ding when it struck twelve noon. The seamstresses stuck their pins in the costumes in an X to mark their work progress, then grabbed their purses and emptied out of the room. All but Rose. She waited for the others to leave the workroom for their lunch break, then opened her carryall to retrieve the satin dress.

Celeste pretended not to see. "You're not getting lunch?" she asked.

Rose held up a sandwich wrapped in paper and shook her head. "I need to stay and finish my other project."

The poor girl would run herself ragged with her ambition. "What's that you're working on anyway?" Celeste tried to keep any hint of overt curiosity out of her voice. "It's very pretty."

"You think so?"

It was the first time she'd seen a genuine smile on Rose's face all day. "It's exquisite." Celeste coaxed the young woman into holding the dress up so she could get a proper look at the garment. A knee-length sleeveless gown. The bodice had been embroidered with flowers stitched in gold thread and tiny seed pearls strategically sewn into their centers to look like dewdrops. It would have been beautiful enough as is, but then panels of chiffon had been sewn into the skirt to give it some flounce. Any woman would be ecstatic to wear such a beautiful one-of-a-kind dress.

"Which movie is this for?" Celeste asked.

"It isn't. It's something I made on my own." Rose laid the dress out on the table, smoothing the material flat as she admired her work. "I'm hoping to sell it so I can afford a new sewing machine. The one I have at home keeps jamming. My father promised to buy me one, but his hours were suddenly cut at the warehouse, so it'll take forever before we scrape the money up from our paychecks alone. It's why I come in an hour early every day so I can use the studio's machines on my own time. Charlie, the janitor, lets me in."

"You've made more dresses like this one?"

"Some, but I want to make more. I get so many ideas, but it's hard to buy enough material." Rose pulled the sketchbook out of her bag. "I don't know why I'm telling you all this. I must be boring you."

"No, not at all," Celeste said. Her mind was spinning with ideas too.

Rose opened the book to show an array of drawings. The sticklike figures were imperfect. Partially drawn with charcoal or pencil. Sometimes the men and women were drawn with eyes, sometimes not. Sometimes with hands and feet, sometimes just pointed lines. The focus was the clothes they were wearing: fanciful knee-length dresses, sleek suits with sharp collars on the men, ladies' headdresses decorated with beads and feathers, long strands of pearls draped around the women's necks. Equal parts costume and couture. The very substance of her heart's desire.

Celeste experienced a light humming deep in her chest, like a tuning fork vibrating against her ribs. Other Gardiennes had told her it would happen when she witnessed a protégé's talent firsthand. That feeling was a key marker for charting her progress. It meant she was on the right track.

"They're just sketches," Rose said, taking the book back. "Practice for someday. Maybe."

"They're amazing." Celeste picked up her handbag to follow through on her plan to leave for lunch. "But if you can do all this, why are you sitting at the back of the room with me working on costumes for peasants and embellishing boots with gold paint and tassels?"

The way the young woman's laugh stabbed the silence was chilling. "Jacobi keeps promising promotions to the other girls. Zelda," she said, nudging her chin toward the empty workstation where the redheaded woman had been sitting earlier. "She can't even sew a straight line, but she's assigned to piecing all the pattern segments together for the gowns in the picture. And Margo's top hats? If the poor actor sweats in it under the bright lights, the glue around the band will come undone, I guarantee it." She shook her head as though to clear her mind of more sinister thoughts. "Anyway, I'm sorry to be abrupt, but I only have a short time to work on my own. Would you mind dropping these boots off in the wardrobe room across the hall? There's a desk near the door where you can leave them. Mr. Jacobi is expecting them." Celeste took the boots in hand with a nod. "Thanks so much," Rose said. "Enjoy your lunch. The cafeteria is in the brick building across the plaza. Just follow the smell of overcooked broccoli and you'll find it."

Celeste assured Rose she'd deliver the boots, then ducked out of the workroom. She was happy to breathe air that didn't smell of cotton, wool, and machine oil. For much the same reason, she planned to avoid a trip to the odorous cafeteria as well. Instead, she wandered into the wardrobe department across the hall where the costumes were stored. She spotted the chaise lounge where she'd been deposited the day before. She'd sensed then the enormity of the room when Nick had disappeared to find a pair of trousers, but walking around she only now realized just how cavernous the space was. The room must have held a hundred closets' worth of costumes. Some gowns and coats preserved on hangers, some shirts and trousers folded neatly on shelves, and beyond that were racks and racks of shoes, headdresses, boas, butterfly wings, turbans, tiaras, and cowboy hats all neatly stowed away. She called out, expecting to hear an echo, but even her own voice couldn't find its way back to her.

Assuming everyone had gone to lunch, Celeste found the desk and set the boots on top, trusting they'd be found. But with no one there, she didn't see the harm in having a look around. Still, she kept an eye out for Gladys and her straight pins while she rummaged through a few racks to get a feel for the studio's aesthetic. The costumes appeared to be organized by purpose, with paper tags pinned to their fronts to indicate which films they'd been used in. Many outfits were already showing their age with a visible layer of dust coating their collars and shoulders. But one costume, a brocaded number done in gold and white, had her taking in a sharp breath of surprise at the heavy memories it triggered. The gown, used in the movie *Holly Goes to Paris* ten years earlier, took her back to when she was a girl still living in the cottage in the woods.

She, like all the sisters, had been taken as a toddler to be raised by a rotating entourage of Gardiennes. For her first eleven years, she'd lived a humble, barefoot life in the two-room cottage tucked under a pair of fat oaks where she'd learned the disciplines of her craft. She'd spent a year with Esmerelda and her levitation spells, a year with Amelia learning the importance of coupling rhyming words, and a year with Desdemona channeling the power of gemstones. Then came Lydia, Gertrude, and Cassiopeia with their books and potions, followed by Beatrix, Myrtle, Charlotte, and Mathilda, each of whom had taught her how to shape her glamour to create illusions within illusions. She'd also learned to cook, sew, and build a fire with Genevieve so that by the time she'd arrived at the eve of her twelfth birthday, she was certain she knew everything there was to know about the world.

And then Dorée had arrived.

Until then, Celeste had considered her everyday wool frock suitable attire for any situation she met. The simple dress was practical, easy to repair, and required only a pair of clogs and a shawl when going outside. Then she met Dorée, and her concept of what sufficed as fashion and etiquette was set spinning like a plate balanced on the end of a broomstick. She was taken to Paris by coach and presented to the fashion houses of Callot Soeurs, Paul Poiret, and Coco Chanel, where haute couture was born. She was introduced to gowns and tiaras, skirts and jackets, well-heeled leather shoes and riding ensembles with boots for when a horse was more practical than walking or riding in a car. In the city, she was taught how to drink tea and maneuver a place setting at dinner and choose wine and style her hair. But it was the clothes she loved the most.

The first dress she fell in love with was a fussy white-and-gold brocade gown with a fur collar and wide, draping sleeves. Dorée was patient yet firm in the matter of selecting appropriate styles for one's age and station. How you presented yourself to the world helped shape the glamour into the vision you hoped to achieve. You were already halfway there if you looked the part that you wanted others to see. The remaining balance of the illusion was wrapped in stardust, aided by a trustworthy animal companion. For Celeste's twelfth birthday celebration, she was introduced to Sebastian, whom she loved right away. *And* she got to keep the white-and-gold brocade dress.

Celeste's mind drifted back to the present. Her education in fashion had no doubt colored her opinion of the craftsmanship on display in the wardrobe room, but something tangible was lacking. There were certainly a few standouts that piqued her imagination, but most of the women's costumes felt too prim and formal, too steeped in the stiffness of the Edwardian period. The designs expressed no passion, no *joie de vivre*. No drama. Perhaps they had been in keeping with the director's vision for his characters, but she rather thought the fallen soufflé of fresh ideas rested on the costume designer's shoulders. Which might explain why Isaac Jacobi might be hesitant to promote Rose to senior seamstress, despite her obvious skills. It wasn't a huge leap to imagine her ideas bleeding through the noise of his anemic designs. A tempting thought.

Celeste was taking a last decisive glance at the rack of period costumes when she playfully pulled out a black feather boa. The card pinned to the end said it had recently been used in a speakeasy flick. She slid the boa over her shoulders, feeling the feathers slink against her skin. A breath of chilly air settled around her. Despite the warm day, the temperature inside the wardrobe room dropped several degrees. Gooseflesh appeared on her arms. Celeste's insides clenched, as though something had begun to slither through her intestines, consuming her body heat until it felt like ice coated her stomach. Alarmed, she dropped the boa and backed out of the room, but when she reached the double doors, they refused to open. She nearly rattled them off their hinges trying to escape and was near the point of calling out for help when they suddenly parted and a man in a three-piece suit strode in.

"Who are you?" he demanded as Celeste backstepped toward the chaise lounge to keep from stumbling. The man moved threateningly closer. "And what are you doing in my wardrobe during lunch hour?" His upper lip was hidden behind a neatly trimmed mustache, and his black hair was slicked back and parted so perfectly down the middle of his scalp Celeste could almost imagine the white line had been carved there with a straight-edged blade. His brows threaded together as he nodded slowly. "I know what you girls get up to in here. But this isn't a place for grubby hands to go through the racks looking for party dresses to wear out to the nightclubs only to spill gin on them and return them soiled."

Celeste shook her head when it dawned on her that this must be Isaac Jacobi. "I'm the new girl, but I wasn't—"

"Don't bother denying it. All of you workshop girls try to get away with it at some point. I'll get a lock for the door if it doesn't stop." He leaned over the desk and picked up the pair of lace-up boots Celeste had just delivered. He examined the gold paint Rose had used to embellish the leather and shook his head. "Blast that girl. I told her to add a touch of gold to the heel to match the laces, not redesign the entire aesthetic. She's painted everything." He let out an exasperated sigh. "Never mind. There's no time to fix them now." He held the boots up in front of

Celeste. "Here. Redeem yourself by taking these to Stage Two. Dolores is waiting for them."

"Dolores?"

"Yes, Dolores Diaz." Jacobi rolled his eyes as though it pained him to speak to one so below his station. "For heaven's sake, she's the new star of the production." He shoved the boots in Celeste's hands and shooed her away. "Go, go, go. They're waiting."

The harsh send-off left Celeste reimagining the bristled end of a besom hitting her behind, the same one Esmerelda had used to chase her out of the cottage after she'd nearly set the furniture on fire with her immature magic. Hugging the boots to her chest, Celeste twirled around, slightly bewildered, until she found the exit, then bolted for the only door onto the back lot she knew how to find.

CHAPTER EIGHT

Diamond Dust

Alone in the hallway, Celeste exhaled in relief. The man's energy was dizzying. Grating in the same way a dust storm kicks sand in your eyes when all you want to do is cross the road. She'd experienced the volatile energy of the creative spirit before, but Jacobi's was layered with the temperament of a rabid dog. His energy was expansive and artistic, yet defensive and full of ambition. His intense craving for recognition and attention had knocked her off center, so much so that she had to walk slowly with one hand pressed against the wall until she recovered her balance.

It was only when she stood in front of the door where she'd sneaked in that morning that she remembered she was meant to deliver the pair of boots she was holding. She had no idea where Stage Two was, but it had to be on the back lot somewhere. She peeked both ways down the hallway to make sure it was empty, then slipped outside. She'd just stepped onto the landing when she spotted the janitor emptying more wastepaper baskets into the outdoor bins.

"You must be new around here," he said, looking up. He replaced the lid on the bin with a slam. "Employees aren't generally allowed to use this as an exit, but we'll make an exception this time. Our secret."

The janitor smiled in the way most unassuming strangers did when they met one of her kind for the first time. "And you must be Charlie," she said, shielding her eyes against the midday sun, thankful he was willing to overlook the infraction. "Rose was telling me earlier about how kind you've been to her."

"Rose?" He scratched his bald head. "Oh, you mean that little sprite of a thing that sews the costumes in the back of the room. Hard worker with a head full of dreams, that one."

"That's right." Celeste surveyed the enormous back lot, grateful for the warmth of the sun as the chill from the wardrobe room hadn't quite left her body. "You couldn't point me in the direction of Stage Two, could you? I'm supposed to deliver these boots to a Ms. Diaz."

"Dolores Diaz. Now there's a rising star, if ever I saw one." The genial janitor pointed toward the center of the lot, where two huge warehouses stood. "Stage Two is the second one." He laughed at the obviousness of what he'd just said.

"Thanks, Charlie." Celeste took a quick scan of his hidden dreams, but he didn't seem to have any filed away in that bald head of his. Not one wish for himself floating around in his humors. Strange, but then perhaps a man like him was already settled into life and perfectly content with things just the way they were. Lucky man, she thought as she traipsed off to find Ms. Diaz.

The stage buildings were thoughtfully marked by huge numbers on the outside walls. Celeste located Stage Two and walked through an open garage door big enough to let an elephant pass through. She considered dropping the lace-up boots on the edge of a set made to look like a tumbledown tavern with rickety tables, a terra-cotta floor, and a faded poster of a bullfighter on the wall. Surely someone connected with the film who knew what to do with the green boots would find them and get them to the right person, but she didn't like leaving the task undone. She ventured onto a haphazard trail behind the set that snaked under ladders, over stacks of two-by-fours, and around fat cables laid out from one end of the set to the other.

Having cleared the chaos, she nearly hit her head on one of three enormous round spotlights big enough to signal a ship offshore. All three of the lights were pointed kitty-corner at a completely different set, where an Old West saloon was set up, complete with swinging doors and a polished wooden bar. Two corners of opposing reality in an artificial world, she thought as she gazed at the unfinished walls and missing ceiling that revealed the warehouse rafters in the open space above.

"At last." A woman in riding trousers, knee-high boots, and a binder tucked under her arm grabbed Celeste by the elbow. "This way," she said and led her in the other direction, down the narrow alley between the stage and the warehouse wall. A man and woman sat in the corridor on folding chairs in near darkness. One chair had D. DIAZ stenciled on the back and the other read O. SINCLAIR. The pair sipped coffee from thermos mugs and laughed as though they were on a picnic, while others busily worked around them adjusting lights, dabbing paint on wooden tavern signs, and running a lint brush over a man's floor-length black cape. The woman, whose sleek brunette hair was parted down the middle and pulled into a knot at the back of her head, set her mug aside and jumped out of her chair when Celeste approached carrying the boots. The green and gold gown she wore was a perfect match to the lace-up boots.

"Costume department finally came through," the woman in riding trousers announced.

"They made it!" Dolores Diaz took the boots from Celeste and set them on the floor. "Look at all the beautiful gold details painted on the sides," she said and slipped her stockinged feet into the insoles. She laced them up, did a little tap dance, and smiled, showing off her white teeth behind red-rouged lips. Her eyes were painted with thick black eyeliner, and her face had been smoothed over with heavy pancake makeup that gave her an otherworldly appearance. The woman dazzled the eye, as though she were made of diamond dust. "You tell Jacobi he did a splendid job on these," she said and winked.

"Actually, it was Rose in wardrobe who thought of the embellishments," Celeste said, thinking there was little harm in planting a few good thoughts about Rose in the actress's head. "She's the one who painted them. Very talented seamstress. Designs her own dresses too."

"Rose? Really. Isn't she the shy one in the back of the sewing room who always has her head down working? Whenever she's assigned to one of my costumes, I always get the feeling she's just passing through on her way to bigger things."

"That's her."

"Well, the details are *perfecto*," Dolores exclaimed. "Exactly what I envisioned for my character. They may not show on camera much, but I'll know they're special."

"I'll let her know you were pleased." Celeste lingered a second longer, taking inventory of the woman's hopes and dreams before any others crowded in with their unspoken desires. The starlet's aspirations soared like a comet across outer space, and for a moment Celeste wondered if she was meant to take on another protégé. But the notion quickly dissolved when the woman walked back to her chair followed by a cloud of spent dreams that drifted to the floor.

The image was confusing, like experiencing hunger pangs ten minutes after eating. Celeste blamed the puzzlement on her inexperience, yet something nagged at her. The woman's strong pull meant something. It was why, on a hunch, she'd planted the image of Rose and her talent in Dolores's mind. Somehow a connection between them would pay off.

Satisfied she'd fulfilled the *true* reason she'd been sent to deliver the boots to the actress, Celeste walked back toward the open garage door. It was there she caught sight of a head full of wavy brown hair and eyes as blue as the summer sky. Nick West was headed her way. She didn't think she'd been spotted yet, so she gripped her pendant and amplified her glamour while she shrank into the shadows. After her long morning of coaxing stubborn events to move in Rose's direction, followed by the odd experience she'd had in the wardrobe room, she wasn't up to facing the charismatic Mr. West. Besides, if he was the Hollywood prince she expected he was, and she was supposed to marry off her protégé to him, his destiny was already spoken for. A thought that caused a minor pinch in her chest.

From the shadows, she observed Nick speaking with another man, who gestured with his hands while he talked. Something about a pitch for a new movie. Before they reached the door to Stage Two, Nick's secretary flagged him down. She had a big smile on her face as she handed him a piece of paper with several rows of figures on it. "Numbers are in. *The Mummy's Tomb* beat Universal and Paramount at the box office for the second week in a row. Looks like you have another hit on your hands."

Nick glanced at the numbers on the sheet of paper, then handed it back with a nod. "Nice to get some good news for a change," he said, though Celeste didn't quite understand the context of his remark. Had something bad happened at the studio? Nick and the other man continued into the building, passing within inches of Celeste. Close enough she could smell the laundry soap on Nick's professionally cleaned and pressed shirt.

Celeste sighed. He was a handsome and successful man, and Rose was clever and ambitious, but she knew in her heart an advantageous marriage wasn't the best use of her imagination in the situation. Nor would it honor the individual desires of her two subjects. There was so much more potential to be had by catapulting Rose's talent. To showcase her designs according to her innermost dreams. But what kind of trouble would she be in if she ignored Dorée's suggestion of making a love match? What could happen to an initiate who didn't follow the advice of the eldest Gardienne? She'd already been banished to another continent after letting her instincts override instructions. What else might they do to her? On the other hand, what kind of Gardienne would she make if she didn't have the wherewithal to follow her own instincts?

CHAPTER NINE

Curses, Plagues, and Other Assorted Maladies

Back at the bungalow, Celeste kicked off her shoes and stretched out on the bed, trying to flush the last remnants of angst from her body. With her head cradled against the pillow, she stared up at the ceiling, replaying her day at the studio as if it were a movie—images of Rose stitching the final touches on her dress, Jacobi sneering at her as though she were gum on the bottom of his shoe, the janitor offering help when her body still shook from the chill that enveloped her. It had been a whirlwind day of new experiences—some good, some confusing. But at the end of it all, it was Nick who filled her head with the most pleasant thoughts, from the cut of his suit on his lean body to his relaxed, confident posture while walking. Funny how she was the one with magic in her blood, yet this prince of Hollywood seemed to be doing all the enchanting.

"What'd you make of Nick after following him all morning?" she asked her companion.

Sebastian dropped the key to the trunk from his mouth onto the bed, then shook out his fur.

"Yes, I know. We'll recharge in a minute, but we need to talk about him." Celeste gazed back up at the ceiling, entertaining impossible thoughts just a little bit longer. "He might be the key to changing Rose's future, you know." He could also change hers if she wasn't careful, but she left that part unsaid.

Sebastian stood on his hind legs and swiped his forearm in the air. His eyes stared straight ahead, sincere but steady.

"Eyes on the prize type." Celeste sat up, considering. "Work is his priority. He's a decision-maker." The stoat nodded. "So, he's busy building a legacy?"

Sebastian ran off the bed and dug in Celeste's bag. He returned with a letter in his teeth. He spit it out on the bed and quickly wiped his face dry with his paws.

"You were very stealthy today." Celeste unfolded the stolen letter and saw it was addressed to Nick at West Coast Studios. Leery of why her companion had stolen the letter, she felt her brows tighten the more she read. It was a notice of collection for overdue payments on the property's mortgage. A threat to call in the loan or else foreclose on the property if the sum wasn't paid within thirty days. "This claims the studio is in arrears," she said, hardly believing it. Just that afternoon, she'd witnessed Nick get surprisingly good news on whopper profits for one of their latest films.

The stoat crawled to the bedside table, where a copy of *Motion Picture Stories* magazine was half-hidden beneath the base of the telephone. He tapped a foot on the title of one of the cover's featured inside stories: **Is West Coast Studios Cursed?**

Cursed?

Celeste could hardly believe it. The author of the article was apparently just as surprised as its reader by the dramatic turnaround of the studio's fortunes. Despite making movies that audiences adored and that brought in huge revenues—including the hugely popular *London After Dark*—financial and logistical problems dogged the physical studio location itself, from faulty plumbing to a mysterious fire that destroyed a new film stage to insurance-coverage mishaps causing the studio to go over budget on building costs for the latest expansion of the lot. Add to that the number of on-set accidents involving cast and crew and it was impossible not to raise the specter of a curse in some of the employees' minds.

"It says the rumors are dragging down the studio's financial prospects and scaring off new investors, with some people blaming the curse on the success of the horror movie itself." A shiver ran over Celeste's skin at the mention of a curse. She set the magazine down in a near trance. Sebastian cuddled closer to her, offering his fur for her to pet. "What if they're onto something?" she asked. "I felt something there today. In the wardrobe department. Something cold and . . ." She paused remembering the icy sensation that had come over her. ". . . hollow. A dark void I thought I was going to fall into. Like standing at the top of the stairs above a dark cellar and getting lightheaded." Her body was sensitive, but her emotions more so. If there was an actual curse, she may have felt the ripples of its effect pass through her. But who in America was capable of such a thing? And why? And how would it affect her work with Rose?

Celeste stroked the stoat's soft brown fur until the dread she'd been carrying all afternoon began to abate. "You did well today," she said. "Tomorrow, you'll have to sneak that letter back into his office. He'll be missing something as important as that, but if you slip it in between the trash can and the desk, he'll chalk it up to a simple misplacement."

People did it all the time. They mistook small interventions by Gardiennes for their own genuine forgetfulness or bad luck—things like missing keys, an expected package not showing up in the post, even a flat tire on the way to work. Some people blamed colleagues and underlings for sabotage and were later humbled when their lost items eventually showed up right where they'd left them. Part of the job of guiding a protégé to their destiny required gathering information on their orbit of acquaintances. A "borrowed" wallet with photos and receipts inside could provide useful information on who and what were important. A walk inside someone's house using "borrowed" keys while they were at work was invaluable for understanding quirks or weaknesses and how they could help advance a protégé's fate. Naturally, stalling someone's arrival to work by giving them a flat tire allowed ample time to snoop through their place of employment to look for similar clues.

Nick's letter certainly proved insightful, if not discouraging. He was charming, handsome, and absolutely dedicated to success, but his "royal" status was showing some tarnish, if this movie magazine article was to be believed. She reasoned the presence of a Gardienne on the studio lot, or at least an initiate, ought to provide some good luck in his future business affairs, but he wasn't—couldn't be—her sole focus for advancing Rose anymore. There was simply too much instability surrounding him to make a good love match for a scrap of a girl with prospects of her own.

There was some relief in the decision, and yet the idea that something was wrong at the studio nagged at Celeste. The chill she'd experienced earlier had felt almost sinister, the way it had tried to snake inside her. If Jacobi hadn't entered the wardrobe when he had and allowed her to get outside in the sunshine to recover, she wasn't sure what might have happened. But a curse? She supposed it was possible.

Back to feeling unsettled, Celeste took the key and unlocked the trunk. Sebastian was right—they needed to recharge their magic. But first she needed more insight on the matter. And since her fellow Fées Gardiennes were over five thousand miles away, and the only way to get in touch was through a telegram, she was forced to rely on the books Dorée's mouse had packed for her.

There were five disappointingly thin books tied up with a red ribbon at the bottom of the trunk. Celeste almost laughed. When she'd been brought up in the cottage, an entire room had been dedicated to reference books. Cassiopeia had needed to conjure up a floor-to-ceiling built-in bookshelf just to house the secondhand editions that Gertrude had found in the back rooms of fashionable Paris salons. Every subject had been at Celeste's fingertips in those days. Now, alone in the far-flung reaches of America, she was relegated to the subject matter a mouse had packed for her.

After evaluating her options, a treatise on curses, plagues, and other assorted maladies with supernatural origins seemed the most helpful. She thumbed through the pages, looking for clues to anything associated with a freezing chill. Ghosts seemed to be the number one cause when it came to dropping temperatures, but it would be remarkable to encounter a haunting capable of affecting the financials of a studio as apparently successful as West Coast Studios had been, even if people did want to blame the continued misfortune on some monster featured in a horror movie. Although she couldn't completely rule it out. Who knew what heap of supernatural rot lay hidden under the glitz and glamour of Hollywood moviemaking.

Sebastian poked his nose in the book, leaving a wet smudge on the page about jinxes, while she continued reading. Mostly toothless, jinxes were small curses that left the victim annoyed and irritable more than anything else. The small setbacks, inconveniences, and feelings of bad luck were what set jinxes apart from full-on curses. "Perhaps that's all we're dealing with," Celeste said, unconvinced by her optimism. "After all, the cold sensation went away as soon as I left the wardrobe department. And Nick did get surprisingly good news on his latest picture soon after. Maybe some of my magic is rubbing off on the place now, and things are already turning around. Maybe everything will be okay."

Sebastian kept his paw on the page and looked up at her. "Yes, I know we still need to be vigilant. But didn't Dorée advise sending us here because she knew we wouldn't run into any . . ." She shrugged at the ether. ". . . interference?"

Her companion tested the air with his nose, then pointed it toward the jar of gemstones.

"Very well," Celeste said, setting up the jewels for their bonding spell. "You know I'm overly sensitive to the energy around me. Always have been. I'm sure the studio is just experiencing the normal ups and downs of a business in the throes of new growth. People gossip and make things up to sell their magazines all the time." Sebastian stretched out over the open book and waited until the gems were lined up in the right order. "Anyway, I started working on Rose's trajectory today. If we can move enough obstacles out of her way, she should start seeing a clearer pathway to a few small career successes within a day or so." Sebastian cocked his head at her. "I know. I'm being terribly optimistic again, and it would have been easier to do some quick matchmaking for Rose like Dorée suggested, but you should have seen the gown she made. It was divine. She really isn't the sort to benefit intrinsically from an advantageous marriage. Her star path is meant to head in a different direction." She was pleased she'd finally said it out loud, a declaration always the first step to turning an idea into reality.

When Sebastian made no objection, Celeste set out the gemstones, preparing to boost their glamour and finally shake off the dread they'd brought home with them. "Of course, the dress she made will be sold by morning. I've seen to that. This change of direction is for the best. We're on our way, Sebastian. We're really on our way."

The stoat did his part in the bonding ritual, then went back to curling up on the page about jinxes and let out a little sigh.

CHAPTER TEN

Borrowed Keys and Old Ghosts

The next morning Celeste and Sebastian were up before the sun. She'd often been warned the hours a Gardienne kept were unconventional, especially when doing reconnaissance on a new protégé. Their work required peeking in on people's lives at all hours of the day and night to understand how they might guide and shape future events. And here she was exploring an unfamiliar neighborhood on the south side of Los Angeles in the predawn hours just as the robins were waking in their nests. She supposed she ought to feel nervous, being in unfamiliar surroundings, but the thrill of discovery overrode caution.

Celeste shut off the headlights on the Pierce-Arrow and parked the car a block away from Rose's house. She and Sebastian watched as a lamp came on in the modest home's front room. The curtains were half-drawn, but shadows moved on the other side. In a back bedroom, the young woman got ready for work by pinning her hair up and tying a scarf around her neck. Meanwhile, her father ate breakfast in the kitchen before heading off to his job at a warehouse near the docks, unpacking crates of coffee, tea, and raw silk—information all gleaned from a morning of sitting side by side with the young seamstress the day before, chitchatting about this, that, and other innocuous details about her homelife.

The quiet American residential street wasn't what Celeste had expected. At home, the city houses were stitched together, one on top of another, all along the narrow cobblestone streets. An apartment could have multiple levels, but the imprint was small and nearly always crowded up against its neighbors. In America, everything was always spreading, growing, expanding. The houses were built on wide streets laid out on a defined grid where two cars could easily pass each other on the road with room to spare. But long stretches of undeveloped plots still occupied the terrain between houses in this part of the city, lending it more of a work-in-progress feel.

Sebastian pricked his ears at a noise in the vacant lot to their left and pleaded for the chance to explore. While he jumped out of the car to go hunt, Celeste reflected on how similar Rose's house was to the forest cottage she'd been raised in, apart from the desertlike surroundings. The house was a humble square shape with a slanted roof to scuttle the rain when it eventually fell. There was a front porch, but not like the neighbors' across the street, with their covered portico and trellis of pink bougainvillea growing up the side. Rose's house was modest in comparison. Someone had made the effort to plant two blue jacaranda trees in front that she intuited would someday be full of purple blooms, but they were still fragile saplings, and the rest of the yard was mostly dirt and rocks. Celeste closed her eyes and listened to the earth breathing in and out. It begged for water, but the grass seeds buried in the topsoil were ready to emerge at the first taste of moisture. "Soon," she whispered, smelling rain coming in off the ocean.

Before the first rays of sunlight cleared the horizon, the front door opened. Rose, carrying a purse and a fabric sewing bag with a wooden handle, called inside to remind her father to leave the back door unlocked. "I must have dropped my keys at work," she explained, then walked toward the next street over to catch the trolley that would take her north to the studio. Sebastian climbed back inside the car, swiping downy bird feathers off his face while they waited for the father to leave in his rusted Model T minutes later.

"Time to go," Celeste said and slipped the stoat in her purse. Using her glamour to appear to the overly curious as little more than morning fog creeping over the sidewalk, she exited the car and walked up the front steps to the house, where the name Downey appeared on the mailbox in hand-painted letters. Using Rose's "borrowed" keys, she opened the front door and stepped inside the modest living room. The space was neatly organized, with a telephone tucked into an alcove by the door, a worn but attractive sofa under the window, two plush chairs that had been reupholstered in a crushed velvet that Celeste suspected were leftover scraps from the studio sewing room, and a secondhand coffee table that had been polished with beeswax. A faint honey scent lingered above the surface.

Celeste took a quick look at the kitchen next, where the morning dishes had already been washed and set out on a towel to dry. She raised a brow in appreciation, seeing where Rose had learned her work ethic from. Next to the clean dishes were a set of graduated glass jars. One filled with rice, another with flour, and a third with sugar half-gone. "Nothing wrong with a sweet tooth," she said to Sebastian, who sniffed around the checkered linoleum tiles. An electric two-slice toaster and coffee percolator—still warm—occupied the other end of the countertop. In the center of the kitchen sat a small table and two chairs. A floral tablecloth had been draped over the top, and a blue mixing bowl with a chip on its rim sat in the center. Unlike the outside, the house's interior was cozy and clean, the reflection of pride and hard work coming together to make a comfortable family home.

The effort stirred a perceptible longing in Celeste for the family she'd never known. All the mornings at the breakfast table she never got to share with siblings. The mundane conversations about school or work between a mother and daughter while peeling potatoes. Or the simple offer of a glass of lemonade to a father just in from doing yard work. She'd been raised by kind people certainly, but the Fées Gardiennes weren't her blood kin and never would be, despite the well-worn emphasis on sisterhood.

"Let's have a look at the bedroom," she said to Sebastian, who peered at her over the top of a trash can, nose twitching.

There were three small bedrooms in the house—two with modest beds and one at the end of the hallway that was set up as a sewing room. Celeste's instincts drew her into the room where a black sewing machine mounted on a treadle table with cast-iron legs sat front and center. It adjoined a longer worktable that held a bolt of fabric, a pincushion, and a sad iron that required heating over the stovetop. A headless dummy stood in the corner with a scarf and string of beads wrapped around its neck.

"Rose claims the sewing machine keeps breaking down." Celeste sat on the wooden stool tucked beneath the table and pressed her foot against the floor pedal. The balance wheel spun as it should, but the needle didn't move. The drive belt had tension, the gears were engaging from foot pedal to balance wheel, but something between there and the needle mechanism wasn't clicking. Sebastian climbed onto the table and sniffed around the bobbin winder. When engaged, the winder prevented the needle from operating, but the pulley wasn't in contact with the wheel. The needle should've been working fine. He scrunched up his nose at the trouble. Celeste peeked at the components too. Everything appeared in order to her, but then the stoat climbed onto the balance wheel for a closer inspection. The knob on the end was loose. "Give it a turn to tighten it," she said. Her companion did as he was instructed and put his front paws on the knob, but it didn't tighten. The dial spun around, tossing Sebastian so he had to scramble onto the table.

"That's not normal." Celeste tried the dial for herself, but as soon as her fingers touched the metal, they were met with a freezing sensation that nearly burned her skin before she pulled away. A second encounter with an isolated pocket of freezing cold? Couldn't be a coincidence. "This machine's been tampered with," she said, scooting away while Sebastian licked his paws on top of the table.

Celeste clasped a hand over her mouth, wondering who had a stake in sabotaging a young woman's sewing machine. It made no sense, but neither did the presence of a bone-biting cold infiltrating a wardrobe department in the middle of Hollywood. The incidents had to be related. The sensation felt distinctly magical in origin, bordering on malevolent as it bit her skin. She hovered her hand over the metal again, careful not to make contact. A detectable pulsing energy embedded in the dial left a prickling sensation on her palm even from an inch away. As a Gardienne, she was naturally sensitive to magical fluctuations around her, but she was certain the cold would be undetectable to Rose or anyone else in the house.

Celeste rubbed her hand again. A jinx? But who could have planted such a specific hex in the young woman's sewing room? Unless the energy somehow hitchhiked home with Rose from the studio? There were, of course, other beings with skills in magic all across Europe—sorceresses, necromancers, occultists. It only made sense they'd have a foothold in America as well. But why aim malicious magic at this particular woman? Why hurt the studio? What did they hope to gain?

Celeste took several steps backward without realizing until she bumped into a chest of drawers against the wall. She turned at the sound of something tipping over—she'd knocked a lamp on its side. Righting it, she noticed a second sketchbook sitting on top of the dresser. Celeste peeled back the cover. Inside were dozens of drawings of women's and men's clothing. While the book Rose took to work was of her own dress designs, this one contained costume ideas for pictures the studio was working on or movies already released. Even with no real knowledge of what was required of a costume for a movie, Celeste could see the inspired details, the flair for the dramatic, the love of design in the depictions. She pulled one loose that she was certain was of the actress she'd met the day before, Dolores Diaz. In the sketch, the actress was wearing the same nineteenth-century-era dress she'd had on while waiting for the boots so she could film the street scene outside the cantina. The boots that Rose had painted were delicately drawn on Dolores's feet complete with the design in gold paint. Seeing the talent displayed in the sketches only reinforced Celeste's belief that the young seamstress was destined for a bright career with her help. A thought that was also terrifying. What if something else was going on besides a few randomly placed jinxes? What if someone else knew about Rose's potential?

But then, of course, someone else *did* know about Rose's talent. The energy had followed Celeste around the home since the moment she'd entered. The house breathed with the electrostatic pulse of the mother still watching and waiting for her daughter to bloom. Celeste didn't know how long dead the woman was, but even old ghosts still carried dreams and aspirations for the ones they'd loved in life. If only she could spill the beans about the source of the jinx.

Celeste stuffed the drawings back in their folder. Something *was* going on at the studio, something that had started before she'd arrived. If there truly was a curse, there had to be an explanation. Likely a rival of Nick's was behind it. Or a disgruntled ex-employee with connections to the city's magical underbelly. Every village in Europe had one. Go down any side street on the dodgy end of any town and you'd find a collection of conjurers with enough skill to cause a little mayhem. They'd set up shop in the back of a pharmacy, or a gas station, or maybe even behind a door advertising an actual psychic. So why not in Los Angeles? But if so, this was the first one she'd encountered who could manipulate temperatures on command.

CHAPTER ELEVEN

Devoré Velvet and Poison

"She'll figure it out soon enough." Anaïs tugged on her bottom lip as she stood on the porch across the street from the seamstress's house. She didn't dare step out from behind the bougainvillea-covered trellis until Celeste returned to her car. "We'll have to move fast once she does," she said to her rook.

Gideon cawed softly from atop her shoulder, so she tossed him a fat beetle for remaining quiet while they'd waited. The rook shook his head as the insect fought against sliding down his gullet. Anaïs petted his soft neck feathers, considering her options. What had Dorée been thinking, sending a novice to a city like this on her own? The young woman made such an easy mark. There wasn't even in any sport in it.

Anaïs waited until she was certain Celeste had driven away. The light came on in the house behind them, so she and Gideon bolted for the Bentley two-seater parked around the corner. Night had hidden their appearance when she and Gideon had followed Celeste to this miserable street at the crack of dawn, but now she had to cloak them both in glamour to get away unseen. She swooped her arm out, letting her gauzy scarf flutter over their heads, surrounding them in a magical camouflage until they were safely away.

The Bentley fit Anaïs like a glove, with its brown leather seats, sporty body, and sleek black paint. She flew down the road, feeling noticeably less wind blow through her hair after getting it bobbed above her collar. The minor rebellion had felt like cutting off a century of patriarchy. Honestly, she was glad the old alliances with the kingdoms had fallen apart. Now her kind were free to do some serious work and start clearing the way for women to achieve a solid place of their own in this man-eat-man world.

Anaïs shifted gears and headed into the scrubland hills above Hollywood. Gideon flew behind her, soaring on morning updrafts as she took the curves, climbing higher. His eye didn't miss a trick. He knew exactly where she was going, and then he was gone, soaring toward their destination in a straight line in the sky.

Gideon was already perched on the roof of the quaint Mediterranean-style house when Anaïs parked in the driveway forty-five minutes later. The grounds along the flagstone path were lush with green ferns and a few native chaparrals. She plucked a wild rose off a stem before walking up the steps and tapping on the door. Her rook squawked in warning as she approached, but he didn't know everything. Holding the pink flower to her nose, she posed coquettishly as the front door opened.

"Well, look what the cat dragged in." A man wearing pleated white pants and a matching tennis sweater with a black V at the neckline stood in the doorway. His posture shifted from relaxed and curious to see who was at his door so early in the morning to outright cocky as he leaned against the doorframe. "Why am I not surprised you found me halfway around the world. Good God, what have you done to your hair?" He waved her in, glancing briefly at his neighbors' houses to gauge who might have seen her arrive. "Come in, come in. What an unexpected surprise."

"That's what makes them surprises, Edward." Anaïs untied her black evening wrap, revealing a red-and-bronze devoré dress beneath. The pattern of the burnout velvet mimicked a flock of birds in flight, appearing to flap their wings whenever she moved. She'd been wearing it since leaving for the speakeasy the night before. "Do you like it?" she asked, cupping her palm against the back of her bobbed cut. "You know me. I just had to try something fun."

"*Très chic*," he said. His tone was too placating, but she understood his effort to be diplomatic. He invited her to make herself comfortable. It was only after she shrugged off her jacket, suggesting her visit wouldn't be brief, that he said he'd find them something to eat. After conjuring up a tray with two coffees and two slices of sponge cake from his kitchen, the occultist sat opposite her, sipping slowly while waiting for her to explain what she was doing in America.

"Did I interrupt your tennis outing?" she asked, nudging her chin toward his outfit.

Edward glanced down at his attire. "A court date with a young starlet eager to be photographed out with a mature and sophisticated man, but never mind that. What do you want?"

Anaïs looked toward the back window overlooking the valley. "I need a favor."

"Naturally." Edward set his cup down. "And how much is this favor going to cost me?"

"Nothing, if we get the results we're looking for."

"We?"

She raised her shoulder coyly. "Well, nothing ventured, nothing gained." Setting her cup down, Anaïs opened her handbag. "You know I'm rubbish at potions and elixirs. I need something that can break a bond." She opened a floral enameled pillbox to show him three pear-cut gemstones inside. On the small side, but still worth a look.

Edward raised an eyebrow. "Between?"

At least he was listening. A very good omen. She snapped the box shut again. "Two people. There's something forming between them that can't be allowed to continue. But if it does, it must be reversed full force."

"Up to your old tricks again, I see."

"You've no idea," Anaïs said under her breath as the occultist, her former lover, stood and went to a cupboard in a small study off the main room. The clinking of small bottles was a positive sign of progress.

"Is the bond chemical or more *mercurial*?" he called.

She interpreted his emphasis on "mercurial" as a slight dig at her kind. Fair enough, she supposed, but she refused to rise to the bait. After considering the question seriously, she answered, "A little of both, I think, but lean more heavily on the mercurial side."

Edward poked his head around the corner and rolled his eyes. "Of course."

While he rattled away in his cupboard, Anaïs stood at the window to take in the view of the city below visible in the notch between hillsides. She almost wished she'd come up during the night. To make love on the deck under the stars with that vista in the background . . . the awkward reunion might have been worth all that she risked in coming to see Edward. It had been three years since she'd last seen him. He'd been a vagabond when they first met, traveling Europe in the years following the war. An American expat eager to wander like so many once the meaning of life had been upended by so much death. Free spirits indulging the whims of human wants and needs. Edward hummed a French tune while he worked in the other room. A deliberate ploy to stir her emotions? Hearing his voice, reminded of their wild youth, she allowed herself to briefly succumb to the spell of sweet memories floating in the ether.

Edward emerged from the back room holding two vials. "I suspect in this case, you're going to need two elixirs." He gave the bottle containing a dark liquid a little shake. "This one will need to be administered first. Each subject gets half of the contents."

Anaïs pulled herself back to the here and now and accepted the bottle cautiously. "What does it do?"

"Think of it like a paint thinner for peeling the magic off enchantments."

She twisted off the cap and took a sniff, turning her face away. "Smells like paint thinner." She quickly capped the bottle again and studied the contents through the glass. "Is it toxic?"

Edward smiled at her with that wicked grin of his. The one that made the span between her hips spasm with want. "A real killer," he said. "*If* used incorrectly. In this case, a half dose will merely loosen the bond between the two people. But both must swallow it for it to work as intended."

A complication, but not impossible, she supposed. "And the other?"

Edward inched closer and opened his hand to reveal an empty bottle. "Alas, I'm all out of the necessary ingredients for this one." She felt his breath sweep over her neck. "You'll have to come back for it. Perhaps later tonight," he suggested as he grazed her shoulder with his finger to slide off the strap of her dress.

"Just how important is the second bottle?" She looked at him with a slight pout on her lips. "It's quite the long, winding drive up here."

"The second potion is for the side effects."

"Side effects?" She slipped her strap back in place before he could kiss her bare shoulder.

He made a small grumbling noise in the back of his throat before stepping back. "Think of the effects of the first bottle like a coat of tar that flows over the skin. That coating dissolves the bond by smothering it, but it can also cause suffocation of the person's magical abilities. A sort of blockage." He waved the empty bottle to tempt her. "This one will restore the person you're trying to help. Worth coming back for, yes?"

Anaïs smiled like a cat about to devour a songbird. "Thank you, Edward. You've been inspirational, as usual."

"Always here when the need gets too great." He straightened his tennis sweater and exhaled. "By the way, how *did* you find me this time?"

"That luscious cologne of yours," Anaïs said. "I'd sniff it out anywhere." It wasn't the case, of course. She'd received a letter from a friend saying they'd crossed paths with him in California recently.

Thinking there might be an occasion to call on him should she ever decide to take the plunge and visit the far reaches of America, she'd arranged for him to "chance" upon the opportunity to rent the perfect secluded house in Laurel Canyon. An offer he couldn't resist. But he didn't need to know any of that. He was much easier to control when uncertain. "I'll arrange to get the second bottle later," she said and grabbed her wrap. "You'll get your pay when you deliver the potion."

It was only when she was back in the Bentley that she second-guessed her quick exit. Edward could be so charming when he was concocting poisons to use on people.

CHAPTER TWELVE

Hokum and Illusion

Celeste stopped the car at an intersection, waiting for the arm on the traffic signal to turn green. The sun had cleared the ridge beyond Hollywood, casting a golden light on the hilltop. She found herself momentarily mesmerized by the simple beauty of nature's magic. It was woven into everything the sun touched, but as she glanced at her fellow drivers on the road, some eating a quick handheld breakfast behind the wheel, she knew few rarely noticed the potency of such quiet, benign magic. It was only when events arrived in the shape of a curse or hex that people took notice of the magic at work in the world. And people were noticing *something* at the studio that was making them superstitious.

There was evidence of that inside Rose's house too, but it didn't make any sense. Curses, jinxes, hexes, they didn't hop around. They weren't contagious like catching a cold. At least she didn't think so. The signal changed and she pulled the car over a few blocks ahead. She was still concerned about Sebastian's contact with the sewing machine.

"Let me see your paws." Celeste took her sunglasses off and held out her hand. The stoat stood on his hind legs, showing off his bloated stomach from the meal he'd eaten earlier. He ducked and bobbed as though nervous, but he eventually settled down and let her inspect his pads. "They appear all right. No blisters. No peeling." She inspected his eyes and found them clear and bright, confirming her belief that nothing was transferred through touch. So how did the same cold curse-like energy she felt at the studio end up at a seamstress's house ten miles away?

In need of answers, Celeste put the car in gear and headed north toward West Coast Studios. Only this time, instead of sneaking onto the premises to work in the sewing room, she intended to drive in through the front gate. Nick had offered to give her the full tour of the studio, and now she planned to take him up on it. Yes, she'd stood him up the day before, but he'd apparently been too busy to notice, based on Sebastian's observations. She tried not to dwell on the fact he hadn't missed her as she waited through yet another traffic signal. But if she could get inside the studio on Nick's arm, escorted by the man himself whose name was at the top of the stationery, she ought to get access to more areas than she'd seen so far. If there were more cold spots designed to sabotage the studio, or Rose for that matter, she needed to know about them.

Celeste drove the Pierce-Arrow up to the gate of West Coast Studios, stopping in front of the security booth. The guard had no record of her being approved to drive onto the lot, but after he shuffled through some paperwork, a note with her name conveniently appeared. The poor man apologized and opened the gate, directing her to park in the "reserved" area.

"You'll find Mr. West's office just through that door," the guard said. While he pointed, Celeste, still gripping her sapphire pendant, arranged for a stray dollar bill to appear in his trouser pocket the next time he searched for his keys.

After parking the car prominently outside Nick's office window, she applied a layer of lipstick using the rearview mirror. Luck and charms were one thing, but a little old-fashioned sex appeal could sometimes be just as effective for eliciting information. Especially when a handsome man was involved. But before she could step out of the car, Sebastian tugged at her sleeve with his teeth.

"What is it?"

Sebastian tugged again and she finally caught on. She was still wearing the plain cotton seamstress smock she'd put on that morning. She'd planned to go straight to work with Rose and continue bonding with her protégé, but the discovery at the house had changed everything. If someone had a grudge against the studio or the young woman, the path forward could be strewn with more obstacles than Celeste had imagined. After a quick check to her left and right, she traded the smock for a flowy dress in salmon pink. The skirt was slightly pleated and hit at the knee, while the chiffon sleeves were sheer and billowy. She wanted to appear flirty yet still be taken seriously, so she rejected the floppy hat and went with a basic cloche instead, though she did add a garnet jewel and white feather to the brim for a bit of polish.

She turned to Sebastian. "Better?" The pair quickly entered the studio's main door and got to work. The stoat hunkered down in Celeste's purse while she faced off with the secretary, who couldn't seem to remember where she'd put her appointment book. When she did finally locate it, her face betrayed her surprise at seeing an entry for a studio tour scheduled for Nick West.

"I could have sworn he was meant to be in a meeting with the insurance adjuster," the secretary said with pinched brows. She shook off her confusion and stepped out from behind the desk. "I'll escort you to his office."

Nick was on the phone when Celeste showed her face at his door. He stared at his desk, rubbing his right temple as if agitated by bad news. She knocked lightly against the doorframe to make him look up. When he saw her, whatever trouble was causing the creases in his forehead to deepen disappeared. His mouth opened slightly as though surprised. She smiled at him, and he pulled the phone away from his ear. "Hang on, Frank. I'll have to call you back." He set the receiver down without waiting for a reply. "I thought you'd given up on me," he said, mildly scolding her.

"I said I'd come by, didn't I?" Celeste had her hands clasped behind her back, gripping her handbag. "You'll find I'm a woman of my word . . . eventually."

Nick smiled in a way that made her insides quiver. "I'm glad to hear it." He stood and came around to the front of the desk and leaned against its side. "I didn't think I'd see you again."

"Well, I'm here now." She sat in the chair opposite his desk and covertly set her purse on the floor, where Sebastian slinked out of the opening with Nick's collection letter in his mouth. "And I'm dying to see the place."

He smiled again, more out of curiosity and confusion this time, so she stood and hooked her arm in his and let him think it was his idea to give her a tour. His hand covered hers, and a little piece of her unexpectedly melted like warm butter and sugar.

"Who are you, Celeste . . ." He dangled her first name in the air, hoping to catch the second, but she leaned into him slightly as they stepped out of the office, and he forgot all about his need to know.

The pair exited the main building after he explained that aside from the wardrobe department in the back, it was mostly offices occupied by writers and publicity people. "Boring stuff," he said as he walked her down the main street within the lot. The grounds were so vast the back lot was like a city within the city surrounded by make-believe. He pointed out many of the structures she'd seen on her own, only this time she got a rundown of what movie they were used in and which big names worked on them. She pretended to be suitably impressed, though she'd never heard of most of the American films he mentioned. But it didn't matter. She was transfixed by his vision of the place as they strolled toward one of the big warehouses labeled Stage Two.

"Now, here's where the magic is made," Nick said. To which Celeste had to stifle a smile.

Inside, Celeste recognized the set where she'd given Dolores the embellished boots. That corner of the stage was quiet now, so Nick escorted her around to the other side of the enormous building, where two other films were being made on two different sets. One stage was made to look like a frozen tundra, while the other was the Old West saloon she'd seen before. A string quartet accompanied the heroic effort of a Klondike miner on the tundra set as he held on to his partner, who'd fallen into a crevasse, while ten feet away on the Western set a raucous piano played in time with a choreographed fight between two cowhands. Above the tundra, a man shook a box of white soap flakes that sifted down over the actors to emulate snow. Back in the Old West, the director called "Cut!" after the fighters fell and broke a table in half right on cue.

"It's madness," Celeste said, covering her ears. "How do they keep it all straight?"

"A little bit of luck and a whole lot of hokum," Nick said with his trademark smile that leaned just a little on the self-deprecating side. "You wouldn't believe the stuff they make up in here."

"Morning, Mr. West," said one of the cowboys, dusting himself off.

Nick waved the man over and introduced him to Celeste as Archie Muller. It was only when she shook the man's hand that she recognized him from a pair of German films she'd enjoyed a few years earlier. "You're American," she blurted out in her own faintly European accent. Linguistics proved no barrier for the Fée. Their tongues could wrap around any language they encountered, though a trace of home naturally lingered in the shape of certain words.

The man laughed, and Celeste felt an uncommon pang of awe. He looked just like he had in the pictures . . . if you took away the ten-gallon hat, six-shooter, and leather chaps and replaced them with a top hat and tails.

"Yes, ma'am." He tipped his hat. "I've done a fair bit of work overseas, which is where you may have seen me before."

"Archie is doing a pair of Westerns with us now," Nick said. "If we can get this first one in the can, that is." The men exchanged a solemn glance. It wasn't difficult to discern the mutual look of determination in the face of a headwind of misfortune. "You'll be shooting the rest of the ranch scenes outside of town," he told Archie. "We'll splice it all together. It'll be fine."

A horn sounded on set that made Archie excuse himself. As the actor returned to the makeshift saloon, Nick directed Celeste back outside, explaining about the newest stage building under construction and how it had burned to the ground a month earlier. "We were set to begin shooting three pictures inside it, including Archie's next Western, when the warehouse caught fire just before dawn. By the time I drove over here, it was a total loss. We're lucky it didn't spread, thanks to a few quick thinkers," he said, pointing to the water tower that took center stage in the middle of the lot.

Celeste expressed as much empathetic glamour as she could, though she could hardly admit to already knowing the depths of his troubles. In response, Nick opened up, describing the list of things that had gone wrong in the past six months.

"It's like someone turned on the tap and a stream of bad luck gushed out," Nick said, not quite defeated, though his words were colored with confusion and disappointment. "First, one of the spotlights fell and shattered, nearly landing on poor Archie. Then there was the fire last month. And last week it was a pair of brand-new cameras that stopped working just as we were getting ready to make the sequel to *London After Dark* with Dolores Diaz and Oscar Sinclair. Cameras just froze up. Had to invest in a pair of rentals until we can get it sorted."

Celeste caught Sebastian's eye and nudged her chin toward Stage One for him to go find those cameras. She suspected he'd discover the same cold trace of jinxed sabotage on the cameras that she'd found on Rose's sewing machine.

"Crew members mutter the word 'cursed' under their breath every time something goes wrong," Nick said. "Investors are even starting to believe the rumors." He shrugged as they strolled past the old pyramid ruin. "And yet, despite everything, our production level has never been higher or more successful. I really shouldn't complain. It's just—"

"You're worried some of it might be deliberate?"

"That's right."

It was hard to quantify the full effect of the studio's apparent run of bad luck. Celeste sensed the energy on the lot was out of balance, but she didn't detect anything else that came close to the prickling cold she'd experienced in the wardrobe department the day before. If there was a jinx or hex behind the misfortune, there ought to be more of a general malaise hanging over the property. Instead, the bad luck appeared isolated to the incidents Nick had just mentioned. Which did make it sound more like sabotage.

Nick kicked a small rock out of the way as they walked along a row of shops and apartments made to look like a residential street. He explained they were mere facades, like half of everything in Hollywood if you dug deep enough. Celeste was accustomed to illusion, but she still had to touch the fake bricks to test for herself that they weren't real. He watched her, hands in pockets, with a grin on his face.

"Here I am rambling on about everything going wrong, and you haven't told me a thing about yourself," he said, suddenly curious.

"I'm merely enjoying the tour." She dusted her fingers off. "Besides, there's not much to say about myself." She didn't mean to be coy. There were things she *could* tell him, but she'd been taught to be wary of saying too much, especially around men. Relationships were fine, but there was only so much you could hide in an intimate setting. And being honest about who and what she was could come only after commitments had been made and certain contingencies were approved by the sisterhood.

"Where'd you grow up?" he asked.

"In a forest cottage outside of Strasbourg."

"Strasbourg? French or German side?"

"French. Do you know it?"

"I was in Chaumont, and later at Cantigny."

"Ah," she replied, knowing it meant he'd fought in one of the ferocious battles of the Great War a decade earlier. She wondered then if that was why he had no outstanding dreams or aspirations that rose up around him. She believed it was Myrtle who'd taught her that those who'd faced imminent death and lived to tell about it would read similarly, because they considered everything afterward a marvel.

"I was orphaned as a child," Celeste said, wishing to give him something real about herself. "So I don't really know where my people come from. Some kind strangers took me in and raised me as one of their own."

"What brought you to the States?" He tugged at his jaw awkwardly, as though he regretted opening his mouth. "Sorry, I'm asking too many questions. A fatal flaw in my character. Hopelessly curious, you see."

"That's probably what makes you a good storyteller," Celeste said, leaving him without an answer.

He held out his hand in invitation, and she took it. They walked the rest of the false street like a reluctant couple at the end of a date, practically dragging their feet so they wouldn't get to their destination too quickly. When they returned to the main building, Celeste thought Nick might try to kiss her, but the minute his secretary caught sight of him, she waved him over.

"It's happened again," she shouted while signaling for him to follow. "Carpentry house this time. I'm calling the doctor."

Nick jogged toward the site of the accident, so Celeste held on to her hat and followed, keeping pace.

Inside the small warehouse a group of workers in overalls had gathered around a man on the ground. He grimaced in pain, gripping his trouser leg.

Nick ducked between the men and knelt beside the injured worker. "What happened?" he asked, pulling his jacket off and sliding it under the man's head. He put his hands on the bad leg, feeling for a fracture.

"He was up on the ladder painting some scenery," a worker explained. "All of a sudden, we hear a crack. One of the rungs just gives way, and poor Tom there loses his balance and hits the floor."

Celeste casually inched closer to the ladder in question. The broken rung was about ten feet up, but the chill hovering over the wood went all the way to the floor. Just like Rose's sewing machine.

"I'm afraid it's broken," Nick said. "Hang in there. The doctor should be here soon."

"Listen, I've been up and down on that ladder a hundred times," the worker said. "Never had any trouble. It's the curse, I tell ya."

When the others began to chime in, agreeing, Nick got to his feet. "Get this straight," he said, staring them down. "There is no such thing as a curse. It's a bunch of superstitious nonsense, and I won't have that kind of talk in my shop, you understand?"

"But how else do you explain it?" a man covered in paint asked. His eyes were glossy with fear.

"Rot, that's how I explain it," Nick said. "Or too much weight. So I don't want to hear any more of this talk. It was an accident. That's all."

The men nodded and sheepishly backed off, but Celeste still detected their growing fear as their eyes traced the walls and ceiling for unseen threats. Nick felt it too, despite his talk in front of the men.

"I'm sorry," Nick said, resting his hand on Celeste's elbow as he urged her toward the main building. "I need to take care of this. Any chance you could stick around so I can buy you lunch later?" When she shook her head, he seemed torn between staying to deal with the latest tragedy and running away with her.

"Thank you, but I really do need to be off." In truth, she wanted to look in on Rose again, but before she left, she removed a conjured card and pencil from her purse and scribbled a phone number on it. "Here," she said, handing him the card. "This is the phone number of the hotel I'm staying at. Call me later."

The smile on his face was worth the risk of revealing where she lived.

CHAPTER THIRTEEN

Silk and Scissors

Celeste waited until both Nick and his secretary had gone back inside the prop house to wait for the doctor. Once they were out of sight, she cloaked her Pierce-Arrow in Model T glamour to make it look like she'd gone, then put herself through a similar transition. Her salmon-pink dress was traded for a work smock in basic gray. Her hair lost its perfect finger waves, frizzing slightly at the ends beneath the matching gray scarf tied around her head. Her rouged lips faded to a natural pink, and the scent of gardenias evaporated in the air. Her transition complete, she hurried inside the building and headed toward the wardrobe department in her practical black Mary Jane shoes.

"Hello there. Where are you off to in such a hurry?" It was Charlie just coming out of a broom closet down the hall from the sewing room.

"Hello, Charlie. Gotta get back to work. Running a little late today." Celeste smiled and waved as she disappeared into the room where the sewing machines were all humming and buzzing at their normal frantic pace.

It was only after she'd slipped into her spot at the back of the room that she noticed something was amiss. "Where's Rose?" she asked.

Zelda, the red-haired woman seated in front of her, turned around, blinking to clear her vision as though she'd only just noticed there was someone at the workstation behind her. "Oh, there you are. For reasons I can't understand, Rose got called up to the formal fitting room about thirty minutes ago," she said. "Apparently Ms. Diaz asked for her herself."

"Did she now?" Celeste could hardly contain herself. The magic was already penetrating through the layers of probability, letting favorable circumstances rise for her protégé. It was one of the moments she'd been told about all her life. When the seed of possibility found purchase in the soil of hard work. When talent met opportunity, and success began to flourish.

And she was about to miss it.

Rose's shears, the silver-handled scissors in the shape of a heron with a long stabbing beak for the blades, sat forgotten next to her machine. They'd once belonged to her mother, Ruth, and still bore the initials they shared engraved just below the fulcrum. Celeste grabbed them and hugged them to her chest. "I'd better pop these upstairs just in case Rose needs them," she said, not waiting to hear any protests.

Celeste had no idea where the formal fitting room was, but luckily Charlie was still in the hallway mopping at the far end. "Which way to the formal fitting room?" she asked, waving the scissors.

The janitor looked up, perplexed. "Formal fitting room?"

"I need to help Rose," she said, unable to hide her enthusiasm. "Our girl was specifically invited to do a costume fitting for Dolores Diaz. Can you believe it? I need to get her scissors to her."

Charlie rested his hands on top of his mop, taking in everything she'd said. "Ah, you mean the room next to Mr. Jacobi's office. That would be up on the second floor, about halfway down the hall," he said, pointing toward a set of stairs. "It's the one with mirrors on all the walls."

"Thank you, Charlie." Celeste ran up the stairs and followed his instructions but still didn't see a fitting room. About to give up, she heard a man laugh politely at something a young woman had said. The sound was so utterly full of false flattery it had to be Isaac Jacobi.

Following the sound, she found the fitting room next to the designer's office as Charlie had said, but to get to the actual space with the mirrored walls, she had to pass through a room filled with elaborate and expensive-looking headpieces decorated with colorful gems, enameled folding fans, silk wraps, and various small accessories that appeared too valuable to be stored in the general wardrobe department where the other costumes were kept. The items were mostly hung on racks or organized on shelves, but there were a few jewelry pieces locked under glass.

Celeste paused, gripping the scissors. She knew she wasn't supposed to interfere when it came to a protégé's talent, but a little insurance in the form of a charm shouldn't be out of line. Touching her pendant, she embedded a little extra spark of dexterity to the scissors to make them cut fast and true. When she finished, she entered the room waving the pair of scissors to explain her sudden appearance.

No one paid any attention. Jacobi stood with arms crossed staring up at Dolores Diaz, who stood on a built-in pedestal before the angled mirrors. Beside him was the woman she'd seen on the set the day before, still wearing her unflattering trousers and knee-high boots. And there, kneeling beside Dolores, was Rose, clamping down on half a dozen pins with her mouth while she tacked on a heavy gold braid along the hem of a long nineteenth-century-style skirt.

"Quite right, my dear." Jacobi came around to Dolores's back to get another view, ignoring Celeste completely. "The dark color suits you better than the baby blue. The contrast will show better on film too," he said to the other woman, whom Celeste had worked out must be the director of the film.

"I don't know," Dolores said, turning from side to side in the mirror. "It was hanging nicely before, but now it's lost its flow."

Rose stood up, taking a glance at the woman from the side. "She's right. The braiding is too stiff for the fabric."

"Nonsense," Jacobi said. "It's a costume, not an evening gown. That's how it's meant to look."

Rose caught sight of Celeste and confided her feelings about the dress with a slight eye roll, while Jacobi strutted to the other side of the actress with his pricked ego. Celeste handed the scissors to Rose, who mouthed a thank-you before slipping them inside her smock pocket.

"It still needs to translate on film like an expensive gown," the director said, pulling the hem away and letting it drop again. "She's meant to look like a famous 1880s Spanish singer at the height of her career, not a carnival princess. I'm pleased with the shape, but let's try a different adornment. Give the gown some expensive-looking accessories. Gild the lily a bit more."

"There's a few yards of lace downstairs that would match beautifully with the silk to make a mantilla," Rose said. "And there are silver hair combs in the accessories room next door we could borrow to give it a lift when her hair is pinned up." She flinched slightly after offering her opinion, waiting for Jacobi to ridicule her suggestion, but before the words could come out of his mouth, Dolores blessed the idea with her dazzling smile.

"Exactly what the costume needs," Dolores said. The actress gazed in the mirror, tilting her head. "You know, you've still got the entire wedding scene ensemble to design," she said to Jacobi. "What if Rose finished off this gown and the two others I tried on. I just adored the gold embellishments she added to the boots yesterday. She seems to have a knack for the little feminine touches we're after."

"Embellishments?" There was a huff from Jacobi, as if the idea were absurd, but then the director chimed in.

"I agree, Isaac. Perfectly splendid idea to call for help so we don't get further behind schedule after all the mishaps on set. Let the young women work on these. The pair of them can get it done while we move on to the next stage."

If Jacobi could have shot fire from his eyes, Rose and Celeste would have become twin piles of ash. Instead, the designer brushed off the dress work left to do as inconsequential. "Yes, perhaps you're right," he said. "This is all apprentice-level work anyway. But I'm warning you two. Stick to the design."

Rose and Celeste both nodded with their lips held firm to keep from breaking out in giddy laughter.

"Now let's go look at your sketches for the final wedding scene." The director grabbed her coat, announcing the fitting was effectively over. "See that it gets done by tomorrow, Rose."

After they left, Rose shook her head in disbelief. "Thank you, Ms. Diaz. It's an honor to work on the dresses for you."

Dolores looked over her shoulder in the mirror to get a view of the dress from the back. "Don't mention it," she said. "We women have to stick together. We're all hoping for that big break. Mr. West gave me mine by offering me this part when a lot of other studios wouldn't touch me." She turned back and stared at her reflection straight on, raising her chin. "I once had a director ask me why I bothered to show up to audition for the lead in a film about a socialite when I clearly wasn't the right *type*. *Dios mío*, he meant I should have auditioned for the part of the maid instead." She raised an eyebrow and stepped off the raised platform. "I recognize what's going on here," she said with a lingering look toward the exit where the head designer had disappeared. "Besides, it's obvious you have talent and ideas. Hang in there. You'll get recognized for them in due time."

Celeste couldn't have agreed more. The talk made her wonder again about the young actress and her suitability as a protégé. If she could have consulted with Dorée about taking on a second charge, she might have, but perhaps Dolores didn't need the help of a Gardienne to get what she wanted. Plenty of men and women in this town had found their paths to stardom. It didn't always take a magical intervention to clear the way to success. Sometimes all that was needed was talent meeting opportunity at the right moment. Sometimes that opportunity was encouraged by the sisterhood, like a midwife helping a woman with a difficult birth. Whatever star path Dolores Diaz had stepped onto, it appeared to be paved with luck and good intentions as she shimmered in radiant light.

"Say, I have an idea." Dolores turned her back toward Rose to be unbuttoned and released from the costume. "Why don't you two come out with me tonight."

"Out where?" Rose asked.

"There's a party at Oscar Sinclair's house. All the gang will be there. It'll be the bee's knees, I promise!"

Rose bit her lip. "I don't know."

Dolores slipped off the stiff gown and bustle with a wiggle, as though happy to be free of the restraint of an entire era. "You must come. Meet some people. Get your name out there, Rose. There might even be a few studio big shots who show up. That's how you get people talking about you. Of course, the regular gang will be there too," she said, reining in her enthusiasm slightly to make Rose feel more comfortable. "Both of you. You must come. I'm planning on wearing that new dress you sold me," she said, standing in her underclothes and swinging her shoulders back and forth as though showing off her shimmy.

"The one Rose made?" Celeste gleamed at her protégé, knowing the magic was weaving in and out of her life like it should.

"That's right," Dolores said. "I stopped by after filming yesterday to thank her for the boots and couldn't resist when she pulled the dress out of her bag to show me. Oh, do say you'll come."

Celeste was inclined to say no at first. She'd been dreaming of landing in her soft bed all day, but she'd been taught not to close off any opportunity that might benefit her protégé. Rose was reluctant as well, but only because she was eager to get to work on the costumes. Celeste could tell by the way she folded the gown over her arm, feeling along the edge where she planned to add her personal touches.

"What do you say, Rose?" Celeste grabbed the two other costumes off their hangers. "We can work on these the rest of the afternoon and then meet Dolores at the party after work. It will be our reward."

"That's the spirit!" Dolores said, revealing a brilliant, wide smile.

Celeste sensed another anomaly on the actress's unusual star path. So bright and yet seemingly on a strange, incalculable trajectory all her own. Maybe that was what a true star was made of around here.

At last, a glimmer of curious excitement caught fire in Rose's eyes. "All right, I'll go. But I can't stay out long. I must get these costumes done or Jacobi will have my scalp."

Dolores clapped her hands. "*Excelente!* And don't worry. I have an early call tomorrow too. I have to fight off that fiend Reginald in our big climactic scene tomorrow." Celeste stared back at her blankly. "Reginald King?" she added. "My costar? Just between us, he's an absolute sweetheart. If he didn't have all that makeup on, I don't know how I'd ever pretend to be afraid of him." The actress laughed, then reached for her own clothes. She dug in her jacket pocket for a piece of paper with the address for the party, and all agreed to meet there by eight. Celeste just knew it would prove to be a pivotal moment in Rose's life.

CHAPTER FOURTEEN

Ball Gowns and Bathtub Gin

Rose got to work right away on the three gowns. Celeste offered to help, but there was little to be done besides handing off scissors, resupplying the thread when the bobbin ran empty, and pressing creases in the gowns with the kerosene-powered iron.

"Honestly, if you want to help, the best thing you could do is finish those beggars rags so I don't have to," Rose said as she tacked on a line of ribbon along the neckline of the first dress. "A few of them still need to be soaked in coffee. The rest need to be ripped up and then restitched."

Celeste could make that happen with a flick of her eyebrow, but she did things the tedious way, if only as an excuse to appear busy while keeping an eye on her protégé. Three hours later, Celeste wrung out the last of the peasant shirts. The breeches and frock coats had all been torn and patched, the shoes scuffed, and the men's cotton shirts all properly stained. Sebastian had helped her with the last part, chewing silently on the loose threads on her lap while she pulled the needle through the trousers to secure the worn patches. Earlier, he'd tracked down the broken cameras, confirming the presence of a cold hex on the metal as expected. He'd also done a bit of eavesdropping, curling up behind a potted palm beneath the window in Nick's office. Her shared psychic power with the stoat had weakened as the day wore on, but she understood Nick had taken several phone calls that portended more bad news. All of it stemming back to the fire. One more disaster and it appeared he might be wiped out financially. She learned this not through words but through an image of Nick holding his face in his hands as seen through Sebastian's eyes, the man's tears real behind the fingers. She'd mulled over the implications of a curse all afternoon as she stitched, wondering about motivations. Who else had a stake in the outcome of life at the studio if it went under? An investor? A disgruntled employee? A rival of some kind?

The last thought struck a chord. There'd been a brief moment at Rose's house when Celeste could have sworn she was being watched. Not just by a curious neighbor but by a wisp of unique energy. And by "unique" she meant "tinged with the supernatural." The energy swirled outside the house like a woman's perfume lingering in the air after she'd left the room. For the briefest instant Celeste's intuition had sensed Gardienne energy, but the feeling dissipated quickly, considering she was five thousand miles away from any of her sisters. And not even Anaïs could hold a grudge so firm and fast that she would travel across an ocean to get revenge for a mostly forgivable offense. Could she? The thought was absurd, so she'd convinced herself at the time it was impossible. And yet she couldn't shake the sensation of being spied on, even as she sat at the worktable watching Rose create the most beautiful embellishments for the gown in addition to the lace trim.

Celeste counted back in her head to the day she'd struck the counter-curse to Anaïs's death wish for the infant. More than thirty days had passed. She put down the needle and asked Sebastian to find the postcard in her purse, the one that had brought her to California in the first place. What was it that Dorée had said about lost mail being attracted to the magic of Fées Gardiennes? An odd thing to say. Celeste had never received a misdirected piece of mail before in her life.

She turned the card over and studied both the sender's name and the intended recipient. The names Edward and William meant nothing to her. And yet the sender had been here in California when he'd mailed the card to Strasbourg, hadn't he? She checked the postmark. The ink had smudged as though it had been swiped with a moist cloth, but she could still make out the stamp from Los Angeles. It had also been sent the week after "the incident." A week was all it took to cross the ocean.

"Is it possible?" she asked as her body flooded with a heady mix of trepidation tinged with disbelief.

Rose looked up from her machine. "Is what possible?"

Celeste hadn't realized she'd spoken out loud. She pointed to the gown Rose was working on. "Is it possible you'll really get them all done in time?"

"With luck." The young woman grinned, then put her head down to concentrate on attaching an elegant flower applique to the bodice of the second dress.

A minute later Charlie entered the sewing room, pushing a broom across the floor. "Mind if I clean up?" he asked. "It's just nearly everyone else has gone, and this is my last job to do."

Celeste looked at the clock and startled at the time. "Half past six! We've got to get a move on." Somehow, they'd worked through dinner, even after the sewing room had cleared out—Rose concentrating on her gown, and she lost in thoughts about a suspicious postcard.

"Yes, of course," Rose said. "Sorry, Charlie, I've been desperate to get this gown done for Ms. Diaz. They're using it in a scene the day after tomorrow."

"Don't apologize," Charlie said. "Stay if you like. I can work around you. Besides, I enjoy your company. The two of you are different than the others, if you don't mind me saying it."

Celeste didn't mind it at all, but they really did need to hurry. "Thanks, Charlie, but we have to get going."

While the janitor swept the loose threads and scraps of material off the floor, Rose pushed her chair back and hung the gown over the dummy beside her station alongside the other two. She tagged the dress to show it was her project and still under construction.

Celeste, too, put her costumes away before grabbing her purse with Sebastian inside. He'd fallen asleep and barely roused as she dug inside for her car keys. Charlie emptied the wastebasket and wished them both a pleasant evening before heading down the hall to clock out. The women followed, turning the lights out behind them, which only made the light still on in the wardrobe room even more noticeable. Jacobi was still working, rummaging through costumes as though taking inventory. He pretended not to notice Celeste leaving, but once she'd passed by the doorway, he confronted Rose in the hallway.

"I know what you're up to," Jacobi said. "With your innocent smiles and 'gee shucks' response to any scrap of praise that starlet throws your way simply because you can stitch a straight line. You circumvented my authority through flattery today, but I'm still head designer at this studio, and you'd do well not to forget that. Furthermore, those gowns had better be impeccable and turned in on time tomorrow or you can start scanning the help wanted pages for another job."

Celeste held her pendant, on the verge of interfering, but to her credit Rose stood toe to toe with Jacobi. She looked him in the eye and calmly replied, "I'll get the costumes finished. And even though I know you'll take the credit for them in the end, I'll always know the extra effort put into making them shine was all mine. Now, if you don't mind, we have a party to attend." Rose turned on her heels, not waiting for a response, and Celeste nearly burst with pride as they exited arm in arm. Talent was one thing, but gumption was rocket fuel for a star on the rise.

The threat of rain hovered over the city as they left the studio to get ready for the party, but it wasn't enough to dampen their spirits. Celeste drove Rose home, pretending to follow her instructions on how to get there. Back inside the cottage-style house, Celeste was struck by how much cozier the home was when the people who lived there hummed about the place. The walls came alive with warmth and love, and the lingering energy of the mother and wife who'd passed on flickered softly in the background.

"Here, you take the midnight-blue dress," Rose said, grabbing a hanger from her closet. "It suits your coloring better, and it will go with that pretty sapphire necklace of yours."

"You made this?" The velvet dress was a plain sleeveless cut with a drop waist and plunging V-shaped drape in the back, but the mercury glass beads that had been intricately sewn in a wide V pattern down the front of the bodice elevated it to stunning. "We'll be advertising your talent to the Hollywood aristocracy with every step," Celeste said, her heart opening wide to the opportunity.

Rose paused with her hand on a second dress. "It's been an amazing day," she said. "I'm exhausted and exhilarated at the same time." She pulled a jade-green outfit off the hanger. "I can't help but think you're somehow responsible. On the level, Celine. Thank you."

"Me? I didn't do anything except bring you your scissors. All the talent and praise belong to you. I'm just the talkative sidekick."

They laughed, and then Rose put on the green dress. The sleeves were fluttery and the waist more cinched than the blue one Celeste wore. Gold embroidery highlighted the neckline and the flouncy pleats in the skirt. It was a dream of a dress. All Celeste had to do was make up an excuse to give the young woman's hair a little tuck here and a swoop there. Gripping her necklace, she added a little sprinkle of glamour and soon Rose's hair went from a naturally curly above-the-shoulder bob to a perfectly sleek marcel curl. Celeste took the liberty of applying a little rouge to her protégé's cheeks and lips, and the transformation was complete. Sebastian poked his head up out of her purse to investigate the use of magic but settled down when he saw the young woman smiling at herself in the mirror. And as the pair waved goodbye to Rose's father for the evening, Celeste thought she felt the energy in the house give a little sigh of approval.

The address Dolores had given them was located just a few streets north of Celeste's hotel bungalow. As they followed the winding road through the palm-lined streets, the houses grew bigger and grander the nearer they got to their destination.

"I think this is it," Celeste said as she pulled into a long horseshoe-shaped driveway that wound around a three-tiered fountain. The mansion could pass for a small country château with its graceful limestone walls, multiple chimneys, and elegant slate roof. Even the enfilades on the upper floor, with each window in the adjoining rooms lit up in warm yellow light, reminded her of her travels through the French countryside. She parked the Pierce-Arrow, still cloaked in humble Model T energy, at the end of the lane and jumped out while her stomach was all aflutter with anticipation.

"Come on, let's go see the inside." Celeste hooked arms with Rose as they strolled up the long walkway to the front door. She got nervous for a second, thinking they might need a formal invitation to enter, until a man she briefly mistook for a butler stumbled out the front door and fell in the bushes dead drunk. His friend laughed at him until he couldn't stand up on his own without leaning a shoulder against the doorjamb.

Celeste hovered over the man in the bushes a moment. "Is he all right?"

The friend took a sip from a small metal flask. "Oh yeah, it's copacetic," he said before struggling to put the cap back on the container. "Great party, come on in."

With a shrug of acceptance, Celeste and Rose slipped past the man in the doorway and went inside. The place buzzed with a frenetic energy that pulsated against Celeste's skin. A live band played from somewhere deep inside the house, the drums dishing out a backbeat while people mingled on the stairs, in the hallways, and outside by a swimming pool surrounded by torchlight. Every direction they turned they bumped elbows with someone whose face Rose said she'd only ever seen on a big screen in black and white.

"Come on, let's go explore the back garden," Celeste said, eager to venture outside, but Rose held back, unwilling to move forward. "What is it?"

"I don't know if I can do this. I feel so out of place. Some of these people are really famous." Rose's eyes filled with genuine distress as she tugged at her dress. "I don't belong here."

"Nonsense." Celeste pulled Rose aside into an adjoining dining room that proved only mildly quieter than the hallway. "Listen, Rose, if you want to design costumes for the movies, you have to talk to the people who star in them. Get to know them. How they move, how they walk, how comfortable they are in their own skin." She gripped Rose gently by the shoulders, bucking her up. "You already know this. It's why you were so intuitive with Dolores. You knew how to make her comfortable in the costume while also meeting the design requirements for the scene and the character she plays. And you know what? She asked for you to work on the dresses. *You*, Rose Downey."

"Who are you?" Rose stopped her fretting long enough to really study Celeste's face. "We only just met, but sometimes I think you know me better than I know myself."

"Well, I know you were meant to do great things with your talent," Celeste answered honestly. "Anyone could see you're going to rise in this industry."

"You really think so?"

"I do. Isn't that what Dolores said too?"

Rose got a funny look on her face. "Why do I get the strangest feeling I've met you before?"

Celeste knew the reason for Rose's feeling of déjà vu came from their intertwined fates, but she could hardly say so. Instead, she gave the young woman a hug. "Let's go enjoy the party by the pool before the rain ruins everything."

They had to cross through a crowded room at the back of the house to get to the pool area, where most people had gathered. A man dressed in tails and a top hat enticed them with suspicious glasses filled with unknown liquids. "What is it?" Rose asked.

"Your ticket to a good time," the man said.

Rose reluctantly accepted, while Celeste took a sniff from her glass and recognized the embalming fluid as a better-than-average bathtub gin. She took a sip, then set it down as a parade of handsome men filed past the patio doors on their way to sit with a woman wearing a fur stole and diamond earrings bright enough to dazzle from across the garden. For the briefest moment she thought maybe Nick West might be in the crowd, but that hope got shot down when Sebastian relayed through a flickering thought that the producer wasn't the partying type. Besides, she was in her Celine glamour, so he wouldn't have recognized her anyway.

She could have sunk into a blue mood, but then she spotted Dolores across the garden chatting with a man in a white suit with a gold tie. Each held a cigarette in a long, slender holder balanced gracefully in one hand, while the other hand rested firmly on the hip. Their pose was half charade, half bold as brass.

Celeste nudged Rose. "Come on, there's Dolores. Let's say hi."

Rose stood on her toes to spot the actress in the crowd. When she found her, she gripped Celeste by the arm. "She's wearing the dress!"

"Of course she is," Celeste said, pride bubbling up inside her. "It's stunning on her. Look how everyone is watching her every move." And it was true. People tried to remain nonchalant as though they had no true interest, but their glances kept returning to the starlet in the buttery satin dress.

The pair got within a couple of feet of the actress, but she didn't turn around. Dolores was too busy telling the man about her new gown. "I know, I know," she said, fanning out the pleats. Rose caught Celeste's eye at the mention and smiled. "It's pretty enough, but now I don't know why I bought it. I guess I felt sorry for the poor girl. She's a little mouse of a thing. Whenever I duck into the sewing room for a quick costume fitting, she's always hiding in the back with her head bent over her machine, squinting at her work."

Something wasn't right. Why was she saying such things? This wasn't the same Dolores they'd laughed with only a few hours ago. Something had changed. Was she acting? Then or now?

A breeze stirred Dolores's hair. Celeste swore she saw a halo of ice crystals form ever so briefly as the actress gave a little shiver.

"She'll never make it as a designer in this business," Dolores said, continuing her rant. "She's got some talent with a needle and a few interesting ideas, but she's off with the fairies, that one. I really only played her up in the fitting room today to make Jacobi angry. I despise working with him. Such an egotistical ass. I may have to tell the studio I won't work with him anymore."

"Wait for your star to rise after the picture is released—and it will," the man assured her. "Then you'll have all the leverage you need to make demands."

"Maybe I'll jump ship and swim over to MGM with you."

The man blew out a plume of smoke while giving the gown the once-over with his eyes. "I won't bother calling the seamstress in for the assistant designer job available, then. Pity, I do love the cut of that dress on you. Absolutely magical design. You're right, she has some real talent."

"Making pretty frocks is one thing, but you need a sheepdog for a job like that. Someone who can keep all the others rounded up so they do as they're told. Not some shrinking violet happy to live in the shade." Dolores rubbed her bare arms. "*Dios mío*, it's getting chilly out here, isn't it?"

Hearing the harsh words, Rose's self-esteem crumpled so hard the impact collapsed a part of Celeste as well. Why had Dolores said such things? Not that she wasn't capable of talking behind someone's back. Everyone had free will. But there should never have been any motivation for it. The actress was under *her* influence. *She'd* induced her to buy the dress. *She'd* planted the seed for her to talk Rose up in the fitting room. Dolores was meant to be a key pivot point in the broader scheme for getting Rose headed in the right direction. She'd felt the connection deeply in her solar plexus. Now the actress was seemingly working *against* her protégé.

Celeste knew something was off. A suspicious chill lingered in the air that was growing altogether too familiar. She cast her eye on the crowd, the trees, and the house but saw nothing remarkable until she sank into her third eye vision. A filament of malevolent energy, like a thread of gray smoke, trailed behind the actress before it snapped and vanished.

The man speaking with Dolores cleared his throat and nudged his chin toward Celeste and Rose when he saw them standing there. The actress looked over her shoulder, and her hand closed over her mouth. Her expressive eyes, so crucial to her success on film, widened in embarrassment.

"Oh, you're here!" Dolores said. She took a step toward them, her worried eyes staring keenly into Rose's. "I've been waiting for you both. I was just telling my friend Adrian about—"

"How could you say such things?" Rose's cheeks had turned a deep shade of red. "I thought you understood. I thought you were different."

"Wait, Rose, I don't know why—"

Rose tossed her glass of gin in Dolores's face and stormed back inside the house. An audible gasp rose up from the partygoers, followed by uneasy laughter as Dolores stood shaking her head and blinking as though coming out of a dream. Celeste reached out a hand to reassure the actress and felt an unnatural chill still pulsating over her skin. She wasn't surprised. Celeste swept the tops of the palm trees with her eyes, looking for the source of the threat as the first drops of rain began to fall, then caught up with Rose and drove her home. The passenger seat practically vibrated from her protégé's resounding anger and humiliation all the way there.

CHAPTER FIFTEEN

Happily Ever Afters Are for Suckers

Anaïs sat in the last row of Grauman's Egyptian Theatre. She'd lost the film's plot already, confused by the actress's waterworks when the man the character was meant to marry hopped on his horse and rode away. She didn't understand the dramatic need for tears. He was a clod, by the look of him. Good riddance. But the theater itself was lovely and dramatic in all the right areas, so she concentrated on her appreciation of the hieroglyphics and decorative pillars while the movie flickered on the screen.

Bored again, Anaïs tore open the box of Jujyfruits she'd purchased on her way in. The man three rows in front of her turned at the sound of the box tearing. She sneered at him with the full glamour of a vamp high on gin, and he went back to minding his own business. She popped one of the chewy candies in her mouth just as Edward spotted her and sidestepped his way to her seat in the middle of the last row. She'd ensured the entire row had remained empty with a touch of her pendant and an arch of her brow, so it was just the two of them when he sat beside her. She touched her ruby pendant again and dropped a veil of silence over them so they wouldn't be overheard.

Edward reached in his jacket and produced a brown vial. "The second potion," he said.

"How did you find the missing ingredients so quickly?"

"For you, nothing is impossible."

"You are a charmer," she said.

"I assume your little trinket there has encapsulated us so no one can hear?" When she nodded, he leaned closer and grazed her low-cut neckline with the glass bottle before letting the vial drop between her breasts. Then he tested her motivations for veiling them in silence by moving his hand to her knee and sliding it under her hem.

"And yet I'm afraid whatever *ideas* you have about us are just that," she said as Gideon flew down from the balcony to land on the seat beside Edward. The rook's sharp beak tapped against the man's shoulder until Edward retracted his hand from beneath Anaïs's dress. She straightened her hem and retrieved the bottle from her cleavage. "Now, tell me how to use this and all will be forgiven."

"A thousand pardons." An irritated Edward backed away from the bird. "It takes a drop or two under the tongue. It's not as stable as the other potion, so you need to act quickly if you want to reverse the effects of the first one."

Anaïs narrowed her eyes at him. "How fast?"

"Within the hour. After that the efficacy diminishes by half."

"And you swear by this?"

Gideon lowered his head and aired out his wings, his black eyes boring into his mistress's former lover while awaiting his answer.

Edward held up his right palm. "On my mother's life, as always."

Anaïs smiled with satisfaction. "I can always rely on you, Edward." She had second thoughts then about shooing him away. There was something seductively provocative about being secluded alone with the man in the back of a darkened theater knowing no one could hear them. Alas, there were more prying commitments that demanded her attention. "I'll let you know if I need anything else," she said and handed him the Jujyfruits as a consolation prize, giving the box a tempting shake when he didn't take it at first. Inside, she'd left one of her gemstones for him to find. The small peridot was the only one she could bear to part with.

He knew better than to ask about the payment outright. Keeping his life intact ought to be compensation enough. Gardiennes erred on the side of duty and justice, but they'd always wielded discretionary power to act in any manner they deemed necessary for their own protection. Anaïs waited for him to take the box of Jujyfruits, then watched him slide out of the row of seats with a hangdog look on his face. Fool. She hoped he wasn't stupid enough to toss out the box of candy on his way home. When he was gone, Anaïs tapped the ruby gemstone in her necklace, dropping the veil around her. Gideon flapped silently to the rafters as she stood and walked to the opposite end of the row of seats. There, she handed the vial to a waiting palm.

"He's a handsy one," the recipient whispered, shaking the bottle to inspect it.

Anaïs gave a flirty lift of her shoulder. "Maybe that's why I've always liked him."

"As long as the stuff works," the voice warned before handing the vial back. "We won't get a second chance."

Anaïs dropped her bravado. She knew there would be grave consequences if they failed to contain the potential damage. "It will work." She'd spoken a little too forcefully and got shushed again by another audience member. Anaïs lifted her brow, and the film snapped and stuttered to a halt. The audience groaned at the blank white screen while the projectionist frantically worked to repair the broken reel in the booth upstairs. "Happily ever afters are for suckers," she said under her breath, then walked out of the theater.

CHAPTER SIXTEEN

Rain and Ruin

The rain came down in a steady staccato beat, flooding the pavement and turning the roadside into a gully. After dropping Rose off at her house and assuring her everything would be okay, Celeste drove around the neighborhood, letting her suspicion that something was very wrong continue to fester. The rain itself was an omen, but she hadn't worked out exactly what it portended. She only knew that a trace of malignant energy continued to move through the atmosphere like static electricity. A feeling of impending disaster that skittered back and forth beneath her collarbone like a flat stone skipping over a pond's surface.

Again, she caught herself wondering how a curse, if that's what she was dealing with, could travel. It was almost as if the bad energy trailed after those connected to the studio, or at least Rose and Dolores. At the same time, the way the so-called curse attacked individuals felt personal. What may have started at the studio as acts of mischief had morphed into something aimed at hurting people. The studio's finances, Rose's prospects, workers' safety, and now for some reason that same energy seemed to want to create a rift between Rose and Dolores. But why?

Celeste sighed behind the steering wheel. Something was very, very wrong. Sebastian agreed, watching the rain fall through his predator eyes. As though something might swoop out of the clouds at any moment and snatch them both in its clutches. They shivered in unison, with Celeste wishing they had more to keep them warm than conspiracy theories.

"It's funny," Celeste said, keeping her voice low. She didn't wish to disturb the ominous static in the air as she followed the trail of some small unseen thing that tugged at her intuition. "Dorée banished me from Europe to escape Anaïs's anger. But she may have marooned me alone with a curse on the loose in a faraway land instead." The wind picked up, driving the rain against the windshield as Celeste cruised north toward Hollywood. "I have a bad feeling, Sebastian. I think we need to go back and check on the studio."

The little stoat chittered and huddled beside her. Traffic was light, but there were a few people out as they drove past a theater decorated to look like something out of ancient Egypt—if Egypt were an amusement park. "Now that was a place steeped in curses," she said as they drove by the entrance made to look like a market square in old Cairo. "You couldn't have paid me enough to work in a pharaoh's palace."

Celeste slowed the car as people huddled under umbrellas walked along the road outside the theater. "You know who else deals in curses," she said with a sidelong glance at Sebastian. As if on cue, a flash of lightning zigzagged through the dark clouds after she conjured the memory of Anaïs. Celeste shook her head again at the reckless disregard for life her fellow Gardienne had shown by cursing a defenseless baby. She wondered if she shouldn't have stayed in France and faced the challenge of combat. Who knew? Maybe she would have survived it.

Lost in thoughts of home, Celeste had to hit the brakes as a man darted across the road in front of her—his dark hair dripping, eyes glowing with disgust. The man slammed his hand against her car, scattering a box of colorful candies across the hood. He stared straight at her as though he might thrust his fist through the windshield. He said something unintelligible, then pulled his collar up with a violent tug and crossed to a shop selling radios on the other side of the street.

At the last moment he turned back and stared at her as if he knew her before heading inside and walking straight to a door at the back.

Celeste waited a beat to make sure he wasn't going to return before pulling the car forward again. As she did, a large black bird soared over the road, its wings captured briefly in the beam of the headlights against the curtain of raindrops.

"Was that . . ."

But it was too absurd. It could be any random bird out flying. At night. In the rain.

A flash of lightning lit up the sky again. Celeste's stomach clenched with dread. She pressed the accelerator and headed for the studio, fearing some invisible threat. She slowed down only when the gate was in sight. The guard was on duty, reading inside his booth under a flickering light bulb. He licked his finger and turned the page as Celeste touched her sapphire necklace and willed him to get lost in the book long enough for her to open the gate with a twitch of her eyebrow and enter unseen.

Once inside the gate, Celeste drove between buildings, making a quick assessment of the lot by looking left, then right. The normal commotion of people hurrying between buildings with ladders, paint cans, a piano on wheels, or an armful of costumes had come to a stop in the wee hours of the night. Stages One and Two were quiet, and the outdoor sets appeared abandoned. Nothing was on fire or knocked on its side. The water tower still stood, and the city facade sat quietly undisturbed. She and Sebastian breathed a small sigh of relief that all appeared normal and parked the car next to Nick's spot in the back.

The lights in the main building were dark except for the offices where the writers hung out, keeping their usual late hours. They worked on the opposite end of the building from the costume department, so Celeste didn't think they'd notice if she manipulated the lock and entered at the far end of the corridor. "It's not burglary if we're trying to save the place," she said when Sebastian gave her a worried look. She swore he sighed as he sank inside her purse so that only his head poked out through the opening.

After hours, when the halls were no longer overrun by the bustle of people working under deadlines, the building grew eerily quiet, apart from the occasional moaning of the windowpanes against the push of the storm. Celeste's heels clacked against the tile floors, so she slipped her shoes off and walked in stockinged feet to the area of the wardrobe room to see if everything was okay.

Even before she peeked through the glass on the sewing room door, the energy in the hallway shifted. A familiar chill snaked over the back of her neck as she pushed the door open. Celeste locked her pendant in her fist, gripping it like a protective amulet. Of all the places she'd checked on the lot, this room's ambient energy held the coldest intensity. The room was dark, so she willed an overhead bulb to come alive softly, just enough to see if anything moved in the corners. When the room remained quiet after the single bulb came on, she flipped the switch and flooded the room with incandescence.

Nothing scurried. Nothing squealed. Nothing attacked. But there was ruin.

The window at the back of the room stood open, propped in that position with a large pattern book jammed between the sill and the sash. Rain must have been pouring in for at least an hour, driven inward by the wind. The gowns that Rose had sweated over all afternoon remained on the rack where she'd left them, but they'd been exposed to the rain. The beautiful red silk was splotched and discolored like a bruise, the stitching puckered, the delicate feathers along the collar emaciated.

Celeste collapsed onto a chair, staring at the mess. Three dresses, beautifully redesigned and ready for their final touches, now ruined. But not just the dresses. This was meant to be a seminal moment in launching her protégé's promising career, as was Dolores Diaz's praise of Rose's work to her colleagues, raising her talent up for others to see and appreciate. But the sabotage was complete. All her magical handiwork had evaporated. And it wasn't merely a matter of starting over. If Rose were blamed for the condition of the gowns and deemed responsible for delaying production, she could very easily lose her position, reputation, and forward momentum. Especially after the way she'd spoken to the head designer. And if Rose failed, so did Celeste.

The depth of the destruction had her wondering again about the bird she'd seen in the rain. Could it have been Gideon? Could Anaïs be behind the curse? Could she really have traveled all those miles to orchestrate Celeste's downfall out of spite? The woman's blood oozed with the vile stuff. But crossing an ocean and two thousand miles of Middle America just to get even? It didn't make any sense. Yet the dresses had been ruined deliberately, of that she had no doubt. Whether by curse or revenge, that was the question.

"I may still be green at this Gardienne business," she said to Sebastian, "but I'm not ready to give up. Not when we're so close."

Celeste set her shoes and bag aside and reexamined the ruined costumes while Sebastian climbed up to the window to knock the soggy, wet pattern book loose and close the window. She knew she couldn't simply replace the gowns with new ones, even though that would be the quickest solution. The rules were explicit on that front. A protégé's work must be their own. There could be no interference in the expression of their talents or interests. Interference was allowed only in removing the stubborn obstacles that stood in the way of them achieving their dreams. And this one was a doozy. Intentional and malicious.

Celeste took a step back, tilting her head to the side. Most of the damage to the costumes was on the material facing the open window, but each one was a total loss. Concentrating first on the sleeve of the green gown, she touched her sapphire necklace and raised her brow to see if there was a way to reverse the damage without altering Rose's work. With a counterclockwise wave of her other hand, she watched as a water stain dried out and disappeared. She tried it again on a larger area and the same thing happened. Feeling a little more confident, she attempted to repair a larger swath and discovered if she overshot with her magic, it could affect other objects in the vicinity. The hands on the clock moved backward, and the tears in the beggars costumes she'd worked on earlier repaired themselves. She reset the time on the wall and went back to concentrating on small palm-size areas until she had most of the dress dried out.

"So far so good where the fabric is concerned." Sebastian agreed, so Celeste turned her attention to the puckered stitches. They, too, straightened as they dried with a little help from Sebastian, who pulled the cloth with his teeth where it remained stubbornly wrinkled. The finished edges would need pressing with a warm iron, but at least the threads held. The glass beading and feathers proved much more difficult. Celeste was forced to go slowly, making sure each tiny barb on every individual plume fluffed back up. Otherwise, the down clumped together and wasn't even fit to stuff a pillow.

It was painstaking work, and her arm was killing her by the time all three costumes had been restored hours later. At least they *appeared* restored to her. She did worry that Rose would still find fault, but that critical eye was part of the young woman's talent, so she let go of her necklace and called it done. If there were a bead or sequin out of place, there was still time for Rose to repair it in the morning. Which, judging by the brightening dawn outside, was on its way.

Celeste's palm buzzed with warmth from the expended magic, but her energy was nearly depleted. Both she and her sapphire pendant were drained. She'd taken a chance exhausting her magic when obvious threats lurked nearby, but she'd had little choice. And now there was no time to go back to the bungalow to rest and recharge. She had to be there when Rose arrived. She had to make sure everything would still work out as planned. Jacobi was an ass, but the endorsement of a respected designer was crucial to getting Rose the exposure she needed to make the leap to the next level of her career, and Celeste wasn't about to let any curse interfere with that progress again.

Sebastian trotted out from beneath one of the canvas trucks used for dumping scraps of material. He had a dead mouse clenched between his sharp white teeth. "I know exactly how he feels," Celeste said. The stoat barely acknowledged her, stealing his prey away to devour it alone in a dark corner. She sighed, knowing their bond had weakened after exerting so much magic. They really did need to get to the gemstones in the trunk and recharge their connection before they ran completely dry. But she wasn't sure she could keep her eyes open long enough to see the way back to their bungalow.

Celeste had started to nod off when a rattle at the door made her eyes flutter open again. "Rose?"

"Just me." Charlie set his bucket and mop down, eyeing her with concern. "You didn't stay here working all night, did you? I thought you and Rose had a party to go to last night."

"Good morning, Charlie." She stretched and yawned before spouting her lie. "Oh, no. I just came in extra early to catch up on a few things. The, uh, guard let me in," she added, remembering Charlie was the one who usually held the door open for Rose in the morning.

He nodded, though she wasn't sure he believed her. "Well, I can see you're a real go-getter," he said, walking between worktables. His eyes swept the room as though looking for evidence she'd slept there. His gaze lingered briefly on the spot where Sebastian had run off to eat his breakfast, but then the janitor grabbed his mop and bucket and said he'd just go sweep upstairs a little before everyone arrived.

When he was gone, Sebastian came out of hiding still wiping his whiskers off. He had the most peculiar expression on his face as he sat on his hind legs and sniffed the air. His nose twitched and his gaze darted to the hallway. Celeste would have sworn it was an alert, but with their connection weakened, she couldn't be sure what he was experiencing. "What is it?" she asked, but he ran off for the hallway before she could stop him. Whatever he'd sensed, he hadn't waited for her to sense it too, so she rested her head against the worktable. She just had to close her eyes for a minute.

CHAPTER SEVENTEEN

Heebie-Jeebies

"Honestly, how could you have been so careless?"

Gideon squawked and strutted along the top of the enormous letter *H*, bobbing his head, while Anaïs sat curled up inside the letter *O* like a woman in one of those studio photographs where they pose with a cutout of the moon.

"And don't use the rain as an excuse." Anaïs rested her head against the patchwork metal. "You should have spotted her in the driver's seat."

The rook shook out his feathers defiantly.

"Yes, I understand there are other black birds flying around the city," she replied to their shared thoughts. "And, true, she may not have recognized you, but you know as well as I do what the stakes are if we fail. It was such an avoidable blunder to fly out in the road at the exact moment Celeste drove by."

Gideon pouted and hopped to the ground to scout for crawly things in the brush to eat. Anaïs wasn't truly upset with the rook. He had always been loyal and done his best. It's why she never complained when he led her to places like this one that soared high above their surroundings. Still, he ought to have seen Celeste coming a mile away in that ridiculous blue car of hers.

Gideon plucked a fat white caterpillar off a yucca bush and flicked it in the air at her. Anaïs tossed a hand at him, done arguing about it. There were more important things to concentrate on now that morning dawned over the city. Vibrations on the wind informed her the day would prove vital toward realizing their ambitions. "Never mind," she said, climbing down. "If she suspects we're here, she'll only grow predictably cautious. That might not be such a bad thing. It'll make it easier to keep an eye on her."

Anaïs strode back to her Bentley, taking the time to admire the view once more before heading down the hill. Gideon spread his wings and followed behind her as she took the curves in third gear. It wasn't that far to Edward's. Less than an hour's drive through the winding back roads of the Hollywood Hills. The temptation burned, as it always did, but when Gideon squawked in protest, she veered downhill toward West Coast Studios. With such potential for change in the air, she thought it best to stay as close to Celeste and her protégé as possible. Now was not the time to get careless, even if she did get only an hour of sleep.

Anaïs was careful to park a few blocks east of the studio's front gate, then waited for Gideon to land on a nearby rooftop to keep watch over the property. Curiously, a line of people waited outside on the pavement, hovering around a man with a clipboard. Actors, she decided. She could tell by the way they all openly vied for a chance to get their face on the big screen, unctuous and full of silver-tongued flattery in their hunt for fame. Most had about as much talent as one of Gideon's slimy invertebrates plucked out of the mud.

The lure of fame and fortune in exchange for a little makeup and a few pulled faces made for the sort of intoxicating elixir even Edward couldn't bottle. One that attracted ten thousand people to the city every month, according to the movie magazine she'd read in Celeste's bungalow. So far in her career, she'd managed to stay away from potential protégés drawn to the stage or screen. It was too difficult to sort through their dreams and desires to find the ones that mattered. Creative types were often an amalgam of ambition and insecurity. Their talents too intertwined with their psyches. Some could skyrocket to the top of the stratosphere on their talent without any help from a Gardienne. But when the inevitable fall came, they were in danger of shattering, too fragile to separate the success they'd experienced from the person they saw in the mirror, once the champagne ceased to flow and the telegrams no longer arrived. They were convinced they were washed up, no good, a bunch of hacks. No, she thought, it's better to leave that sort of protégé to Dorée, who excelled at plucking up young, talented artists and entertainers destined for a place in the celestial sphere.

Gideon cawed from above. The handsome studio owner had arrived for work.

"He's an early bird, coming in at this hour." The rook screeched at her choice of words. "You're growing too sensitive," she said as she closed her eyes and relied on Gideon's vision to show her Nick West's arrival in detail.

He drove a Rolls-Royce two-seater convertible, a Silver Ghost with an engine that purred. The roadster was sporty but far from showy. "Fun" was how she would describe it. The car must have been wonderful to drive on the winding hillsides with one arm outstretched to feel the air rush by. The line of actors spotted him driving in. A flurry of squeals erupted until he gave them a wave and passed through the gate, leaving them behind to wonder if he noticed their hair, eyes, or smile enough to make them a star.

Anaïs's stomach contents curdled in disgust. With his power he could pluck any one of the women out of the line and make her promises of fame in exchange for certain favors. A few of them hoped he would, craning their necks to see which way he'd gone. She watched, waiting for him to signal the guard to let one or two of the pretty ones through. Incredibly, he didn't bother to even entertain the thought, driving onto the lot without a second look back.

Curious.

"I think it's time we explored this movie studio from the inside," Anaïs said, opening her eyes. Disguising herself with a bit of glamour, she emerged from the Bentley wearing a sleek black dress with a fringed hem, a shawl made of embroidered Chinese silk, and a silver comb in the shape of a bird's wing tucked into her short bob. When she reached the group of people in line outside the studio gate, she mingled with a few of the young women until she got the gist of the background parts up for grabs that day. Their desperation for a lucky break floated like musk in the air. She didn't dare let her guard down to listen in to any wishes around so many hopefuls. It'd be like sticking her head inside a bell and waiting for the gong to knock her out. *No, thank you.*

Gideon swooped in and perched atop the gate's pillar with instructions to watch for the sneaky little stoat, while Anaïs crept closer to the man with the clipboard who acted as judge and juror over who got to go inside and who got turned away. It would be easy enough to slip past him using her magic, but she was in the mood for a more organic introduction to the world of moviemaking.

"Name?"

"Anna Louise Parker." Anaïs thought it sounded flatly American.

"Auditioning for the part of Sofia in *The Madman of Madrid*?"

"Yes, that's right."

The man looked her body over as though she were a goose hanging in a butcher's market, so she extended her leg through the slit in her dress to let him get the full view, including the rolled top of her stockings. "Yeah, all right." He pointed to a line of women along the wall. "You're number seven."

"My lucky number," Anaïs said with a slick smile, though luck was something a Gardienne was never obliged to rely on.

Despite the slight yet undeniable thrill she'd felt making it past the initial gatekeeper without using any additional glamour, Anaïs had more important business to attend to than checking that her stockings were straight and her lipstick wasn't smudged before miming some woe-is-me tale of lost love for the cameras. Two more actresses joined the queue, and then the man with the clipboard shut the gate and ordered the women to follow him. He led them to a huge building labeled Stage One. Anaïs was just about to slip away when Nick West came around the corner, a script in one hand and a cup of coffee in the other, to welcome them inside. Had she got him wrong after all?

The stage building was a flurry of activity. Men climbed ladders to secure lights above sets—though they appeared awfully cautious about it—while camera operators cranked the levers on their machines and a woman shouted directions at a man dressed as a king, telling him when to sit or speak or roll over as if he were a trained Alsatian puppy. Out of curiosity, Anaïs remained with the group of actresses while Nick explained the part one of them would be asked to play.

"We invited you nine in because you best fit what we're looking for in the Sofia character," Nick said. "She's a hardworking girl. She's waiting tables at a cantina in the city when the young Salvador shows up, twisting his mustache, and lures her outside under the full moon. Of course, turns out he's a real monster of a customer."

The other women laughed, but the joke went over Anaïs's head. The blonde next to her took mercy and whispered in her ear, "It's a horror flick set in Madrid. The main character's fiancé is secretly a ghoul of some kind. That's the hook. The Sofia character is his first victim."

"Is that so?" Anaïs was aghast. She'd met many women like Sofia while traveling through Spain. She hated to see the character portrayed as a victim of some fiend who was too cowardly to prey on his own sex.

"After the success of *London After Dark*, this one is sure to be a hit too," the blonde explained.

"What was *London After Dark* about?"

"Do you live under a rock? The movie only brought in about a million bucks," the woman hissed. "Vampires. Ghouls. They came out after midnight to terrorize the city, but the chief vampire was after one woman in particular. But"—she raised a finger triumphantly—"her brother happened to be a professor who specialized in the occult, so he knew what to do. The movie gave me and my girlfriends a real scare, but that Oscar Sinclair who played the brother is just so dreamy to look at. He's back in this one as the premier expert on monsters."

So, Nick West was trying to replicate the studio's success by giving people the heebie-jeebies again. Anaïs got a little chill up and down her backbone that said it must be true. But the information gleaned from Ms. Know-It-All also put her on edge when she'd raised the specter of the occult. Anaïs didn't sit well with uncertainty. So, despite the temptation of landing the role of Sofia and being immortalized on film as the very first victim of the madman of Madrid, Anaïs took the opportunity to slip into the shadows when an actor in a cloak and top hat arrived onstage to play against the actresses during their auditions.

Good luck, ladies!

Anaïs touched her ruby pendant, spreading a veil of glamour that rendered her functionally invisible by making herself a shadowy void so the workers would ignore her presence in the stage building. Being overlooked wasn't a state she was generally comfortable with, but it had its purposes. She needed to stroll through the warehouses and outbuildings on the lot unencumbered. Observing, listening, and sensing. If she was going to pull this off in the way she hoped, she needed to be prepared for the inevitable interference she'd face from certain factions. Anaïs wanted no surprises when it was time to go in for the kill.

After wandering around the sets, there was little to recommend inside Stage One that would aid their objective. Too many active areas. Too many people. Too many potential witnesses. What Anaïs needed was to find a quiet place that wouldn't raise suspicion but that was also sturdy enough to withstand a little drama. Venturing outside to get the lay of the land, Anaïs found the open lot proved slightly more promising, so she waved at Gideon to follow. She walked along a strange city street, where the buildings revealed themselves to be flimsy and hollow when she knocked against them to test for sturdiness. A house on rollers farther ahead made her pause, and she saw the burned remnants of a structure beyond that, which still carried the stench of mischief on it.

It was the burned warehouse that seemed to have caused the most damage to the studio. Both physically and financially. The aftereffects were plain to see on the owner's face. Nick West put on the airs of a carefree, successful man, but he was hanging on by his fingernails. One more hard blow and he'd fall into the abyss to be torn apart in a hell populated by insurance men, debt collectors, and lawyers.

Anaïs headed back toward Stage Two. Inside, things were quieter than Stage One, as though productions hadn't fully taken over the space yet. There were two sets on the far end and an odd winter scene in the corner, but the rest of the real estate was vacant, used instead to store large set pieces, spare lights, ladders, and a pair of plaster lions painted gold.

"This might do," she said when Gideon swooped in through the open door. He landed on top of one of the lion heads. "We get the two of them in here, shut the door. Cloak the whole thing in glamour. Set up some rigging." Her gaze swept the room, taking in all the advantages and disadvantages, shadow and light, massive heights and sneaky hidey-holes. Her mind filled with possibilities. "It could work."

Gideon squawked and stared at the other end of the huge warehouse, where a crew was busy building up the walls of what looked like an apartment or hotel.

"Oh, well, we can create a mishap of some kind to get rid of them," she said to the rook. "We'll put them behind schedule by breaking a light or camera they have to replace. Or maybe I'll have you parade around their set as a skunk when the time comes. That'll flush them out."

The bird shook out his feathers and threw his head back in what Anaïs took for laughter. She chuckled softly, ready to move on, when a blood-freezing scream echoed down from the main building.

CHAPTER EIGHTEEN

Thread of Life

Celeste startled out of a dream, wondering where she was until the smell of wool and machine oil hit and she remembered she was in the sewing room. She glanced at the clock. Half past seven. Odd. Rose was usually in front of her machine by now. She stood and shook off the pains of having dozed off in a chair when she realized Sebastian wasn't there either.

"Sebastian?" When Celeste didn't see the stoat, she went out into the hallway to investigate where he'd gone. There was no trace of him on the first floor, and he didn't answer when she called for him outside by the car. With worry creeping in about what might have alerted him earlier, she retraced her steps and ran upstairs to the second floor, drawn by an instinct she didn't yet understand. Halfway down the hall a woman's scream shattered the quiet.

Celeste hurried toward Isaac Jacobi's office. A light was on inside the vestibule where the accessories were housed between the office and the fitting room. Gladys stood inside with her back to the hallway and her hands splayed out before her as though trying to hold back some unseen threat.

"Gladys?" Celeste hastily cast as much glamour as she could muster over herself to make certain she appeared as Celine.

Hearing her name, the supervisor turned and gripped the doorjamb, barely able to hold herself up. Her skin had gone pale; her breathing caught in her throat so that she gasped for air. When she saw Celeste, she lurched forward into the hallway, leaving behind a smeared handprint on the jamb.

"What's wrong? What's happened?"

Gladys made a noise like she was choking. "She's dead." She swallowed and gasped again, pointing to the room surrounded by mirrors. "I came in early to get the room ready for a fitting." She pressed the back of her forearm to her mouth as though she might be sick. "She was just lying there. I tried to help, but there's so much blood. Oh God, we have to call the police!"

The woman looked down at the gore on her hands and began to shake. Celeste eased Gladys against the wall for support, with her own body flooding with adrenaline. "Stay here," she said and ventured into the fitting room.

Every hair on Celeste's body went erect with dread as she passed Isaac Jacobi's office. She gripped her pendant, worried about her diminished power after a night of repairing dresses for Rose. Would she have enough energy left to defend herself?

Something skittered across the floor in the accessories room. Knowing her magic was iffy, she reached for a brass stand that had been holding up a beaded headdress. She hefted it in both hands in case she needed to hit someone over the head. Pushing against her desire to flee, she crept around the corner and entered the fitting room.

Celeste's gaze latched on to the body on the floor. A pool of blood radiated out like a full moon around the woman's head. A pair of scissors jutted from her neck. The thread of life snipped in two.

Sebastian scampered into the room with paws tinged reddish brown. He stood on his hind legs sniffing the air beside the body. His whiskers twitched as he leaned in toward the woman's face.

Dolores Diaz still wore the butter-yellow dress she'd bought from Rose for the party, only now crimson flowers bloomed across the bodice.

The delicate beading had been slashed at the throat. Celeste didn't need to ask Sebastian to check if the woman was dead. Her slack gray skin was proof enough.

"I don't understand. How did she get here? When did this happen?" It was difficult to reconcile the lifeless figure splayed out on the fitting room floor with the young, vivacious starlet she'd seen a few short hours ago at the party.

Sebastian scurried closer. He lifted his head and pointed his nose toward the woman's injury. Celeste's connection with her companion had weakened, but it wasn't yet depleted. His eyes told her to concentrate on the scissors, and that's when she focused on the heron-shaped handles sticking out of the woman's throat with the initials *RD* highlighted in blood. A shudder rattled through Celeste knowing she'd charmed the scissors to make them cut sharp and true. And now they had.

What had she done?

For a brief second she was tempted to pull the scissors free of the woman's neck and hide them away so no one would know what she'd done or read the lie they were meant to tell. She was bent forward, hand outstretched, when footsteps from behind halted her.

"I called the police. They're on their way!" Gladys shouted. The poor woman didn't dare enter the fitting room again. She stopped short just outside the door, panting while she caught her breath. "That poor girl. God rest her soul."

Celeste straightened and staggered out of the fitting room with her hand pressed under her nose to avoid inhaling too much death. Once the scent got inside you, the transformative energy that clung to the recently deceased tugged on your spirit, spiraling your thoughts ever inward. And right now, she needed a clear heart and mind if she was going to sort this out.

"We should go wait in the sewing room," Celeste said, urging Gladys to walk with her. "You need to clean up before the rest of the girls show up for work. The death will be a shock to them all. We must be ready to meet them."

"Yes, you're absolutely right," Gladys said, holding her hands out from her body as though they were foreign to her.

They'd gone halfway down the stairs when they met Nick West and a handful of his crew rushing from the other direction. "Someone said they heard a scream," he said, breathless from running.

Celeste avoided looking Nick directly in the eye, praying that her glamour would hold up to his scrutiny long enough for her to pass by as just another seamstress from the sewing room. He barely looked at her.

"It's Dolores Diaz," Gladys said to him. "Oh, Nick, I think she's been murdered."

"Murdered?" Nick pushed past them. He ran up the remaining steps, followed by the other men.

Celeste listened to the men gasp and swear to a God they no longer understood as they discovered the body. She urged Gladys to go find the washroom and get cleaned up while she lingered a moment longer on the steps. Two minutes passed. The men finally scattered into the hallway at the sound of approaching sirens on the street below. She hunkered down in the stairwell, clutching her pendant to squeeze out an ounce of glamour to make herself blend in with the bricks and steel. Nick and the other men walked past her on the steps, oblivious to her presence, their skin blanched and sweaty.

Sirens blared on the street outside. Nick galloped down the rest of the stairs, then ran to the far exit, shouting to the guard to let them in. Celeste followed, watching him knock Charlie and his bucket over in the process.

The janitor straightened his uniform, then called out to Celeste when he spotted her coming off the stairs. "Why are the police here?"

"Something terrible has happened, Charlie. A young woman has been killed."

Before Charlie could respond, he was forced to steer his mop and bucket out of the way again as Nick and three police officers rushed inside. Celeste pressed her back against the wall as they ran past and headed upstairs. One of the officers remained downstairs, securing the area once the women began arriving for their morning shifts. Carpenters and electricians from the lot poked their heads inside the building to see what had happened too, and then Oscar Sinclair pushed past all of them as the investigating officers came back downstairs wearing grim faces.

"What's happened?" Sinclair asked. "What are the police doing here?" The actor stretched on his toes to see over the heads in the crowded room as though looking for someone. "Where's Dolores?"

A policeman singled out Sinclair. "Are you a friend of Ms. Diaz's?"

"Yes, we're working together on a picture."

After a brief exchange between the officer and the actor, the basic circumstances of the grisly crime were revealed. A collective gasp erupted in the hallway.

"I don't understand." Sinclair collapsed into a chair beside Gladys's desk while the officer pulled a notebook from his pocket. "We only drove onto the lot forty minutes ago," he said in a daze. "You must be mistaken. Are you sure it's her?" He looked around again as if he might find Dolores among the faces staring at him.

"We?" the officer asked, scratching out a note on his pad. "So you two arrived together? That makes you, what? Married? A couple?"

Sinclair hedged on answering the question outright until the officer ordered the curious bystanders out of the room. When they'd gone, the actor shrugged as he retrieved a polished silver case from his breast pocket and took out a cigarette. "We were nothing official. There was a party at my place last night. Things ran a little late. One thing led to another." He lit his cigarette, hiding his nervousness behind the smoke.

"I don't suppose there was any alcohol involved at this party?"

Sinclair answered with the sincerity of an altar boy. "Of course not, Officer, that would be illegal. But you know how it goes. The hour got late, people were loose, and I believe there was a wet dress that needed removing so it could dry out." Sinclair gave Celeste a curious glance as he slid an ashtray closer to him from Gladys's desk.

"Why so early?" the officer asked. "I mean, if you were partying last night, I'd think you'd both be sleeping it off."

"That would be my preferred routine, but Dolores and I both had early starts on the call sheet this morning. I had a costume fitting set for eight, and she's scheduled for a pivotal scene with Reginald first thing. *Was* scheduled, that is."

"Reginald?" The police officer looked up from his notebook, barely able to conceal his smile. "You mean Reginald King?"

"That's right. New picture we're making together. He plays a marvelous murderer in this one." Sinclair stubbed out his cigarette, eyebrows cinched tight in response to his unfortunate choice of words.

The officer nodded as he made a note. "But if you were the one with the early fitting, what was Ms. Diaz doing here in wardrobe? By the way, where were you prior to arriving in this building?"

Sinclair made a quick glance at his captive audience—Nick, who'd returned from upstairs, Gladys still drying her hands, and a handful of uniformed officers—as though gauging how serious the question was. "I was in my dressing room," he said, face neutral.

"Anyone see you there?"

"I don't know. Maybe."

The officer made a quick note and tapped his pen against the paper as he asked, "And Ms. Diaz? Tell me again. Did she go straight to the fitting room? Or did she stop by her dressing room first?"

"I parked the car, and she came straight to wardrobe. She said she had to speak to someone before reporting to set. She and one of the costumers, a young woman, had a misunderstanding at the party, you see. Some harsh words were exchanged. Words she wholeheartedly regretted. Later in the evening she was angry at herself for having said something cruel. She said it wasn't like her at all. She was desperate to apologize to the poor girl. Dolores seemed to think the young woman had a reputation for coming in to work early, that's why she came straight here."

The officer looked around as though waiting for someone to volunteer who the costumer was.

"I think she said her name was Rose," Sinclair offered. "Yes, I'm sure of it. I saw her name sewn on the label of the dress."

The officer lifted one brow. "The dress that needed drying?"

Sinclair gave a sheepish nod.

"Rose?" Gladys covered her mouth with her hand as the color drained from her face.

The officer pivoted. "Is she here?"

"No, but . . . there's something you should know." The mention of the missing seamstress prompted a worried glance from Gladys as she walked to the back of the room to search Rose's workstation. She opened a drawer beside the sewing machine, then closed it slowly.

The scissors. Celeste's throat constricted knowing the story they told.

"She usually does arrive at work before everyone else." Gladys glanced at the clock that read half past eight. "I don't know where she could be. She's never late."

A man in a gray suit and broad-brimmed fedora pushed through the onlookers to the back of the room. He introduced himself to Gladys as Detective Stan White, then did the same quick search of Rose's workstation. "This gal happen to use a pair of scissors with handles shaped like herons?"

Gladys nodded and confirmed the scissors were missing from Rose's workstation. Celeste shrank back against the wall, too ashamed to be seen. How could she have failed her protégé so badly? How could she not have seen this swath of shade in the young woman's path? Using a final pulse of glamour from her pendant, Celeste veiled herself once more just as Rose entered the room, unusually bedraggled and begging forgiveness for being late. She tried explaining how her trolley had broken down on the tracks but stopped when she noticed everyone staring at her with their mouths hung open.

CHAPTER NINETEEN

Home Sweet Home

"You heard the scream too?"

Gideon swooped down from his perch, landing on a ladder while Anaïs stuck her head outside the warehouse door. The men hammering away inside Stage Two hadn't heard the scream with their plugged-up mortal ears, but the particular shriek of fear associated with the discovery of death had traveled to Anaïs on a chord of sound still vibrating with alarm.

"Our hand may have just been forced early," she said to her companion, feeling the air simmer with misfortune and rising consequences. "You'd better fly and get the word out. I'll wait here as long as I can."

While Gideon ducked out the door and soared over the main building, Anaïs concentrated on forcing the men out of the warehouse. She was in a hurry and didn't have time to be clever. She gave a little sigh, knowing shoddy work couldn't be avoided, then touched her ruby pendant. A small pile of rags kept in a metal bucket in the corner began to smolder until the undeniable scent of smoke wafted under the men's noses. With the studio's recent loss of a building to fire, she assumed it would chase them out.

It didn't. They merely stomped out the smoking cloth and went back to work, shaking their heads and muttering about curses.

Time to try a little harder.

Anaïs, still under the veil of her glamour, remained practically invisible to the humans around her. Her mind raced for a solution as she dug through crates and piles of wire until she came upon a length of rope coiled around a sawhorse. "That will do," she said. With a lift of her brow, she transformed the cord into a six-foot rattlesnake, a species she'd learned about while reading up on the dangers of the American West. Not a real snake, of course, but close enough to fool the ear with its distinct rattle, which supposedly had the power to make a grown man tremble. She sent the snake slithering across the floor until the men jumped against the wall at the sight. The snake coiled in front of them, its body set to strike while flicking its tongue in the air. The men sidestepped toward the elephant-size door, then ran, swearing they'd be back with a pistol.

Once they were gone, she sealed the place with a veil of glamour in case the workmen really did try and come back with a gun. Alone at last, she searched her purse for the first of the two vials she'd bartered for with Edward. She held the contents up to the light, watching the ingredients swirl inside, fighting to be free. If they'd finally arrived at the moment the elixir was made for, she had to be ready. The timing was crucial. She gripped the first vial and tucked it in the sash tied around her hips to keep it handy.

Anaïs supposed there would be hard feelings when this business was all done. It was inevitable when deception was involved. But any perceived harm would blow over. Eventually. If things turned out okay. If no one got hurt. She suspected the fight over the man would be the biggest hurdle to overcome. The attachment between them was strong, however brief a time their bond had had to form. Anaïs shook her head, knowing there was no other way. She reasoned they'd been relatively lucky up to this point—a fire, a few near misses with falling lights and broken cameras, a sketchy sewing machine, a broken leg, all followed by some unflattering press that threatened the livelihood of the studio boss and his backers.

But that scream changed everything.

Already sirens wailed in the background. The scent of blood and fear swung in the air. How would Celeste react? How would she decipher the threat in flux all around her? Would her instincts recognize the danger she was in? Doubtful. It was why Celeste was inside those doors of the main building and she wasn't.

Anaïs moved a few set pieces around the stage to clear the area of the most obvious deadly projectiles—light stands, ceramic pillars, and a few medieval-looking spears leaning in a corner. She was relatively certain the spears were made of something less substantial than iron, but with enough velocity, they could still be as deadly as the real thing. Trouble was unpredictable, and so every precaution taken was another brick in the wall of defense.

The silence outside the stage building became unnerving. There'd been people milling about here and there when she'd arrived, like a sleepy village coming to life. But ever since the scream, the innocuous background noise of people walking, talking, and clearing their throats had diminished to an eerie ghost-town level of silence. She suspected someone had swept the lot for her, and yet she couldn't risk going outside to check. Not when Gideon was still on the move and danger percolated beneath the ground like those ghastly tar pits that bubbled up, tainting the air with their fetid odor.

Anaïs wiped off her hands, one against the other. She hadn't done anything to get her hands dirty per se, but a thing was never done until you wiped yourself free of it. Feeling disjointed while she waited, she wandered over to the set the men had been working on before jumping at the sound of her rattler. Based on the arrangement, it was an American-style living room, with a sofa, two chairs, a coffee table with a magazine with the title *Life* spread on top, a Victrola in the corner, and a set of false stairs built in an outer hallway that led to nowhere.

The ceiling was nonexistent, leaving the top of the room open to the warehouse's rafters and lighting rigs.

She sat on the sofa and crossed her legs. The cushions were uncomfortable and gave off a damp odor, as though they'd been left in the rain and now suffered from mildew. But it was the pillow on the chair opposite with the phrase HOME SWEET HOME cross-stitched into the fabric that left the sour taste. Such quaint domesticity sewn into those three little words. The saccharine expression set her on edge until she was forced to look away for fear of burning the damn thing with a lift of her brow.

Though the workmen hadn't built actual bars around the quaint set, the matrimonial constraint was implied. An invisible cage built for women, camouflaged in the promise of domestic bliss. Alejandro had tried it on her. Maurice too. Even Edward had once proposed to her in a moment of weakness, hoping to keep her tethered to him and no one else till death do them part.

"No, thank you," she said to the pillow, knowing there was too much flight in her blood to settle on any one branch for the rest of her life. She'd rebelled against the restraints the Gardiennes put on her when she'd been younger, thinking a normal existence had been stolen from her before she even had a chance at life, but now she thought she was the luckiest woman alive. Relationships were messy and only ended up interfering in their work. She simply couldn't stay in one place or with one man for very long. A final lesson Celeste needed to learn. If that meant the hard way, so be it.

Anaïs flipped the pillow around so she wouldn't have to look at the trite words again. When she did a little pivot on the rug to double-check what else needed to be done to prepare, she got a small surprise. Climbing out from under the sofa with the fake rattlesnake in its mouth was Celeste's little brown stoat. He proceeded to chew the head off his victim while she calculated how long it would take for Celeste to figure out how much trouble her companion had just stumbled upon.

CHAPTER TWENTY

The Weight of Suspicion

Given the revelation of the argument the night before by Oscar Sinclair and the discovery of the distinctive heron-shaped scissors in the victim's neck that everyone swore to the police belonged to Rose Downey because of the engraved initials, the young woman was handcuffed and led away to be officially questioned at the precinct station house.

"You have the wrong person!" she protested as they led her away. "It wasn't me! How could I do such a thing?"

Gladys folded her arms and smirked. "I always knew there was something off about that girl," she said, then took over completing the finishing touches on the three gowns hung up near Rose's workstation. Celeste nearly collapsed from the disappointment.

The police officers, having corralled the dozens of potential witnesses who'd entered the building into various offices, began interviewing them one at a time about what they knew. Nick appeared to nurse a headache, running his hand through his hair and wandering the long hallway between the wardrobe department and his office as though lost in thought. Sometimes he rubbed his chin. Sometimes he inhaled as though he'd forgotten how to breathe. Once the coroner had removed Dolores's body from the premises, Nick ordered all the employees on the property to go home. Afterward, he informed Gladys he was going to sequester himself in his office and pour himself a drink from the flask he kept hidden behind a stack of scripts if anybody needed him. It was ten o'clock in the morning.

Celeste sobbed as she watched the fallout from the shadows. She knew everyone was wrong about Rose, the police most of all. They had to be. It would have been impossible for her to choose someone with a temperament toward murder to bestow her favor on.

Unless she was the world's worst Fée Gardienne and she'd somehow got it wrong.

Celeste leaned her back against the wall, then slid to the floor when her legs refused to hold her up any longer. The homicide detectives walked past her, never noticing the puddle of a woman at their feet. She'd already erased her existence. She'd been forgotten in everyone's minds. The seamstresses would never remember working with someone who went by the name Celine. Isaac Jacobi would never recall seeing anyone attend to Dolores in the fitting room besides Rose. And Charlie would forget he ever looked in on a pair of giddy seamstresses on the day of their biggest break.

Celeste sniffled and wiped her eyes. She'd never heard of a Gardienne failing so miserably. She didn't know what Dorée or the others would do to clip her metaphorical wings after the mess she'd created. Would they make her give up her sapphire pendant and work as a scullery maid at the cottage? Would they confiscate her gemstones? Take Sebastian away from her? Cast her out of the sisterhood? Maybe they were already thinking she should just stay where she was and adopt the tarnished Hollywood dream like every other human crawling from casting call to casting call.

Celeste was on the verge of accepting her failure when she overheard two detectives talking about the crime scene.

"Other than the scissors, there's not a lot to go on. No one, except the lady supervisor and someone named Zelda, had a bad word to say about the kid. All of them claim she was a hard worker with bright ideas. But there was always a little hesitation when asked if they thought she was capable of something like this." The officer checked his notes. "They all said they think the place is, and I quote, 'cursed.' And if the young woman *did* do it, it probably wasn't her fault. Can you believe that?"

"That's movie-business types for you." Stan White, the first detective on the scene, rolled his eyes. "I'll send someone to speak to the father and check out the girl's alibi. And you need to track down the costume designer and get a statement. Guy by the name of Jacobi."

"Didn't turn up for work today?"

"He initially told his assistant he wouldn't be in today because he was ill, but then she admitted he had an interview over at MGM this morning. Looks like he was getting ready to decamp for greener pastures, but we better double-check. Word is he was a little envious of the girl's talent."

"The seamstress?"

White examined the fabric on the three costumes hanging near Rose's work area with an appreciative eye. "Seems she recently showed him up with a few of her ideas."

The detectives gathered their papers and cleared the area, leaving Celeste alone in the corridor. So even the detectives had their doubts about Rose's guilt. The only real evidence they had against her were the scissors, which would obviously contain her fingerprints, and Sinclair's recollection of the argument between Rose and Dolores at the party the night before. After letting it all sink in, the facts were just a little too tidy and contrived—the murder weapon being a pair of scissors everyone knew belonged to Rose, Dolores provoking Rose into throwing her drink with out-of-character talk, Rose arriving late to work in a disheveled state for probably the first time in her life. None of these things should have been happening to the young woman while under her protection. The magic ought to have been impenetrable.

But if Rose didn't kill Dolores, who did?

Celeste got to her feet, shaken by a deep-rooted suspicion that had finally been given the space it needed to bloom into a full accusation.

Who was the one person who might benefit by pointing the blame at Rose for a ghastly murder? What was there to be gained from seeing a woman fall from grace just as she was meant to find her star path? And whose heart was corrupt enough to kill an innocent woman to get the revenge she craved? The same woman who was willing to curse a child to death in retaliation for a minor trespass.

"Anaïs?" Celeste's blood quickened in her veins. She paced the hallway, thoughts racing. "Could she really have followed me here?" She tuned her perception, sampling the energy around her while focusing on a certain spirited vibration she felt whenever she was around Anaïs. She desperately needed to recharge her magic, but even in her depleted state, she sensed a faint tremor unique to the woman's energy somewhere on the premises. The prospect sent a chill through her body. "She's here."

But could a Gardienne plunge a pair of scissors into a young woman's neck? How shriveled did a heart have to become to be willing to commit murder in the name of retribution? How pinched did an ego have to feel to travel thousands of miles to even a score that never existed in the first place?

Celeste pounded her forehead with her fist. "How could I have made such a terrible mistake by coming to America all alone? Of course she found out where we went. And now we're as good as marooned with a madwoman. Maybe I could send a telegram to Dorée. What do you think?"

Celeste expected Sebastian to be at her side as usual, but when she looked to him for an answer, he was nowhere to be seen. "Sebastian?" She searched under the stairs, in her purse, and in the corner of the sewing room where she'd seen him with the dead mouse, but he wasn't there. He wasn't anywhere.

Something was wrong. He wouldn't have wandered that far without reason. He wouldn't ignore her calls either. Not after what had happened to Dolores. Celeste closed her eyes again, inhaling and exhaling until her breathing aligned with his. His heart was pounding fast. He'd found something. Some kind of wriggling snake. His heartbeat knocked against hers like a telegraph tapping out an SOS. He was in trouble. Was the snake poisonous? Or was it something else he was afraid of? Or *someone* else?

Celeste's eyes shot open. Sebastian had to be on the lot somewhere. She burst out of the back door and played a game of Hot or Cold trying to find him based on the strength of his tiny heartbeat. The lot was eerily empty, yet a strange mix of energy swirled in the open air. A visible cloudlike wisp that was there one moment and gone the next. A full Fée Gardienne's aura was radiant, like the refraction of gemstones in sunlight. Even Anaïs's. But this was different. More muddied. Like brackish water in sunlight filtered through leaves. Unable to pinpoint if the energy was natural, like a mini dust devil or a puff of car exhaust, or not, she kept searching for her companion.

It was only when Celeste approached the outer wall of Stage Two that she caught Sebastian's quick heartbeat thumping away again. She was certain he was inside, but she didn't dare call out to him. The building had been cloaked in a veil of glamour. Most passersby would never notice, but spangles of prism light danced along the roofline and the stage door that were meant to mesmerize the eye and make it look away. Celeste wasn't fooled. She wore a weak variation of the same kind of glamour around her now to keep from being noticed by any stragglers still on the property. It was common Gardienne magic, which meant her suspicions about Anaïs were correct. The implications froze her to the pavement.

Now it was Celeste's heart that raced. She had no doubt Anaïs was on the other side of the door. She swore if the woman did anything to harm Sebastian, she'd squeeze out every last ounce of magic she had left to slam the gussied-up witch from the floor to the rafters. She gripped her sapphire pendant, letting her anger drill down to find the remaining magic, then flung the door open, nearly knocking it off its hinges.

The stage building was bathed in low light. A single light bulb suspended on a wire swung in the air above a sofa and two chairs. The swinging action sent dizzying shadows sailing across the space. Celeste lifted a brow and increased the light. "I know you're in here," she said.

Anaïs stepped out of a false hallway where a staircase led to the rafters above. She held Sebastian in her hands, petting the top of his head as he chittered wildly. "You shouldn't waste your energy like that in here," she said as though Celeste had walked in on a private meeting. Predictably, Anaïs was dressed in black with fringe and gaily embroidered Chinese silk. Did she think a silver comb tucked in her hair made the perfect accessory for committing murder?

"I knew it was you." Celeste's body shook from the confrontation. "I knew I'd seen Gideon last night."

"That was unfortunate timing," Anaïs said. She cooed in Sebastian's ear as she stroked his fur.

Celeste took a step closer, clutching her pendant while she let her anger override everything else. "Put him down!"

"As you wish." Anaïs never took her eyes off Celeste as she slowly lowered the stoat onto a chair that was part of the set. She gave him a final peck on the top of his head before releasing him.

Anaïs had obliged a little too easily. Had she taken a page out of the stoat handbook on distraction? A little fancy dancing to hypnotize her prey, all the while moving closer to sink her teeth into the jugular. Sebastian was a killer, certainly, but at least his bloodletting was born out of the need to survive, not an act of petty revenge because of some perceived slight.

Unnerved by the quizzical look in Anaïs's eye as she straightened and wrapped her shawl closer around her, Celeste beckoned the little stoat to her side. "It's all right, Sebastian. You did well in locating her. I'll handle things now."

The stoat was rightfully upset. He chittered almost nonstop until Anaïs hushed him with a quick click of her tongue. "I can understand what you might be imagining, discovering me here like this," the Gardienne said.

"I haven't imagined anything." Celeste's anger boiled over until her eyes filled with the heat of hot tears. "I know it was you who killed that young woman today. A promising actress with a bright future." Squeezing her pendant for all it was worth, Celeste brought the set wall down behind Anaïs, intending to splinter the wood and plaster in a show of force. Instead, Anaïs transformed the wall into a curtain that folded neatly to the floor.

"Careful, Celeste."

"And why her? Because you were offended that I didn't let you kill an innocent child? That I somehow made you look bad? What's *wrong* with you? You're a Fée Gardienne. You're supposed to better people's lives, not ruin them."

Anaïs hadn't moved, so Celeste sent the prop lamp flying at her. The Gardienne redirected it in the air with a twitch of her eyebrow, turning it into a papier-mâché bird that sailed just over her head.

"Celeste, stop!" Anaïs slid behind a pillar to avoid being hit by any more thrown objects. "The actress's future was already cast in shadow," she called out. "You know that. Sebastian told me you both sensed it."

"You'll use any excuse to murder someone." Celeste scowled and tipped a heavy klieg light, making it crash at Anaïs's feet. The glass smashed and the bulb exploded with a loud pop. The strike looked and sounded worse than it was, but she relished the way Anaïs jumped back with a squeal. "You really traveled thousands of miles to ruin my chance to succeed and destroy an innocent woman's life?"

Anaïs poked her head out from behind the pillar. "Actually, two women, if you're going to keep count."

Celeste's anger mixed with the energy of her pendant to send an eighteen-foot ladder hurling through the air, but her energy flagged, and the ladder clattered to the floor several feet short of its target.

"Well, now I don't think you're even trying to hit me," Anaïs said in a voice entirely too tolerant of the situation. "I'm happy to let you air your grievances, but I think that's quite enough." She stepped out from behind the pillar. Playfully swinging her pendant on the end of its chain, she made a chair slide across the floor. It hit Celeste in the back of her calves, forcing her to sit. Celeste attempted to stand, but her body was held firm in the seat by an invisible force that strapped her down.

"That's better." Anaïs swiped a stray hair out of her eyes and came closer, holding her shawl in place around her shoulders. She sat on the sofa opposite Celeste and crossed her legs, exhaling as though she'd needed to discipline a small child who'd acted out.

Celeste struggled in the chair. "What did you do to me? Why can't I move? Sebastian, do something!" Her companion climbed up on her shoulder, then rested his head against her ear, purring softly as his warm breath pulsed against her skin.

"I need you to calm down," Anaïs said. "If you don't, I have no compunction against taping over your mouth to make you do so." A roll of masking tape flew into her hand from the workbench on the other side of the stage. She pulled a length of tape free and raised an eyebrow.

Celeste stopped struggling. Sebastian's behavior had her confused, as did Anaïs's. "What have you done to Sebastian? What are you going to do to me?"

"To you?" Anaïs sat back, a pouty smile on her face. "You really are as naive as everyone claimed you to be."

"What's that supposed to mean?" Celeste tried again to move her arms, but they wouldn't budge. The Gardienne went quiet. A shadow swooped over Celeste's head as Gideon flew inside the stage building and landed on the seat beside Anaïs. He shook out his glossy feathers as another figure entered on foot behind him.

"It means Anaïs isn't your enemy."

CHAPTER TWENTY-ONE

The Downfall Effect

Celeste felt the woman's presence before she saw her face. "Dorée?" The eldest Fée Gardienne walked onto the stage carrying a carved wooden staff that looked like something out of a prop room for a medieval fairy tale. She wore a hooded cloak over a full-length gown with her diamond pendant the size of a quail egg hung prominently around her neck. Her silver hair was pinned up in its usual cornucopia, with Benoit poking his nose out to sniff the air.

"I don't understand," Celeste said. "How did you get here?"

Dorée sat beside Anaïs, keeping to the edge of the cushion as she held her staff upright before her. "I arrived on a steamship bound for New York, the same one as you. Followed by a grueling train ride through the most remarkably diverse landscape. I had no idea America was so big. I'd barely packed enough cheese for Benoit for the journey."

Celeste began to think she was hallucinating. That handsome man in the tails and top hat had slipped her a mickey in her drink at the party. Yes, she must be under the influence of some strange concoction and hadn't woken up yet. Dolores was fine. Rose was fine.

Dorée gave her a pitying sideways glance, as though she knew exactly what Celeste was thinking. "No, my dear, you're not imagining anything. That poor young woman truly was murdered. And our job is to find out by whom."

Celeste's gaze shifted to Anaïs, who smirked in response. "You're barking up the wrong tree, sister."

"Yes, as for that little misunderstanding, I owe you an explanation," Dorée said. "But first we need to add another layer of security to this unusual setting." The Gardienne gripped her staff and made a stirring motion. The air swirled around the three women and their animal companions until they were encapsulated inside the calm eye of a whirlwind. Celeste couldn't see anything past the cloudlike wall of churning energy that surrounded them. It ought to have made her dizzy, but it didn't. Instead, she felt cocooned and safe. "Now, that should keep us protected so we may speak freely."

Dorée tilted her staff toward Celeste. A band of prism light touched her skin, and her arms were freed from their invisible bindings. "Please, somebody say something to make this make sense," Celeste said, rubbing her arms.

"I have a small confession to make." The eldest Gardienne wasn't the least bit contrite, despite beginning with words some might use to preface an apology. "You have been ill used, my dear, but it couldn't be helped."

"Ill used? A young woman died today. My first-ever protégé has been arrested for the murder."

"Yes, that was unfortunate." Dorée raised a hand to silence Celeste when she tried to protest the lack of compassion shown yet again. "But what you must understand is there was always a high probability there would be bloodshed." The Gardienne tapped her pendant with her free hand. A set of scales appeared on the coffee table, though unlike any Celeste had ever seen before. A golden woman served as the fulcrum holding up two bejeweled pans suspended on chains that hung from her hands. But then the arms rotated, and on the other side was the featureless form of a man carved out of lapis lazuli who held a pair of onyx pans. One side of the scale tipped to his right, weighed down by a dark glob of tar, before the arms rotated back to reveal the female side once again.

Even though she didn't understand the meaning, Celeste felt the first tingling of truth invade the periphery of her intuition. There'd always been something extreme about being forced to go to America. Something unjust in her punishment and not Anaïs's. She pulled the postcard out of her purse, seeing it in a different light. "My coming here to Hollywood wasn't my choice at all, was it."

"Oh, you kept it!" Anaïs reached for the card, then examined it front and back, smiling as if she were in a shop picking up a souvenir. "How charming."

"The postcard was Anaïs's idea." Dorée glanced at the sender's name and did a poor job of hiding her disapproval. "It was embedded with a small enchantment to make you curious enough about Hollywood you'd be motivated to make the long journey alone."

"But why? You told me the travel was for my own good." Celeste stared daggers at Anaïs. "That I was in *danger* if I stayed in Europe."

Gideon squawked like he'd been insulted, while Anaïs raised an indifferent eyebrow at the remark. She handed the postcard back to Celeste. "The truth is, we're all in danger, sweetheart. But, yes, I suppose you most of all due to your lack of experience."

It might be true, but it still landed like an insult coming from Anaïs.

"Ever since the end of the Great War and the decline of the royal houses, there's been a growing imbalance between what we do and what the *others* do," Dorée explained. "A rise in the instability in the way things have always been. You see, there are certain unspoken rules in our line of work. The good-fortune work we do is only one side of the scale. On the other there has always hovered the specter of misfortune." Dorée had the scales rotate again to show the blue man on the other side. "There were never any formal contracts written per se, but agreements were made, all the same, that everyone accepted as fair. Fair to us, to the others, and to the protégés themselves. A matter of balance, you see. For nearly two centuries this has gone on without any issue."

Celeste recalled her lessons in the cottage under Beatrix's tutelage. She'd been taught from her earliest memory about the powerful fate the Fées Gardiennes granted when they selected a protégé. As benefactors of that remarkable gift, they had to be mindful of who they bestowed such rising good fortune on, because there was always the inevitable fall from grace. The shoe drop. The footfall of shadow. Once the protégé found their star path and followed it to their pinnacle of success, there awaited the inevitable slide down the back side of fortune. It could mean good luck in business, bad luck in love. The gift of brains and beauty, the curse of addiction and scandal. Celeste never quite understood why this downfall had to happen, only that she was taught that whoever she chose as a protégé should be someone who would have the emotional fortitude to withstand the inevitable lead weights that would pull against the next phase of their life. Not everyone bore such resilience.

"You're talking about the downfall effect," Celeste said solemnly as Sebastian climbed off her shoulder to nestle in the crook of her arm.

"Just so." Dorée gave a curt nod, as if she did not wish to linger on the term.

"But the downfall effect isn't an inevitable occurrence like tossing an apple in the air only to have it fall again under the power of gravity," Anaïs said. She shrugged off her shawl to reveal her bare shoulders—powder white against the straps of her black dress. The contrast only further accentuated her bold red lipstick. "There are forces that are attracted to success, happiness, victory. All the good fortune we dole out. But they crave something more sinister from the attraction. The opportunity to cause harm and see the person's fortunes tumble. Quite often the higher the business success of a person, the bigger and more public the personal downfall."

Celeste knew this. It was all part of her lessons growing up. But being encapsulated within the whirlwind with the eldest Gardienne, and the nearest thing she had to a nemesis in Anaïs, made her suspect something more serious was happening than the usual give-and-take of both sides of the scales of fortune. Especially since her own protégé hadn't even been positioned on her star path yet.

"Do you know who the others are?" Dorée asked.

At one time Celeste had half suspected Anaïs was one of them. "The Skulks are like shadows that sniff around the successful looking for vulnerabilities to exploit?"

"Yes and no," Dorée said. "That's more of a derogatory term some people use. No doubt Mathilda is responsible for passing that pejorative along." There was a slight eye roll but no further reproach. "The Infortunii are much more than shadows."

Dorée raised her staff and pointed it at the whirlwind. Several likenesses of well-known figures from the past swept by on the wall of swirling air. The famous faces were known as much for their successes in life as for the tragedies they later become infamous for: a child musical prodigy who'd played his compositions before kings but later died a pauper; the last czar of Russia and his family shot in a basement; a Victorian playwright who'd been the talk of the town only to be sent to prison for indecency; a stage actress lauded as the greatest of her generation who lost a leg after an agonizing accident.

"The work of the Infortunii," Dorée said as more faces went by. "None of it done in the shadows, though you weren't completely mistaken. The Infortunii's natural form is one of mutability. But they are quite capable of taking on the appearance of a man, a woman, a fish, a cloud even. They use the art of disguise to get close enough to study our protégés before exacting the payment due to balance the scales."

"Payment?" A chill cascaded through Celeste, as she'd never heard it explained in terms of a debt owed.

"Our agreement with the Infortunii. We are allowed to raise certain individuals up, and later they get to take a bite out of that luck. Sometimes a little. Sometimes a lot. Not out of spite or jealousy. It's simply their nature to suckle at the teat of misfortune. They serve a purpose in nature, the same as any bottom-feeder. Keeping balance.

Imagine if people never had anything to worry about but enjoying their happiness and success? Their heads would float off their bodies into a cloud of entitlement. A dose of humility keeps one grounded."

Celeste regarded the scales on the table. "I recognize clearly enough the importance of equilibrium in the relationship our kind holds with Skulks . . . I mean, the Infortunii." She pushed a finger against one of the scale's jeweled plates to see it move. "What I don't understand is why you've traveled five thousand miles to tell me something I already know."

The faces on the whirlwind vanished. The air inside their cocoon of glamour went still as the Gardiennes settled back in their seats.

Dorée smiled grimly. "Three months ago, I was contacted by a gentleman named Barnaby. My counterpart in the Infortunii. He came to me asking for a favor."

Agreeing to a favor for someone who drinks the milk of human misfortune couldn't be good, Celeste thought. Sebastian thought so, too, as he shivered in her arms. Celeste sneaked a peek at Anaïs. She hadn't spent a lot of time around the woman. There was an eight-year difference in their ages so that by the time Anaïs had graduated to living in the larger world outside the cottage in the woods, Celeste was only just learning the fundamentals of their kind. Their one meaningful interaction was the day she believed Anaïs had tried to murder an innocent child. But she could honestly say she'd never seen anyone stay so still or go so pale for so long as Anaïs did while listening to Dorée's account of being contacted by the Infortunii.

"Spring had not yet poked its head up out of the ground when I felt a chill so deep it nearly froze my liver." Dorée squirmed slightly in her chair. "I was sitting in my salon wondering if I should see a doctor, when a man in a pin-striped suit and fedora approached my front door. Normally I would have had a servant send him away, but the shiver in my liver said otherwise. Barnaby introduced himself with such charm." Dorée scoffed in disbelief, as if she still couldn't believe it. "I invited him in for tea, which he accepted. The conversation was pleasant while we stuck to the weather, but then he set his cup down. Overtaken by what I took for embarrassment, he looked away while explaining that he'd lost track of one of his own. An entity named Liam.

"Barnaby said this fellow Infortunii had complained incessantly about their lot in life. Too many celebrities. Too many artists. Always forced to hold off for months or years before casting their misfortune on our famous protégés. This Liam fellow didn't see any reason why things shouldn't be reversed. Let the Infortunii have the first bite at the apple and the downtrodden could find their arc of success with us afterward." She shook her head at the state of things. "When the royal houses fell, tradition went right out the window with them."

Dorée paused, turning her head toward the door as though she'd heard something. Celeste and Anaïs locked eyes and shook their heads to say they hadn't noticed anything. Dorée checked with Benoit to see if he'd been alerted to a sound, but when he yawned and scratched his ear, she continued with her tale.

"Barnaby came to me because he was afraid this missing colleague had gone rogue. Well, you can imagine what kind of havoc that would create, if one of the Infortunii decided to get proactive with their misery. The entire balance between fortune and misfortune might break down if none of us were expected to stick to the unspoken rules any longer. The idea!"

At news of a rogue Skulk on the loose, Celeste's instincts tingled with suspicion. "Earlier you said I'd been ill used. What did you mean by that exactly?"

Anaïs gave Gideon's neck feathers a scratch. "Well, you'll never guess where the missing Skulk miscreant finally turned up."

"Liam is here?" Celeste experienced the chill she'd felt in the wardrobe room all over again. "That's who's been jinxing the studio?" She sat up straighter. "And my protégé?"

"We can apparently add murder to the mix now too," Anaïs said.

A stern look from Dorée made Anaïs turn an invisible key against her lips. "Barnaby's purpose in seeking me out was to ask for our help in locating this missing Liam. The Infortunii are the worst cowards, but they're dangerous and unpredictable nonetheless. Due to their intrinsic nature and proclivity toward violence, the tendency for the situation to fall into a downward spiral of worsening events is nearly guaranteed if a confrontation between two or more of them were to occur. And if the confrontation were to take place in public, can you imagine the consequences?" Dorée produced a fan from her cloak and waved it at her face. "It was suggested our glamour would make a better and safer defense against an Infortunii in a city of one million people."

"So how do you stop this rogue Infortunii?" Celeste looked from Anaïs to Dorée, wondering what training they had that would prepare them for such an encounter. "How do you even find him?"

"See, that's where you come in, toots." Anaïs plastered a wicked grin on her face.

"Me?"

"Being of the same general ilk as we Fées Gardiennes—believe me, it pains me to say it—the Infortunii can see us for who we truly are, even when disguised in our glamour. All of the older sisters are known to them. Some even follow us around plotting the exact moment they'll inflict a protégé's downfall. Like a wolf sniffing out a weak fawn. But you, Celeste, are different. As an initiate, you're still an unknown to them. You haven't yet established your first protégé on their star path, and so your light, your magic, is not yet powered from within. Your aura radiates at a lower frequency, closer to that of ordinary people. And yet, because you were born to be one of us, this stray Infortunii would naturally be attracted to your small but bright inner light."

"Wait, are you saying you sent me here to act as bait for a murdering shadow?" Celeste sprang out of her chair.

"Look at that, she's finally catching on," Anaïs said. "Almost sounds worse than traveling halfway around the world to get away from *my* murderous instincts, doesn't it? Which, by the way, that business at the christening was all part of the ruse. I'm on very friendly terms with Fontaine and his wife. That's why they agreed to the charade." She leaned back, crossing her legs, unperturbed. "I mean, did you really think I'd curse a child to death?" she asked, rubbing the underside of Gideon's neck until the rook cooed and purred.

Yes, actually.

At the revelation, Celeste had to question whether her life had become a mere illusion. That was the only explanation that made sense. She sank back down in her chair with the urge to reevaluate her entire existence.

Dorée fanned herself while Benoit squeaked from inside the curl of her hair. She shook her head in mild apology. "The truth is, Celeste, we did lead you astray on a point or two, but we needed you to believe that avoiding Anaïs's wrath was the sole reason you were sent away. The only direct information Barnaby could provide was he'd detected an anomaly in the flux and flow between our energies." Dorée directed their attention to the scales again to demonstrate the imbalance on the Skulk side. "I did some deep scrying and felt very strongly the source of the imbalance was concentrated on the west coast of this country. Too many outcomes here had tilted toward despair and iniquity lately. Well, more than is normal for the region. Barnaby and I surmised the Hollywood area was the most likely place Liam had fled to, given his attitude toward celebrity and the spike in negative energy. With that as our only lead, we couldn't take the chance of him sniffing out one of us before we had the chance to find him and flush out his motivations. He simply must be stopped."

"He needs to be stuffed in a gunnysack and drowned in the ocean," Anaïs said, then locked her lips again and threw away the key in anticipation of another reprimand.

Celeste wasn't convinced their ploy had worked. "But he could be anyone. Anywhere in the city."

"Because the Infortunii and the Fées Gardiennes are linked on the spectrum of fate and fortune, we were confident you and he would ultimately be attracted to the same energy of potential," Dorée said. "There aren't that many truly worthy candidates for a protégé, even in a city of a million."

Under the weight of Dorée's practical logic, Celeste was forced to sort her understanding from her anger, like lentils from ashes, but it was her anger that won out. She felt used. Like a cheap stage prop. A means to someone else's ends. She began to worry her life would always follow that same pattern. She'd been taken from her home as a babe, denied knowledge of who she was or where she came from, and raised to serve the hopes of others. Then her own people had the gall to send her halfway around the world to search for her first protégé alone, knowing she'd have a target on her back, only for the mission to end in the callous murder of an innocent woman. For ones so closely aligned with the benevolent side of fate, they sure had a talent for deceit.

A thread snapped inside Celeste. Maybe the Skulk's influence had somehow infected her blood like a virus and she was the cursed one now, or perhaps she was just worn out from the subterfuge. All she knew was that she was done being manipulated and exploited.

"In that case, he's definitely here," Celeste said. "I don't know who he is or what he looks like, but I've felt his shadow form, here and at Rose's house. He could be posing as someone who works at the studio. Someone who has access to the lot." Celeste's intestines formed a hitch knot as she thought about Dolores again. "I only wish I'd known what I was looking for so I could have stopped him."

"Your instincts about the seamstress led us here," Dorée said in her typical muted way of showing approval. "We're in the right place. Now all we need to do is flush the murderer into the light and end this loathsome affair."

Celeste settled Sebastian in her arms and stood. "I wish you the best of luck with that, but I'm done with this carnival ride. I wish you'd been on the level with me. Or at least have let me known the danger I was walking into. Instead, you dangled me out there like a worm over a hungry toad. So now I'm going back to my bungalow to consider my options for how to get home." Celeste walked to the edge of the cyclone swirling around them and tested the boundary with her hand. "Open it," she demanded.

"Celeste, don't be absurd." Dorée tapped her staff on the stage. "Sit down. We still have much to discuss."

"I'm done talking. You've lied to me for weeks. Now open it!" Celeste pressed her hand against the wall of spinning air. Suspecting the energy was meant to keep others out rather than keeping her in, she took a chance and jumped through the cloud wall without looking back.

CHAPTER TWENTY-TWO

Shrouded in Frost

Dorée stared in disbelief at Celeste's dramatic exit, but Anaïs sympathized with the young woman. They'd used the inexperienced initiate instead of trusting her, just as she'd claimed. They'd set her up in a dangerous situation and expected her to take the news in stride once they explained that it was all a ruse for the better good. They might have gotten away with a heartfelt apology before, but not after the murder of a young woman.

"She'll be back," Dorée said, stubbornly optimistic in her assessment.

Anaïs wasn't so sure. Knowing the part she'd played in the deception, she suffered an unusual flutter of conflict over the way the scenario had unfolded. To be safe, she sent Gideon after Celeste to keep an eye on her. They should have anticipated how she might react. Fées Gardiennes were all afflicted with the same wound. The older women had the benefit of time that perhaps allowed them to forget, or at least make peace with their history, but for her and Celeste, two of the youngest, the wounds were still just a little too tender, the scars just a little too new.

Anaïs remembered the day they brought Celeste to the cottage. She was wrapped in a blue blanket and laid in the crib beneath the window so she could absorb the morning sunlight. Anaïs was nine at the time and still didn't quite grasp what had happened—to her, to Celeste, to the older sisters. But she welcomed the new little one with a kiss on the forehead. Desdemona had said she'd done the right thing. When Anaïs asked if Celeste's mother and father would miss her, Beatrix got a wistful look in her eye and said, "No, they've had to leave her behind, dear. She's in our care now, but her parents send their love." As proof, she'd pointed to the window and the shaft of golden light that hit the babe's curly locks.

Years later, Anaïs had been in one of her ever-growing defiant moods and sneaked into the attic to hide from Charlotte and Mathilda, ignoring their pleas to come out. There she discovered a dusty scrapbook with all the Gardiennes' names listed in it, from Mathilda, the living eldest, to Celeste, the newest and youngest. Sometimes a letter, a card, or a newspaper clipping was affixed next to the name with a dab of glue. Sometimes just a written notation. But for each woman and their predecessors, there was an entry for how they came to be orphaned and later were brought to the cottage to fulfill a place in the roster of Fées Gardiennes. None of them had families anymore. No parents. No siblings. Their family members had all died in tragic accidents, leaving behind a single child, always a girl, to be swept up and taken to the cottage to be raised by the sisterhood. From that moment on they had only each other, their mission, and a gnawing ache to know who and what they once belonged to and who they might have been under different circumstances.

"We should have confided in her," Anaïs said, leaning forward to study the dual scales for herself. "She isn't a child any longer."

"Be that as it may, she's acting like one now." From the look on Dorée's face, her true emotions betrayed her as soon as the remark left her mouth, as though they'd pinched her insides.

"We're the closest thing she has to a family, and we lied to her. Used her, even. You know how tender the subject of trust is for most of us."

Dorée gave a little ground. "Yes, yes, I know you're right. I understand we all wrestle with the demands of our calling differently." The elder Gardienne took a packet of sunflower seeds from her cloak pocket and poured them into her hand. Benoit scurried down from his safe space inside her hair and nibbled at the offering. "It took me years to settle into the cottage and understand my place there. Of course, I was nearly six years old when I'd arrived."

Anaïs had studied every page of the hidden scrapbook and knew everyone's story by heart. The steamship Dorée and her parents had been on in 1850 had sunk in the English Channel. There were no survivors save for the five-year-old girl the Gardiennes had scooped out of the sea and stolen away to raise as one of their own.

"None of us have had to add murder to the list of things to contend with on our first job."

"The news of the woman's death was grim," Dorée admitted. "Which is why it's so important we flush out this Infortunii. He's here somewhere. It's time to lure him out into the open before he does any more damage. Certainly, we can feel justified in our actions on that front."

"And then what?" Anaïs put the weight of her finger on the scale. It didn't move. "I persuaded Edward to mix the bottle of elixir as you asked easy enough, but I haven't got a clue how to get it down this Skulk's throat. Our glamour won't sufficiently fool him, so how can we get close enough to hold him down?"

"That's why we still need Celeste. Though loathsome, he may have already formed a bond with her. Well, as much as any Skulk is capable of. Hopefully he hasn't figured out why he's attracted to her yet. Our best scenario is that he glommed on to her hoping to cause mayhem in her life like he did with Rose. But that's why we need Celeste to lure him out."

"You mean to wiggle her like a worm in front of his hungry toad mouth?" Anaïs couldn't help twisting the knife a little.

"This fight is hers too. As soon as she realizes it, she'll come back. She must, if we're to have any chance of breaking the bond between them. I'm not sure there's another way, short of knocking both her and the Skulk unconscious so we can pour the elixir down their throats. Which I'll do, if I must."

They hadn't had the chance to mention that part to Celeste before she'd stormed out. Anaïs wished it could be her instead to lure out the Skulk. She was the one who'd always had nerves of brass. But she already had a well-known reputation with the Infortunii after kicking one of them off a bridge when he'd followed her from Paris to Bruges. Wasn't her fault a barge just happened to be chugging down the canal when he fell in. Besides, he got what was coming to him after trying to interfere with her protégé's grand opening as the city's first female chocolatier. Sometimes a little cockiness was needed to make the bastards keep their distance so a girl could breathe. Nonetheless, the incident with the Skulk had made her a target.

"I'll go check on her," Anaïs said. "See if I can get her to look at the bigger picture." She reasoned Celeste's feelings were only temporarily hurt. The young woman's sense of justice ran deep, so she ought not to need much convincing that what they were trying to do was for all the right reasons.

"In the meantime," Dorée said, gazing at the enormously tall ceiling. "I'll see if there's another location where we can lure this Skulk to. This stage building is too large for my comfort. It's contained, but there are too many places for things to go wrong."

Dorée leaned on her staff as Anaïs helped her step off the stage platform. They were prepared to go their separate ways under the veil of their glamour, but before they made it to the exit, the building's walls rumbled and shook as though struck with an enormous force.

"That wasn't the wind," Anaïs said, staring at an indentation made in the wall.

Dorée tightened her grip on the elder staff. "It's him. He's discovered we're here."

"How?"

"He must have followed Celeste. Skulking is what they do, after all."

"We're not ready for him." Anaïs shuffled Dorée to the other side of the building, searching for a back way out. There wasn't a door, but that didn't mean they couldn't make one. Anaïs gripped her pendant and drew an oval in the air with her finger. A section of wall fell away, just big enough for them to slip through, until a large, bladed pendulum swung across the opening, threatening to cut them in two if they dared go forward. Anaïs attempted to transform the pendulum into a revolving door, but her magic crystallized in the air and sifted to the ground like snowflakes.

"Try the front again," Dorée said.

They hurried back to the other side, only to be met by an advancing German shepherd that foamed at the mouth and snapped its teeth.

"Is it real?" Anaïs asked, hoping the dog was somehow an illusion. But it was a false hope. The Infortunii didn't rely on any trick of the eye to inflict their brand of terror. They cast their pain in flesh and blood.

"Real, and it apparently has a master," Dorée said as a man stepped out of the shadows, a ghastly grin splitting his face.

"Well, well, well, two precious fairies caught like moths in a trap," the Skulk said with eyes cold as ice.

Dorée straightened her back. "We prefer to be addressed as Fées Gardiennes, if you please."

Anaïs wasn't sure it was the right time to be arguing over titles.

The Skulk scoffed. *"If I please?"*

"What is the meaning of these obstacles you have surrounding us?" Dorée tapped her staff, tipping it slightly toward the yapping dog, but the animal only snarled more viciously. "I am the eldest of the Gardiennes, and you will show me the respect I deserve. Now, let us step outside and we can have a chat about all this."

The hideous smile vanished. "The old country and its ways are dead. In this new frontier *I* make the rules." His tone left them no illusions about his intent, nor did the intense cold that crept in off his breath like a spell as he spoke. "You want to chat? The young woman is mine, and I get first bite. That's all I have to say. Sleep well." And then the Skulk slammed the door shut.

Anaïs's fingers went numb. Her reservoir of magic slogged like winter sap in her veins as she pounded on the door. "Liam, wait!"

Dorée lifted her staff to stop the Skulk, but there was no flickering energy to force the door open, no flash to blind him, only an intense cold that shrouded the women in a layer of frost.

CHAPTER TWENTY-THREE

The Illusion of Magic

Celeste put the Pierce-Arrow in gear and drove. She was eager to get as much space between her and the studio as she could get on a half tank of gas. She felt wrung out. Used. Lied to. Outrage and fury churned inside every time she thought about how she'd ended up driving the streets of a crowded foreign city five thousand miles from home. She shoved the gearshift into third and hit the accelerator.

The farther south Celeste drove, the heavier the traffic grew until she was forced to slow down or crash. A feeling she was getting overly familiar with lately. A few blocks ahead she came to a busy road where dozens of Model Ts jockeyed for position in their lanes. The "stop" arm on the semaphore ahead popped up, so she halted the car a few feet behind the intersection and rested her head against the steering wheel. While not ready to forgive, she understood the dire need to confront an unchecked, murdering Infortunii. She could even justify Anaïs's instinct to do whatever was necessary to stop him from causing any more harm, including her deep deception. At least *she* hadn't turned out to be a murdering Infortunii out for revenge. A small bright spot. But then Dorée had to go and say the Skulk would be attracted to her for reasons he wouldn't grasp yet. He would have been drawn to the energy of her glamour, even though he couldn't see her as a Fée Gardienne. He would have wanted to be near her. Revive her when she fainted. Hang up on a colleague so he could walk with her down a studio street surrounded by false buildings. Take her to dinner. Maybe even kiss her when he took her home.

The light changed to green and the "go" arm sprang out from the signal. Three cars honked at her before she let off the brake and pulled forward. At the last minute she decided to turn right onto Wilshire Boulevard. She and Sebastian were both wiped out. They desperately needed to return to the bungalow and recharge so they could go check on Rose. Despite everything, Celeste still hoped to see her protégé protected and set on her path. If it wasn't already too late.

The area surrounding the boulevard was aggressively being developed, but large swaths of land were still populated with oil derricks. And tar pits too. Such curious pools of asphalt that bubbled up through the earth. An acrid odor lifted off the blackened ponds as she drove past, making her cover her nose with the back of her hand. Sebastian concurred, wiping his face against the seat.

When Celeste returned to the hotel, she left the car with the valet, then took the narrow garden path back to her private bungalow. She'd deliberately avoided the hotel lobby and the chipper front desk clerk, too worn out to make light conversation with anything more animated than her pillow. Rodney caught up to her anyway, flagging her down to deliver a message along with a bouquet of flowers.

"These arrived for you yesterday," he said, handing her the flowers and a card in an envelope with her first name written in fanciful script on the outside. "From Nick West himself," he said, shuffling his eyebrows. "I was just about to put them in your room for you."

What he didn't say was that he'd noticed she hadn't returned to the hotel last night. She was sure he had all kinds of ideas about that.

Celeste tucked the flowers in her arm and thanked the clerk, giving him a coin from her purse. He waited around as though hoping she'd open the note, but she didn't want to read it just yet. Not out in the open. Better to get inside her room, away from lurking spies. Oh, yes, she'd seen Gideon flying about from tower to cornice to rooftop once she got out of the car. Naturally, Anaïs and Dorée would want to keep her under their watchful eyes since they already believed they had her under their thumbs. She pulled her scarf over her head to hide her face from the rook's penetrating glare, then escaped inside her bungalow.

Exhausted, Celeste kicked off her shoes and set her purse and the flowers on the bed. Sebastian escaped from her bag and shook out his fur. His nose twitched in the air as he explored the bedspread while Celeste sank into the mattress, resting her heavy head against the pillow.

"How did this happen, Sebastian?" Celeste stared up at the ceiling, fanning herself with the note she hadn't yet opened. "Our first chance to fly solo and we sailed right into a trap." When the stoat didn't reply with a reassuring nudge, Celeste lifted her head to look for him. "Sebastian?" She thought he'd curled up on the edge of the bed near the flowers, but instead he'd jumped down on the floor. After searching either side of the bed, she found him sniffing around the area near the trunk. "What is it?"

Even before he began trilling in alarm, Celeste sensed disaster. The scent of hair pomade and something else that reminded her of bitter herbs hung about the corner of the room. Sebastian inched closer to the trunk, and his nose twitched as though he'd inhaled something pungent and deadly. She noticed then the latch on the trunk appeared bent and the hinges sat somewhat wonky, as though they'd been forced apart. The residue of some sticky substance coated the latch.

Celeste sprang from the bed and tugged on the trunk's broken lock. "Oh no, no, no." She flipped the latch open and swung the lid wide. The trunk had been ransacked. Her personal belongings had been sorted through and stuffed back in their drawers randomly. Her books were splayed and torn at the bottom, and her bottles of ointments, herbs, and medicines had been opened and left to dry out. But the thing that made her sink to her knees was the missing jar of gemstones.

Celeste covered her mouth with her hand as her blood drained to her feet. "Oh, Sebastian, we're in real trouble. They're gone. They're really gone."

The stoat ran around the room in a frenzy, poking his nose inside the trunk, behind the trunk, behind the sofa and curtains. But the stones were gone. Stolen.

"He was here in this room, Sebastian. It had to be him. The Skulk figured out where we're staying. If he didn't know who or what I was before, he knows now."

Fear gripped her heart and squeezed until her imagination began conjuring up everything that could go wrong. Without the gems, she couldn't recharge. Sebastian couldn't recharge. They would still have some connection, some magical skill at their fingertips, but it would be severely weakened. Celeste gripped her sapphire pendant. There was still a mild thrum there, like a car on its last ounce of fuel.

Why had she wasted so much energy throwing ladders at Anaïs? It might have been worth it if she'd hit her, but she'd missed each time. *Almost* on purpose. Celeste wiped a tear away and started pulling everything out of the trunk. Maybe they'd missed the jar of gems beneath all the other items on their first search through the damage. Surely a thieving Skulk wouldn't know what the gems were for. Though he would know their monetary value. They'd be an easy thing to pocket and sell.

Celeste gave up when she'd sorted through the trunk for the third time and all she'd accomplished was making a messy heap on the floor of things she had to put back. She slumped against the wall with her legs spread out in front of her. "How did he get inside? How did he get around our protections? Oh, Sebastian, what are we going to do?"

Her eye landed on the card from Nick. Had he really been capable of this? She grabbed the unopened envelope, slit the seal, and read the note.

Thanks for making my day a little brighter. I'll call you later.

—Nick

She burst into tears. Was this part of some plan to torment her? Flatter her, make her feel wanted, then cut her legs out from under her by stealing her gemstones. Then what? Finish her off like he did Dolores? She knew Skulks were devious, deceitful, malicious, but toying with her heart was low even for an Infortunii.

That is, if it was Nick.

But it had to be. He *was* unusually attracted to her, just like Dorée had said. He had been almost from the moment he first set eyes on her for no other reason than she appeared on the studio's doorstep in a vulnerable moment. She could understand how that might have happened—she was endowed with a certain glamour—but what confused her was that she'd felt the same about him. How could her instincts allow her to feel that way about someone of his ilk? *If* he was of that ilk. Her head spun with questions of what if.

But if it *was* him, she wasn't going to let him get away with murder.

Celeste wiped her face. She and Sebastian needed a plan. There had to be something they could do. Some other way to call up their energy. Some means for getting their hands on a few gems. "We're in desperate straits, Sebastian. I don't know what we're going to do."

The stoat didn't respond. Not even a sympathizing head bob in her direction. She picked him up and gazed into his eyes. He pushed against her arm, his whiskers twitching like crazy, searching for an escape. The spark she usually found in his eyes was fading, which meant the magic between them was fading. Their thread of communication would fray if they didn't recharge soon. But without gemstones she didn't know what to do. She cradled him in her arms, rocking back and forth, desperate to figure something out. Her heart clenched, forcing an involuntary whimper to escape her throat when nothing came to mind. Without her magic, who was she?

Celeste no longer recognized herself. All her life she'd questioned where she came from, yes, but she'd never fully doubted who she was meant to be in the care of the sisterhood. She'd been shaped and molded to be a Fée Gardienne since she was a baby. A woman with the power to encourage aspirations, fulfill the heart's deepest yearnings, and grant long-held desires. But that same energy the Gardiennes used to benefit their protégés benefited them as well. For a full-fledged Gardienne, the magic became embedded in their hair, their skin, their blood. Wherever they went, some diffusion of magic followed, radiating around them for the benefit of someone nearby. And while their purpose was to cast about favor, there was no question the glamour proved equally advantageous for them. By any measure, they lived a charmed and privileged life as caretakers of the magic they carried inside them.

Only now it wasn't working. Not for her, at least. And just when a Skulk was prowling the city looking for people he could drag into misery.

The smart thing to do would be to admit what had happened and get a message to Dorée and Anaïs, but Celeste wasn't ready to start groveling before either one of them for help. Not yet. She wasn't fully convinced the whole adventure hadn't been some plot to subvert her chance to become a Fée Gardienne. She certainly felt set up. Did they think her lacking in enough skill to serve? Enough discernment? Or maybe they thought she didn't possess the right poise? If so, she might as well pack her broken trunk and sell her sapphire pendant for the fare home on the next steamship.

Celeste's spiraling thoughts were disturbed by a rapping at the window. She was so used to observing Gideon spying on her from afar she was startled to see the bird up close. He tapped urgently against the window with his beak, pausing only to gaze at her with one eye to see if she was responding. In no mood to deal with Anaïs's bully bird, she snapped the curtains closed on him. "Go away!"

The bird pounded his beak against the window even harder until she thought he might break the glass. After ignoring him for all of ten seconds, she peeked through the curtains to see what his problem was. "What do you want, Gideon?"

The rook dipped and bobbed, nearly frantic. He flew off the window ledge to the top of his tree and stood pointing to the northeast with his beak. Celeste glanced out the window but didn't see anything out of the ordinary. Gideon flew back, did his frantic dance again, and then returned to the tree to point with his wing. This time when he nearly smashed into the window, she thought she might have an inkling of what he was on about.

"What's wrong?" she asked.

He hopped up and down, squawking as though he had some mad crow disease. There was only one thing that could make Gideon that agitated. "Is it Anaïs? Has something happened?"

Gideon flapped his wings and bobbed his head before jumping into the air, urging her to follow. Celeste shared a confused look with Sebastian. They'd just left Dorée and Anaïs within the hour and they had been fine. Condescending and disrespectful of her as an aspiring Gardienne trying to do her best, but in good form nonetheless.

Gideon beat his wings against the window again, only this time he pressed his eye up to the glass and froze, panting through the stress of having to hold still. His bizarre behavior focused Celeste's attention. She leaned in and opened the window to see if there might be something physically wrong with him, when she caught a flicker of light in his dark eye. She peered closer and her jaw dropped when she spied a fish-eye view of Anaïs inside Stage Two. She was as frantic as her bird, pounding the flat of her hand against a door, then kicking it when it didn't open. Dorée raised her staff and placed the crystal tip against the door, but whatever she was expecting didn't happen. Then Anaïs turned her head to stare straight at Celeste through Gideon's eye and mouthed the word "help." As she said it, her breath rose in the air in a silver cloud. Her lashes were tipped with frost, and she trembled slightly as though trapped in some macabre snow globe.

Celeste pulled back. Anaïs had employed a form of scrying magic she'd never attempted herself, though she knew the communication coming through the companion to be authentic. She also recognized that cold breath and what it meant. It hadn't been a curse that afflicted the studio—it was the Skulk. The memory of his cold presence still caused a prickling sensation under her skin that now warned her she had to do something. Grabbing her purse, Celeste scooped up Sebastian and dropped him inside. They were going back to the lot.

Gideon sagged in relief as the image of Anaïs faded from his eye. Then, just as he leaped off the ledge to take to the air, the window disintegrated as though the wood and stucco were made of sugar that had been left out in the rain. The ceiling of the bungalow vaporized into a view of blue sky just before the bed, sofa, and tables dissipated into mist.

"My magic is fading." Celeste spun around, watching the walls disappear around her until she stood in the middle of a vacant patch of grass beside the metal trash can that had been at the center of her enchantment. She paused a moment to consider dragging her trunk with her, but there was little of value left inside and no time to haul it, and so she ran to her car with only her purse and her companion tucked inside before time ran out.

Celeste and Sebastian hopped inside the Pierce-Arrow, desperate to race back to the studio. Yes, Anaïs and Dorée had used her and put her in harm's way without the benefit of foresight, but they were still her sisters. They were one and the same. Or soon could be. Celeste ordered the car to start as she'd always done. The engine purred to life, only to gasp and gurgle before sputtering to a stop. A rear wheel fell off, and then the other. Once the back end fell, the hood, windshield, and doors shriveled like wadded tinfoil. The rest of the car quickly collapsed until Celeste found herself sitting on one of the hotel's bell trolleys used to haul luggage for guests instead of the driver's seat of her car. Without the gems to recharge, everything she'd created was falling apart. All her glamour coming undone. All her enchantments fading from sight. Just when she needed her magic the most.

CHAPTER TWENTY-FOUR

Brushstrokes and Stinging Nettle

Anaïs kicked the door for the tenth time. "Let us out!"

Dorée had already tired from the effort of trying to open the door with her staff and sat on the sofa on the stage. "It's no use. He's sealed us off."

"How did the bastard figure out how to do it, that's what I want to know."

"Language, Anaïs." Dorée pulled the hood of her cloak up over her elaborate hairdo. Her tiny mouse, who'd refused to leave her side to save himself, shivered inside the curl at the top with his tail wrapped over his nose. "I imagine any and all information is for sale for the right price," she said, tucking her hands under her arms to keep them warm.

Anaïs studied the ceiling of the warehouse, searching for a chink in the Infortunii magic. Hoarfrost coated the beams above like hairy mold. "How many do you think there are out there to be able to do this kind of magic?"

"I only saw the one, but I'm beginning to believe Barnaby may not have been completely honest with me about this rogue Skulk we were conveniently warned about. He seems to know a little too much about us."

"I'll say," Anaïs agreed. While they'd gathered inside Stage Two to explain to Celeste that the real danger on the lot was an entity that thrived on misfortune, the Skulk had outmaneuvered them by exploiting the one weakness in the Fées Gardiennes' magic. Their individual power to enchant was enhanced by exposure to the light refracted in faceted gems. The spark and spangle of mirrored light, rays of pure sunshine, and even the glitter of starlight could enhance their power. Initiates like Celeste had to keep their gemstones protected and nearby to constantly recharge their magic, but once they successfully set a protégé on their star path, the magic fused with their physical being, and it was with them always. But lock a Fée Gardienne in a space without sunlight or warmth, or cut an initiate off from access to a source of jewels, and their powers retracted. The ember of magic burning inside them retreated to the center of their bodies, protecting the tiny flicker from harm until ignited by the spark of either strong light or the radiance of gems.

"How could one Skulk do this?" Anaïs slammed her hand against the frost on the wall again, taking satisfaction from the resounding echo inside the warehouse. She could feel despair trying to seep into her psyche under the Infortunii's influence, needling its way into her mind. The tactic might work on an ordinary human, but she was made of more mercurial stuff than that. She mentally dodged whenever the sensation dipped, refusing to give in to defeat.

Dorée brought out the small bag of sunflower seeds from inside her cloak and fed them to Benoit one at a time. "Did you happen to notice a peculiar odor about this Liam when he spoke?"

"What do you mean?"

"I don't know exactly. Something seemed off, something unnatural about the air around him. Like cheap cigars perhaps. And alcohol. The scent of whiskey."

Anaïs shrugged it off as she dug through a box of props to look for something useful to help them escape. "Nothing unusual about that.

There's a half dozen illegal gambling dens in the area that serve bootleg whiskey. Drunks, gamblers, prostitutes. He'd be attracted to all of it, if only to drag as many as he could toward a life of depravity. Skulks are detestable creatures, the way they generate misery in others so they can feed the black holes they call hearts."

The eldest Gardienne brushed off the pile of seed shells Benoit had discarded on her lap. "They, too, serve their purpose."

"Necessary, I suppose, in the larger picture and all, but vile nonetheless." Anaïs found a sword at the bottom of a crate. It felt a little light for fighting, but it might give her enough leverage to force open the door. She jimmied the pointy end in the gap between the door and the jamb and put pressure on the sword. It snapped in two on her first try, splintering to reveal the wooden interior beneath a thick layer of paint.

Anaïs tossed the broken sword on the floor, then bit her lip, feeling the need to admit something that had been bothering her since the Skulk had trapped them inside. "Listen, I did something earlier you may not like."

Dorée had started to nod off in the cold but lifted her head at the promise of a confession. "Oh?"

"I sent a message to Celeste asking her for help."

The old woman's eyes darted to the door where Gideon had flown out just before they were trapped by the Skulk. "She's on her way back? She's not equipped to deal with an Infortunii on her own."

"No, she's not, but we can't just sit here and freeze to death."

"She'll be walking into a trap. You heard what he said—he can't wait to get his claws into her. He must think we're here for her. To elevate *her* as a protégé." Unsettled by the news, Dorée reached for her staff again. She strode off the stage, aiming the tip at the frozen hinges on the small door. The tiniest spark splintered off the crystal before it evaporated in a puff of frail mist. Her posture sank, revealing a fragile eighty-two-year-old woman. "We might as well be toadstools, sitting in the cold and dark."

"Don't count her out yet," Anaïs said. "She's got gumption. Remember, she stood up to me when she thought I'd cursed a child, and that's a hell of a thing for an initiate to do."

"Hopefully she had the sense to recharge before you had Gideon make contact with her." Dorée sat again to catch her breath. "I sensed she was nearly tapped out when she left. She needs to get her protégé settled soon. This can't go on much longer."

Anaïs didn't think Dorée was talking solely about their situation inside Stage Two. Ever since she'd found the scrapbook in the attic, she'd had time to think about each of the thirteen Gardiennes and the arc of their lives from tragic beginning to bestower of dreams. And it had always been thirteen Gardiennes at a time, even while one or two initiates were brought to the cottage to begin their training. Always, just as the eldest of the sisters' spine began to curve under the pull of time and gravity, a new initiate was ready to take on her first protégé. Dorée was the oldest now. Anaïs knew what would happen once Celeste successfully set her protégé on her star path. There must always be thirteen Gardiennes. Only now, two of the thirteen were trapped by a Skulk's contemptible magic, and very likely they'd both die of hypothermia if they didn't get out soon. Anaïs kicked the wall one more time just to make sure the universe heard her punctuated thoughts.

"I remember my first protégé like it was yesterday." Dorée's eyes shimmered in the chilly air as she revisited her memories. "He was a painter."

Anaïs hauled over a rolled-up tapestry she'd spotted behind the prop trunk. She sat next to the old woman and covered their laps with it. Everyone knew about Dorée's first protégé. He was infamous. Several of the artist's paintings hung in the Musée d'Orsay for all to admire. He was gone now, outlived by his benefactor, but esteem for the man had been engraved in time.

"Did you know immediately he'd be your first?"

"Oh yes. I was drawn to him from the first sighting. He couldn't even afford to buy paint when I found him. But the spark of rebellion in his eyes combined with the deep reservations he held about his talent and his future were irresistible. You can really make the start of something special with a combination like that. Our magic strikes like a match to oil." Dorée's frosted breath rose in the air, adding an aura of fascination to her wistful recollection of the famous impressionist.

"He painted me once," Dorée said in uncharacteristic boastfulness. "Well, a version of me in my glamour. I was still so young then. But I remember there was a group of us at Le Moulin de la Galette in Montmartre. Laughing, drinking, and dancing. He was there with his canvas and captured the moment perfectly, as he always did." She pulled up the tapestry as her body shivered. "I'll miss that sensation of discovery terribly when I'm gone."

Anaïs didn't say it out loud, but that end could be sooner than either of them anticipated if they didn't get out of their refrigerated state soon. "What do you think he means to do to us?" she asked.

"The Skulk? Oh, I imagine he's just playing with us. Literally keeping us on ice so we don't interfere with his agenda. His real prey is Celeste, I'd think. As I said, he'll have attached himself to her without knowing who and what she is destined to be. To him, she's just a shiny object he can tarnish. She's going to require the elixir to be rid of him."

Anaïs took the two bottles of elixir out of the sash around her hips. She wanted to double-check the first one Edward had made, the one that would break the bond, to make sure it was still viable. She pulled the stopper out and took a sniff. The liquid smelled just as toxic as the first time she'd inhaled it, so she put it away and uncorked the second, the one meant to address the side effects from swallowing the first one. The fluid had changed color, and it smelled off, but she didn't know if that was normal or not. She'd never had any need for the type of secondary potion he'd recommended, though she did know a few of the ingredients it ought to contain—a dash of aniseeds, ginger, a little castor oil to purge the system. All distinct in taste and smell, yet the contents smelled nothing like licorice or ginger. She put a drop of elixir on her finger to taste it. Her tongue and finger blistered at the touch.

"Good heavens, what's the matter?" Dorée asked when Anaïs winced.

Anaïs spit out the dab of elixir and wiped her mouth with the back of her hand. "We're in bigger trouble than we thought," she said, glancing at the bottle. Edward's betrayal was clear. She'd trusted him based on their history together, but she suspected he'd substituted some nasty ingredients for the real thing. "I could kick myself for not keeping an eye on that two-timing quack while he made this," she said. "He's given us some horrible blistering potion." Anaïs pressed her tongue against the roof of her mouth, trying to quell the burning sensation.

Dorée took the bottle and inhaled carefully. She turned her nose away when her eyes watered. "That's stinging nettle in there. I'd wager your occultist friend coated the tiny spines in some spell to make their stinging property remain dormant until you'd departed as a satisfied customer."

"But why? Why would he interfere in something that doesn't concern him?" As she said it, a nagging little detail from her past scratched at the back of her brain. Things hadn't ended between them as well as her ego preferred to remember it. There'd been a broken vase and threats of ruination, before a door was slammed shut for good. But the nagging detail she'd let slip from her memory was that Edward knew about the effect of cold on Gardienne magic.

"You paid him well, didn't you?"

Anaïs nodded. "I placed a small peridot gemstone in the box of Jujyfruits for him to find." But perhaps she'd been too clever for her own good. It was very possible he'd missed the stone altogether and thrown the box away. Dolt. Who offered a box of candy as payment for a sophisticated potion they couldn't make themselves? Unless he'd been legitimately hoping for a payment in the flesh? He ought to have known better.

"Well," Dorée said, hugging her arms as she looked around helplessly at their refrigerated prison, "I think we'd better consider the genuine possibility we're in a tight spot."

Gardiennes were ever the optimists, but Anaïs thought that was too polite a way of putting it. They were in the shitter, and she had only herself to blame. She'd let her guard down by trusting Edward. He was an opportunist who'd sell his grandmother to pirates for the right price. She just hadn't counted on him selling *her* out.

Anaïs remembered now where he'd learned the inconvenient truth about Fées Gardiennes and their weaknesses. It was two years earlier, and the sangria had been flowing while she and Edward visited Pamplona for the running of the bulls. He'd been worried she'd wilt in the heat, but in her inebriated state she'd confided that her only vulnerability was the cold. Drop the temperature below freezing and the magic turned to sludge in her veins. They'd drunkenly laughed about it at the time. Later, she was certain he'd chronicled the information in one of his notebooks, though she hadn't dared admit the slip of the tongue to the sisterhood at the time. They'd have been mortified by her breach of conduct. She couldn't help feeling she was paying the price for it now. Oh, but later, if she survived, it would be Edward's turn to feel the consequences of crossing her.

Anaïs pulled the tapestry up on her lap and tried to fend off the negative thoughts that rode in on each wave of frigid air to corrode her mind: *You're worthless. You're a failure. If you and the old woman die, it's your fault!*

Beside her, Dorée's eyes fluttered closed as she sank with her head against the HOME SWEET HOME pillow. Benoit tumbled out of the old woman's curls, landing on his back with his feet in the air on the armrest beside her as the cold closed in.

CHAPTER TWENTY-FIVE

Sunset Boulevard

Celeste stood up from the bell trolley and dusted herself off before the bellman had a chance to give her a curious look. It had been a very long time since she'd had to move through the world without her magic. Not since she'd been invited to visit Paris for the first time as Dorée's guest ten years earlier, during the height of the war. Out of extreme precaution, the sisters had her forgo charging her gemstones for a week to prevent any awkward mishaps in the bustling metropolis. The city had been bombed by German zeppelins months earlier, and there'd been hushed talk between the sisters over candlelight about Celeste's ability to restrain herself should danger find her, given her brief training. So she'd been forced to endure her first Parisian tour in a vulnerable state just as she did now.

And yet Celeste had still found magic at every turn on her trip to Paris—in the grace of the architecture, the aroma of baking bread, the trail of perfume that seemed to follow every well-dressed woman, and in the delicate details of a gold lamé dress in the salon of Callot Soeurs. The dressmakers had been a favorite of Dorée's, so she'd taken Celeste to teach her about the importance of appearances and to have her first dress made by a true designer rather than poor old Myrtle, who couldn't even see to thread the needle anymore. The Gardienne had also wanted to show off the sister protégés she'd nurtured for nearly twenty years, although by then the downfall effect had already begun to take its toll.

But what was she going to do now?

Celeste checked her appearance in the reflection of the hotel's front door. But at least her clothes hadn't fallen apart, since they hadn't been magicked into existence through enchantment like everything else. But how would she get to the studio without a car? It was too far to walk, and she'd not seen a streetcar or trolley roll by the hotel in all the days she'd been there. And even if she had seen one, she had no funds to pay for the trip. No gems, no magic, no more lavish lifestyle.

Except . . .

Celeste dug a little deeper in her purse. She had to push Sebastian aside to reach it, but there at the bottom, beneath a tube of lipstick, was the bronze coin the father of the boy on the steamship had given her. The father had said "for luck" when he gave it to her. Again, she felt the energy of a thousand unrealized dreams fused with the metal. An odd coin. Old and worn as though dozens had rubbed their thumbs against the embossing, hoping and wishing.

What if?

Closing her eyes, Celeste held the coin in her open hand, sliding her thumb over the side with the palm trees. "I need help," she said to whatever energy inhabited the coin. "I wish to get back to the studio. I have to find my sisters, but I have no way to get to them." She opened her eyes, not sure if she should expect anything from a coin that was likely little more than a souvenir, but she'd take any luck she could get. When nothing happened, she decided her only option was to go inside the hotel and humiliate herself by asking the clerk for cab money. But then a rumble sounded from the driveway, and a sleek maroon two-seater sports car approached from the back of the hotel, headed for the exit.

Reading the opportunity as a sign her plea had been heard, Celeste frantically waved down the driver, who turned out to be a young woman with dark hair and startlingly blue eyes. She was dressed in a smart black-and-white checkered suit with a dazzling diamond on her left hand. After Celeste explained her urgent need to get to West Coast Studios, the woman invited her to hop in.

"I'm headed that direction myself," the woman said. "Hold on." After a wide swing onto Sunset Boulevard, the woman began sneaking worried glances at her passenger every few seconds, sizing her up, until she finally asked, "You've heard the horrible news, right? About the murder at West Coast today?"

"Yes." Celeste bit her lip, remembering. "I was there when they found her."

"You were there? Well, what happened? Did you know Dolores? I'd only just met the poor girl a few weeks ago, but everyone is talking about her. I heard they arrested a seamstress who works at the studio, is that right?" The woman had taken her eyes off the road briefly, then had to slam on the brakes to avoid hitting the car in front of her.

Celeste gripped the dashboard, silently cursing the thief who'd stolen her gemstones, forcing her to rely on a talisman to hitch a ride in a stranger's car. "The police have the wrong person," she asserted, sitting back in her seat again. "She'll be released. They have to let her go. Rose couldn't have done it."

"You sound pretty certain," the woman said, not bothering to hide her skepticism.

"I am." Celeste held on to her hat as the woman sped up and shifted gears. The driver had a powerful aura that radiated around her. Celeste would have taken a reading on her if she'd had the energy, but even without the ability she could tell the woman had something special about her. Others seemed to notice it, too, as they waved to her from their cars, honking their horns. The woman waved back and smiled, then concentrated on maneuvering through traffic again as though it were a normal occurrence to get so much attention on the street. Celeste knew she couldn't be a Fée Gardienne, but how else did a woman retain such glamour about her?

The woman winked at her, as though reading her mind, while they continued down Sunset Boulevard. A few minutes later they pulled up in front of West Coast Studios, where a small crowd had gathered to lay flowers outside the gate in remembrance for the murdered actress. Two uniformed police officers also hovered near the guardhouse, reminding Celeste of the horrible crime.

"Here we are." The driver looked up at the guard standing inside his booth at the gate and waved as if she knew him. "I heard they shut down production today," she said to Celeste. "Are you sure they'll let you in?"

Celeste had no idea but nodded with confidence. "I know the owner."

"Oh, in that case, tell Nick that Gloria said hello." The woman's ring sparkled in the sunshine, making a kaleidoscope of light that hit the dashboard. "Let him know I'm thinking about him. I'll check in on him later, when the dust settles."

Celeste lied and said she'd pass on the message before thanking Gloria for the ride. And just as quick as the stranger had shown up in her two-seater sports car when Celeste needed her most, she sped away again down the boulevard as more people honked and waved.

"Sorry, miss, the studio is closed today," the guard said when Celeste approached. The two police officers crowded around her to make sure she got the message.

Her first instinct was to camouflage her appearance so she could walk right past them, but of course that wasn't an option so long as her energy was still on the fritz. "I'm a friend . . ." She had to stop and contemplate how to present herself for her best chance of gaining entry. Was she a friend of Nick's? A potential lover? A new nemesis? While she was making up her mind, she noticed Gideon swoop in overhead. The rook circled, dipping his wing once, before gliding toward the back of the lot. Celeste kept her eye on him while the guard stepped out of his shack to shoo her away. Before the man got the satisfaction of reading her the riot act, Gideon channeled some illusion magic of his own, turning his wings into wisps of black smoke that billowed up from the back of the lot.

Celeste pointed. "Is that a fire?" she asked. The guard spun around on his heels. The cops were more jaded, keeping their hands near their holsters as they craned their necks to glance behind them.

"Not again!" The guard ran back inside his booth and picked up the phone to call for help. The two officers ordered Celeste to stay where she was, then scrambled toward the smoke to investigate. While the guard was busy on the phone with his back turned, Celeste slipped past the gate. She darted between some bushes, but she needn't have bothered. The guard was so distracted by the mayhem of "the curse" unfolding on the lot again, he never gave her a second glance. She waved at Gideon, then hurried inside the main building.

The plan, if she had one, was to first rescue Anaïs and Dorée, who seemed to be trapped inside the Stage Two warehouse. But she couldn't just walk out in the open on the lot. Not without her glamour. And definitely not with a murdering Skulk prowling the grounds, possibly waiting for her to show up. She had an inkling of a solution to her magic problem thanks to her encounter with the popular Gloria, but she didn't have the experience to know if it would work. Still, she had to try.

There was movement inside the building. Voices, camera flashes, and the sound of boot soles marching up and down on the stairs. Celeste peeked around the corner. A handful of police officers were still working on their investigation of Dolores's murder. She recognized Detective Stan White among them from earlier in the day as he spoke to someone on the phone.

Celeste listened to the men run through their theories about what had happened. Rose was their primary suspect. The murder weapon belonged to her, she'd been seen arguing with the victim the night before, and she'd always rubbed a few of her fellow seamstresses the wrong way, according to the interviews.

But there was one small problem.

"Bad news, fellas." Detective White hung up the receiver. "Just got off the phone with the chief. The girl's alibi checks out. The father says she was home at ten last night and didn't leave again until six-thirty in the morning."

"Of course he's gonna say that," one of the officers said.

"Yeah, but we also got a neighbor who was out walking his dog early this morning who saw her running for the trolley at the same time. There's no way she could have made it to the studio in time to commit the murder. Not according to Sinclair's story of when they arrived."

Celeste whispered to Sebastian, "I knew it!"

"Damn it." There was a long exhale of breath before a second officer slammed a chair into a desk.

Detective White tamped down the man's outburst by offering him a cigarette. "Let's wrap it up here. Grab the last of the statements. We'll reconvene down at the station."

"So it wasn't her? Are you certain?" The man's voice rose a note higher on the second inquiry.

Isaac Jacobi. So, he'd finally returned from sneaking off to interview with MGM. Celeste hoped he got the position. That would be one more roadblock out of Rose's way.

"Thank you, Mr. Jacobi, for speaking with us," the detective said without answering the question. "You've been very helpful."

"But if it wasn't her, who was it?" Jacobi asked. "Are you certain she couldn't have done it? She's trying to ruin my reputation, you know. That's motivation enough, isn't it?"

"We'll be in touch if we need anything else."

The men came out of the wardrobe department, where they'd presumably remained since early that morning. Celeste backed into Charlie's janitor closet, leaving the door open a mere crack so she could see, and waited for them to leave. "I hope we never have to get used to physically hiding ourselves," she whispered to Sebastian. Glamour was much more convenient.

The police exited the building, but she never did see Jacobi leave. Which meant he must have returned to his design studio upstairs. Another complication, but they were too close now to turn back. She wondered briefly if Nick was still in his office too. Would he have stuck around while the police kept working? She didn't like to dwell on the possibility he might be the one out there waiting for her. But if he was, she'd be ready. At least she hoped she would be.

When the coast was clear, she and Sebastian ducked out of the closet and headed for the back stairs at the end of the corridor. She worried her connection with her small companion had frayed beyond repair. Without each other, what were they? At the top of the stairs, she closed her eyes and tugged on her necklace, making one more plea to let the little stoat understand. A flicker of energy, no stronger than a snap of static electricity, struck her palm. She opened her eyes, desperate for the spark to carry her message.

Sebastian, with his sleek body, slipped out of her purse and onto the floor to sniff the air around the corner. He looked back at her and dipped his head once. "The Swarovski crystals," she said. "On the beaded headdress. You know the one. We need to borrow it." She made a shooing motion with her hand, and the stoat ran to the storeroom, where Jacobi kept the more valuable accessories used in the movies. The room next to the place where they'd found Dolores's body. Celeste held her necklace and willed her companion the grace of invisibility just in case Jacobi was nearby.

Two minutes passed. Then three. She began to fear Sebastian might be stuck somewhere, when she was distracted by the sound of a man clearing his throat. Jacobi came out of his studio with a portfolio tucked under his arm. Celeste hunkered down in the stairwell, clutching her pendant to try and make herself blend in with the bricks and steel, knowing it wouldn't work.

Please go the other way. Please go the other way. Please go the other way.

When no one came down the stairs, Celeste poked her head around the corner. Jacobi had headed for the other end of the corridor, his skin blanched and sweaty, while being escorted by a young uniformed police officer. She had to wonder if the designer had something more to feel guilty about than hoping to land a job with MGM. He did see Rose as a threat, that much was clear. But could *he* be the Skulk in disguise instead of Nick? His pallor and demeanor said yes, but he certainly displayed no outward attraction toward her. He'd barely taken notice of her except for the day he'd chastised her in the wardrobe room. She was grateful when he and the police officer disappeared down the hall just as Sebastian ran out of the accessories storeroom with the headdress clenched in his teeth.

Celeste scooped up Sebastian and the headpiece and desperately hunted for a space filled with strong sunlight on the far side of the building. Nick's office was obviously off limits. The writers' rooms appeared empty, but the blinds were drawn, and the desktops were tainted with ashtrays full of cigarette butts. Definitely not the ambiance she was looking for. There was another janitor's closet on the second floor, but it was a dark, windowless room that smelled of bleach.

"Maybe this way," Celeste said, hurrying toward the end of the hallway with the headdress gripped firmly in one hand and the stoat in the other. Sebastian had begun to squirm to be free, as though his wild side grew more aggressive. She had to hurry. Opening and closing doors as silently as possible, they'd traveled from one side of the second floor to the other. Finally, at the far end of the hall, she came across a publicity department office that looked out over Stages One and Two on the back lot. Sunlight gleamed through the window, hitting a pair of healthy houseplants sitting on top of a filing cabinet. "This will do," she said. Sebastian pushed against her arm, his whiskers twitching like crazy as he searched for threats.

Celeste closed the door and secured the lock. She moved the plants aside and set the crystal-studded headdress on top of the filing cabinet just as the sun's rays hit the spot in full.

"They're not gemstones, but we can still harness the energy from the refracted light," she said, setting Sebastian down beside the headdress.

"At least I hope we can. I've only ever read about it in a book, but we must do something before our bond is broken. I'm so sorry it went this far, Sebastian." Her companion stayed where he was, though there was a noticeable tremor beneath his ruffled fur.

Celeste tapped her foot nervously while she waited for the sun to charge the Swarovski crystals. Would they react like diamonds? Or emeralds? She watched as the sun glinted off the individual facets, scattering dots of light, but the radiance of the crystals paled in comparison to her gemstones. It wouldn't be enough.

Unless . . .

Celeste undid the clasp on her necklace. She held the chain up, letting the blue sapphire catch the sunlight, then suspended the pendant just above the headdress. Shards of radiance sparked against the crystals, making sequins of refracted light dance on the walls.

"It's working." Celeste drew down the energy with her invocation as Sebastian chittered and stomped his paws. The magical light encircled them both. The energy played over her face, seeping under her skin, infusing her hair, dazzling the eyes. She saw the magic working in Sebastian too. His fur shimmered like the northern lights, and the spark reappeared in his eyes. He stood on his hind legs, letting her know their connection had been reestablished.

The union felt wonderful, but there was no time to waste. Celeste peeked out the office window overlooking the lot. The place was eerily quiet. There was no one hauling ladders, or lights, or set pieces on trucks in the lanes between buildings. No one giddily rehearsing their dance routine before going before the cameras. And no Nick walking the grounds to take the pulse of his life's work. Other than the two police officers walking back toward the front gate while cursing the jumpy guard and his delusions about random fires, the place was empty. But not abandoned.

Nothing stood out about the exterior of Stage Two, but if Gideon's eyesight were to be believed, that's where Anaïs and Dorée had been locked inside. But how could a Skulk get the drop on two experienced

Gardiennes? And more importantly, how could she prevent it from happening to her?

"We gotta get down there," she said.

Sebastian unlocked the office door with a twitch of his whiskers, then ran out. Celeste followed, her mind racing with possibilities. Why couldn't Dorée use her staff to free herself? Why didn't Anaïs raise the giant door with that dangerous arch of her eyebrow? Something had gone all kinds of sideways.

"Celeste?"

The voice stopped her in her tracks.

"What are you doing here? Did you get my note? I tried calling last night, but the hotel clerk at the front desk seemed to think you weren't in." Nick stood holding his coat casually over one shoulder. Celeste faltered briefly at the sight of him. Tall, broad shouldered, and with a face that could have drawn in record crowds at the theater if he'd chosen to be an actor instead of the man pulling the strings behind the scenes. But a killer? Not one instinct inside her responded with a shiver of truth.

"Yes, I did receive your card." She fumbled with her purse, trying to think of some excuse for why she might be roaming the upper hallway of West Coast Studios when everyone had been sent home. "I came by to thank you and got turned around in the maze of offices."

Nick glanced down the hall toward the fitting room where Dolores's body was found. The officer who'd escorted Jacobi downstairs hadn't returned, but the fitting room was still cordoned off to discourage anyone from entering or interfering with the investigation. He had to be wondering if the scene of the murder was what she'd really come to see and not him. But if so, he didn't let it show.

"Well, here I am," he said with a reserved smile. He held his arm out to escort her down the stairs. There was no aggression, no air of misfortune hanging over him, just a tinge of confusion and overwhelming relief to see her. She knew then he really was smitten with her. Not obsessed, or drawn inexplicably to her aura, but genuinely interested in getting to know her.

She leaned in and kissed him.

Nick reacted with a startled blink of the eyes followed by a smile that suggested he'd like more. Which made it such a shame that she had to color his memory over with her glamour to make him forget he'd seen her. She hoped it wouldn't be forever. Her regret was palpable as she touched her lips to remember the feeling of their kiss, but there was somewhere else she had to be, and someone else she had to confront. She knew that now without a doubt.

Displaying no more physical presence than the scent of evening primrose that wafts in through an open window and then is gone, Celeste gripped her pendant and disappeared from Nick's sight and thoughts. His forehead wrinkled briefly, as though he were trying to remember why he'd come onto the second floor of the building. He scratched the spot over his left brow, shook off whatever it was he'd forgotten, and then turned toward his office with a tired sigh, just as he would have done had he not caught her coming out of the sunny room behind him. And while it was gut-wrenching to watch him walk away, it felt good to have her magic back.

Celeste ran down the stairs to catch up with Sebastian. He'd kept going while she'd stopped to say goodbye to Nick, and now she wasn't sure which direction he had gone. Something was blocking their linked vision. Instead of seeing him prance down the hallway, all she could sense was the scent of cold metal and the taste of blood.

CHAPTER TWENTY-SIX

SHIVER ME TIMBERS

Anaïs patted the old woman's cheeks. Dorée had gone pale, as though all the blood had receded from the skin's surface. "You must wake up," she said, slapping a little harder. "We can't give in. Not now. It's not time."

The cold had become nearly unbearable. Anaïs's fingers grew stiff, and the tip of her nose was numb to the touch. When Dorée didn't rouse, she paced back and forth in front of the sofa, rubbing her arms, trying to work up enough magical friction to ignite a spark. She wished now she'd taken up smoking. At least then she'd have a lighter. She'd happily burn the entire warehouse down if it meant getting a little warmth.

Dorée moaned and shivered on the sofa. At least she was still alive. But for how long? And where was Celeste? Maybe she'd put too much faith in the young woman's loyalty. Maybe she really had left and wasn't coming back. Anaïs had been cut off from Gideon ever since she'd used her last burst of unfrozen magic to send her message, so she had no idea if he'd flown the coop too. But, no, he was a devoted bird. Had been nearly all her life. He, at least, would return. Until then, she had to stay focused. Alert. Alive.

The hoarfrost had turned into icicles that grew like stalactites from the ceiling and along the walls. Anaïs tracked one of the longer dagger points with her eyes. Curiously, it stopped just above a row of three electric lights with lenses as big as the wheels on a steam engine. Her magic might have been put on ice, but her brains hadn't. Feeling a hint of optimism again, she stepped off the stage to investigate, only to learn the damn things weren't plugged in. A quick search along the wall revealed there weren't any outlets big enough to plug them in anywhere. So how did they work?

Her curiosity drew her even closer to the lights. She followed the cables to their plugs, but the prongs weren't like those on a table lamp or a percolator. Yet they plugged into something. But what? How could a film studio not have outlets big enough to support the massive lights they used for moviemaking? There had to be another power source somewhere. The lights certainly weren't enchanted. "Not even Hollywood magic is strong enough to make lights work without electricity," she said, then laughed out loud. She was getting delirious from the hypothermia. But there had to be a normal, mundane way to make the lights come on.

Beyond the row of lights, she spied a large contraption draped with a tarp. She tossed the cover off and discovered a big, scary machine with all kinds of knobs and wires. And on the side was a row of sockets that looked custom made for the plugs on the long cables trailing off the lights. Her wicked grin returned, thinking of the revenge she might yet have on that Skulk.

"Now, how to get you going." Anaïs took one sniff and knew the generator ran on gasoline. "Can't be any more complicated than operating a car, can it?" She plugged in the cable from the nearest spotlight, then fiddled with a few of the gadgets and whatchamacallits on the generator, pushing buttons and moving levers, in between blowing warm breath on her fingers.

At last, the thing rumbled to life. She stood back in awe, eyes alight. But her Prometheus moment proved short-lived when the light didn't come on. Not ready to give up, she jiggled more switches and knobs on the units themselves. She swung a lever to the right and pushed a button above. A lightning crack sizzled inside the housing. Smoke came out of the top of the arc lamp, and a brilliant white light shone across the room.

Even from two feet away, she could feel the heat coming off the lamps. If they could get in the light, get warmed up . . .

"Dorée! Wake up! We're getting out of here."

The old woman kept sleeping, so Anaïs plugged in all three lights. They were aimed at the opposite wall, which affected the hoarfrost but little else. With a little maneuvering she was able to tip each contraption so that they all shined at the base of the stage with three crossbeams making spotlights on the floor. She carefully stepped into the light, exposing her body while shielding her eyes with her forearm. The warmth of the spotlights tingled against her skin as it oozed into her blood. A wave of static flowed through her hair, and the fog lifted from her mind.

Thinking like a Gardienne again, she held her ruby pendant up to a beam of light. A burst of color radiated around her. It encircled Dorée too, blanketing her in warmth. The old woman started to rouse. With her magic flourishing, Anaïs got behind one of the lights and aimed it at the ceiling. The beam of light spread out at her command until the icicles sublimated into mist and the frost retreated.

"Oh, you've done it at last," Dorée said. She lifted her head, wobbling slightly and falling to her right before catching herself. Her little mouse wiggled his tail. The old woman gathered her strength and reached for her staff before getting to her feet. She exhaled a cloud of breath, then dipped the crystal-tipped staff into the light. A shower of warm magic ignited like a lit flare, cascading over her and Benoit until the rosy color returned to her cheeks, her back straightened, and the gleam in her eye gave fair warning her powers had been restored. "Now, I think we better go find this Skulk," she said and aimed the staff's energy at the main door. The frost on the hinges melted away, and the giant door disintegrated, taking the guard dog on the other side with it. And there, circling in the sky against a blue backdrop, flew Gideon.

Dorée scooped up Benoit, warming him in her hands until the mouse perked up enough to jump on top of her head and settle into her hair. She gripped her staff firmly as Anaïs helped her off the stage and into the sunlight outside. They had only a moment to close their eyes and soak in the natural rays before Gideon squawked a warning above.

"He says Celeste is here, but something is wrong." Anaïs shaded her eyes as she glanced down the roadway between buildings. The back lot was still eerily quiet, but not completely empty.

"Can you feel his energy?" Anaïs asked with a shiver. "It's cold and damp. Like a wet towel in a dark cellar."

"The Infortunii draw their power from the deep places in the earth. Caves and tunnels. Mines. Lakes and pools too. This one must have a potent power source nearby to be able to create the frigid conditions in the warehouse and cut us off from our magic like he did."

Anaïs had to wonder what earthy darkness he could possibly be drawing from in a sunny place like California, but there were always pockets of shadow hidden in the world.

Dorée clicked her tongue against her teeth. Benoit crawled out onto her shoulder. "Where do we confront him?" she asked her companion. The mouse twitched his whiskers, sniffing the air. He rose on his hind legs and squeaked in alarm. The eldest Gardienne peered down the long canyon of buildings leading away from the front gate. "That way," she said to Anaïs and headed toward the back lot, where the main mast and tattered sails of a pirate ship rose above the other structures defining the skyline.

Anaïs hurried to catch up, instantly regretting her high heels. "Wait, what's the plan?" she asked. "What about Celeste? Once we find her and the Skulk, how will we administer the unbinding elixir?"

Dorée stopped in her tracks and swung around. "We don't need any potions to remedy the situation if he's dead. Believe me, that will do the unbinding for us."

The blunt statement punched Anaïs right in her conscience. Since when were they going to kill the Skulk? "Doesn't that violate about ten different laws? Or, at the very least, our unwritten agreement with the Infortunii?" She didn't really care about any of that, but she thought Dorée ought to give it just a little more thought, being the eldest.

"*They* broke their word first when they failed to tell us one of their own hadn't just gone rogue but also carried the glint of murder in his eye. We're well within our rights to defend ourselves and any others in harm's way, even if that means striking this Skulk down. Unless you'd like to experience being left to freeze in cold storage again."

Anaïs resisted the urge to point out the killing had only been a recent development and the Infortunii might not have been aware of Liam's murderous intentions, but even she didn't have the mettle to confront Dorée on technicalities when the woman was in her diva mood. "Don't we still need a plan?" she ventured.

"What we need is action to get things back on track." Dorée swept her cloak up and marched toward the back of the lot.

For a woman of eighty-two, she moved with surprising agility as she climbed the ladder onto the pirate ship. It wasn't a real ship, of course. Anyone could see that once they got within ten feet of the thing. The entire backside was only half-finished, but it was a remarkable reconstruction. Simply made yet detailed enough to fool the eye temporarily from the right camera angle, and with a deck long enough to film a decent swashbuckling scene. Perhaps even Douglas Fairbanks himself had swept down from the rigging to battle a rival ship's captain in one of his films. But what on earth was Dorée up to inspecting the deck of a fake ship?

"Have a look," the elder Gardienne said. She pointed her staff toward the lane they'd just walked down, while her other hand rested atop one of the three prop cannons made of tin with rust eating away at the rivets. Following the sight line between the cannon and the main building, there was a clear shot for the equivalent of three city blocks.

"What are we going to do? Challenge him to a duel?"

"Don't be ridiculous," Dorée said. "We're going to shoot him with the cannons."

"Well, shiver me timbers," Anaïs said, keeping her eye on the horizon.

CHAPTER TWENTY-SEVEN

The Misery of Life and Bliss of Death

A phantom taste of blood flooded the inside of Celeste's mouth. She didn't think it was from Sebastian killing his prey. It felt more like a wound. A broken tooth, maybe, and his own blood. She hurried down the stairs to search along the corridor for her companion. Wherever he was, it was dark. A room without windows. Closed off. Dank. And he was trapped. She sensed Sebastian was alone, but she couldn't be sure of what she was perceiving anymore. Was the uncertainty due to a faulty connection between them because they'd used crystals instead of gemstones to recharge? Or was it because he was no longer conscious?

Celeste sent out a silent signal from her solar plexus. An SOS made up of bursts of light that emanated from her core being. If their bond was still strong, the light ought to emit near his presence. After listening for signs of the police still milling about, she ducked into the sewing room. "Sebastian?" When she got no answer, she tried the wardrobe room. The cold entity she'd felt before crept back in, stinging her skin with ice crystals, so she backed out quickly when there was no pulsating light evident in the dark. Standing in the hallway with her ear tuned to the sound of a heartbeat, she tried once more to connect with Sebastian, but all she heard back was emptiness.

She was on the verge of giving in to heartbreak when a tiny spark, no brighter than the static on a blanket in the dark, flickered under the door to the janitor's closet.

Celeste flung the door open and found the little stoat lying at the bottom of a metal mop bucket. A splotch of blood covered his nose. He didn't lift his head or open his eyes when she entered, but his little chest still expanded with each inhale. She bent closer and discovered a tinge of frost on the tip of his fur that made her insides coil in fright. Knowing Sebastian had to get warm as quickly as possible, she scooped him up and hugged him close with one arm, urging him to wake.

Celeste blew a warm breath over Sebastian as she shivered from the chill rattling through her own body. Her companion obviously hadn't knocked himself out and shut himself inside a closet. She didn't see anyone in the hallway, but the goose bumps on her neck told her the Skulk was close. Nick had told his employees to go home, and the police had escorted everyone else out, so did Skulks have the same ability to make themselves unseen as her kind did? Was that why Dorée had said he would still recognize her in her glamour? She tested the theory by going full shimmer. To the normal eye she would appear invisible as the light reflected and refracted off her body, bending the shape of reality. She dropped into shadow as her clothes, hair, and skin no longer absorbed the light and she melded into her environment.

A clatter in the sewing room, like a spool of thread hitting the floor, caught Celeste's attention. She took a deep breath and entered the space. A number of items had been disturbed by the police—boxes of ribbons and lace that were usually in easy reach on a table had been stacked haphazardly in a corner, the canvas trucks used to haul heavier items were all pushed up against one side of the room, and the worktables had been swept clean of their sewing projects only to be replaced with coffee cups, broken pencils, and dirty plates of cafeteria food.

Three things that hadn't changed, though, were the costumes Rose had designed for Dolores to wear in the monster picture. The dresses that had been mysteriously ruined in the night and then repaired with her magic twisted on their hangers as though fluttering in a breeze. Then one of the dresses jerked and fell to the floor as if yanked off the hanger. The sea-pearl buttons popped off the bodice of another dress one by one, scattering in all directions. The feathers were plucked off the neckline, and a sash came loose from the bodice.

"He isn't dead, but near enough," a floating voice said near the once more ruined gowns.

The Skulk thought he was invisible, but he wasn't. Aside from ruining the dresses, an outline of frost gave away his position in the low light, though Celeste couldn't make out his face. But she didn't need to see him to know his voice. All the sympathy had been stripped away from the janitor's words, but the tenor was the same.

"I shouldn't be surprised you're so practiced at kicking small, helpless animals." It was only because Sebastian was still alive that Celeste hadn't driven a shaft of light through the Skulk's brain. She took a step closer to position herself in the sunlight coming through the window while trying to ignore the creeping chill closing in around her.

Charlie matched her approach by taking a step nearer and stared straight at her out of the shadows, eyes glistening like ice. "And I should have known who and what you are from the start." He materialized in full sight, but he'd lost the amiable expression he'd worn when she'd first met him. "I'd never encountered an initiate on their own in the world before. Your light doesn't shine from within like the others. Clever, sending you."

"I suppose neither of us had enough experience to see the other for what they truly are at first blush," she said.

Charlie grinned at her remark, but then his eyes sank into their sockets and his teeth protruded over his lips, gray and pointy. It was no friendly smile. She'd been warned about the mutable quality of Skulks, but the change still caught her off guard. His appearance reminded her of a demon contemplating the taste of its eviscerated victim's flayed flesh.

Celeste had no intention of fulfilling her end of *that* scenario. She wasn't one hundred percent confident in her recharged magic, but she didn't dare show any doubt. She'd been taught that the Infortunii were necessary. Healthy, even, for a protégé's personal growth in the grand design of a person's life. But Charlie was her first face-to-face Skulk encounter, and while intellectually she understood the meaning of "necessary evil," being in proximity of an Infortunii she knew had committed murder triggered all her primal self-defense mechanisms. Her nerves geared up to put her in a panic. It took all her concentration, and a healthy dose of sunlight on her face, to ignore those fight-or-flight instincts so she could stand her ground.

"Where are my sisters?" she asked, with an eye toward the studio's lot.

Charlie ignored her question and raked a hand over the green dress hanging beside him, tearing it to shreds with claws that seemed to extend from the tips of his fingers. "We both spotted it in Rose, didn't we? The talent. The potential. We've both touched the same life with our magic. Two sides of fate and all that." He split the dress in two, ripping the seams that had been so carefully stitched together. A piece of Celeste's heart ripped at the sight as well. "My kind go back to the beginning, you know, when the world was still being shaped by suffering and woe. The festering sores, starvation, sickness and disease, broken limbs with no relief, deformities with no remedy. Half the babes died before their first birthdays, others were orphaned and left on their own." He plucked another button off and flicked it across the room. "To be a human alive in those days was to bargain in bread with us to spare a child, forgive a debt, or heal a wound. The Infortunii were the barrier between life and the long drop of death. That was our reality before your lot were birthed in the dawn mist. The Dark Ages are viewed as bleak times to the modern eye, but the people coped, they really did. They found ways to scrape by. And they were grateful to us for any relief, however small." He inhaled as though agony were a kitchen scent to whet the appetite. "Aspirations had no hold on a man's heart outside of his weary nighttime dreams. Such nonsense drowned the common man in false hope, you see."

Coming out of his beastly mouth, the descriptions rang truer than Celeste would have liked. "Is that what they taught you? That grievance makes right? That suffering is somehow more honorable than carrying dreams of a better life?"

"There's nothing more noble than knowing you carry a person's suffering in your hands." Charlie flashed his teeth at her and gestured to his ghastly appearance with a wave of his clawed fingers. "It's why we were given these bodies so different from your own. To wear the skin of misfortune was our reward for maintaining our virtuous position in the world order with dignity."

Even though they were the same ilk, Celeste had never been told why the Infortunii manifested so differently. She'd assumed that a Skulk's repulsive appearance was due to the accumulation of negative energy they carried, which once coalesced in physical form had no choice but to express itself as something grotesque. She had no idea if what he'd said was true, but she believed it was *his* truth. She petted Sebastian's back to settle her nerves and noticed her fingernails had turned a pale shade of blue.

The Skulk emerged from the shadows to reveal his full hideous form. His skin glistened with the sheen of sour meat as he continued. "But as the world grew brighter and the fleck of dreams sparked in people's eyes, we had to learn to cover our faces when walking among humans because of the way women and children began to recoil from the sight of us, as you do now. We had to disguise what you call the misshapen body that offends so deeply even dogs run away with their tails tucked between their legs." He snarled, showing a fang, then turned his back on her before using his glamour to make himself shimmer into the form of the janitor she'd first met, a humble man with a genial smile whom she'd trusted because of his outward kindness. She could see the similarity between the faces, but this Charlie was all illusion.

"This *veneer* is how we're expected to walk in the world these days," he said with clear blue eyes. "After the Fées Gardiennes arrived, the world grew soft and intolerant of imperfection under your ideals of beauty and splendor." He spit the last word out like it were a poison on his tongue.

"What happened to you?" Celeste almost pitied him, seeing how his twisted logic had been built on a scaffold of lies made to support his worldview. "How did you lose all perspective? All sense of balance?"

Charlie let the shimmer around him fade. His sunken eyes returned, and his pallor dulled into the color of cold clay. "People used to know their place," he said. The Skulk picked up a strand of crystal beads from Rose's workstation and tested their weight in his hand. He let the string of beads slink back and forth, rattling against each other. "Your kind. My kind. We had become two equal sides of a scale until people started believing they *deserved* favor. Expected it, even. And then kings and queens all over the world arranged for grace and fortune to be just another set of commodities that were bought and paid for with gold and gemstones."

The accusation stung. Though the events he complained about had happened in another age, he wasn't wrong. The bargain *had* been struck. Favor *had* been given to the royal houses of Europe. And in exchange, the Gardiennes weren't cast out and hunted throughout the forests as fey or witches for their magic. Instead, they were revered and sought after for the benevolence and honor they could bestow. They were gifted thirteen gemstones and the carved staff of the eldest to mark their status. The very staff Dorée carried now, as well as the sapphire and ruby that she and Anaïs wore around their necks. Celeste cringed, wondering what bargain the Infortunii had struck, and with whom, in those dark days of war and bloodshed.

"Have you ever been in the room during a birth?" he suddenly asked, still weighing the beads. "With the blood and the agony? The screaming of mother and child. The rending of flesh. That is life in its purest, most honest form. New life is most precious when tempered through pain and suffering."

"And what about the tender love that allowed that life to be?" Celeste's nature compelled her to challenge his remarks. "Or the well-wishes and blessings bestowed upon the newborn for a life of health and happiness? How do those figure in to your purity test for what gives life value?"

He brushed off her comment, continuing with his bruised line of thinking. "Death, on the other hand, is silent." He squeezed his hands around the string of beads and pulled. "You would expect life to thrash and bellow like an animal being sucked down into the mud, and yet I find it simply slips loose and is gone."

Celeste involuntarily took a step back, watching the hands that had driven the scissors into the neck of an innocent young woman stretch the string of crystals until it snapped. The beads scattered across the floor, serving as a timely reminder not to let her guard down. "Are the Infortunii so sunk in their own misgivings that they can't even see the wonder of life anymore?" she asked. "Or is your kind so riddled with bitterness that beauty has no place in your vocabulary?"

"Beauty is an illusion. Dust on the fingertips. Here and gone. What does anyone ever remember of beauty when they're in the grip of death? Do you think that actress was thinking about how beautiful she was while the blood spilled out of her? Do you think she was hoping I might spare her life because people thought she was *attractive*?"

Celeste didn't know how to react. She'd been taught the Infortunii served a purpose. They brought balance to the equation of fortune and misfortune. They kept the arrogant and ruthless in check by making them eat crow. But this one was making his own rules as he went.

Celeste hugged Sebastian a little closer and noticed the color of her fingernails had deepened into a panic-inducing shade of indigo blue. With the threat of cold creeping in, she wanted nothing more than to run and be rid of this Skulk, but her curiosity screwed her feet to the floor. "Why did you kill Dolores? And why frame Rose for her murder?"

He let the last of the crystal beads fall from his hand. "You saw what was happening with Rose. Her potential shone brighter than all the rest of them put together. It's why you're here. I'll wager the energy of her dead mother begged for favor, and you decided to grant it. Set her daughter on her star path, is that it?"

"I'm not a genie."

Charlie guffawed. "And I'm not a devil. But this city is full of hearts bursting with starry-eyed kids all hoping they're the next Valentino or Clara Bow. Skewering those dreams is what I throw on the stove to eat for breakfast now. Dolores was just another casualty of my hunger."

Celeste grew heartsick over their back-and-forth. A woman was dead, and he was making jokes. "But why murder her?"

"You know why." He was beginning to tire of her questions. He picked up a jar of straight pins and dumped them in his palm. He closed his fist and smiled as black oil oozed out of his skin. "The old European order is over. Look at this country. It's all virgin territory. Souls for the taking. Lives to be played and strummed on a guitar in any tune I choose. Until you showed up, that is. You thought the old rules would apply here, too, because that's the way it's always been done, but I was here first. And *I* make the rules." He swept his hand free of the pins, then licked his palm.

"You're mad."

"Why shouldn't the dreamers have a taste of misfortune first before they go collect their accolades? Why shouldn't they have to rise from the ashes of my handiwork first? If they're truly worthy, talented, and destined for glory, they ought to be able to overcome adversity first. The struggle, Celeste. That's what ought to be prized."

"You've been sabotaging Rose since you met her." Celeste's anger had her magic rising in her veins. "You thought you could ruin her future. Leave her mired in the scandal of a celebrity murder. Ruin the studio. Ruin Nick West."

"No, no, darling. Their downfall was your doing. It's your fault the girl is dead. I was happy to keep Rose and the rest of them in a constant state of frustration. Little annoyances that made life just a little more difficult for them. A car that wouldn't start when they're running late, a fire on the back lot that makes investors look twice, a sewing machine that doesn't let you create the one thing you're good at making. But *you* upped the stakes when you came here and singled out Rose to be your protégé. *You* started improving her prospects. *You* boosted her confidence so that the little slights meant nothing. *You* got her noticed by the people who could give her a hand up. And *you* left me no choice but to balance the scales by pulling her and the rest back down."

Celeste planted her feet. "You can't just change the way things have been done for centuries because you don't like coming in last."

"I was curious why they sent you, though," he said, assessing her with his sharp blue eyes. "I'd wager you're still so new you're relying on your gemstones to keep your energy levels up. I admit I didn't see you for who you are at first because of your dull shine. Not until you restored the costumes I'd deliberately left in the rain. Only one of your kind would have done that. And, of course, I knew the Gardiennes wouldn't have sent someone as green as yourself all alone. There had to be at least one other full Gardienne watching over you in the shadows. Turned out there were two."

"What have you done to Anaïs and Dorée?"

"So, you see, it's really your fault the actress is dead," he went on. "You left me no choice but to flush out your accomplices. And how else to lure two Fées Gardiennes to their death if not through the affront of an innocent's death? Your kind always rises to the bait of injustice," he said with a callous shrug.

Celeste didn't see the Skulk move, yet he was suddenly only a few paces in front of her. He came so near she could smell the black oil scent rising from his wounded palm. The lines of his forehead deepened as he studied her. Was he reading her? Could he do that?

"You've recharged since this morning, but you haven't got your gems, have you?" He flashed that ghastly smile of his, as though he knew about the theft. "But you must have found a substitution."

Celeste was careful not to back away and trigger any sort of instinct in him to chase. "You stole my gems."

He threw his head back in delight, snorting out a laugh. "Ha, so I was right. He did get to them."

He?

Confused, Celeste thought it best to inch her way toward the door. If there was another Skulk around, she had no desire to meet him.

"But if you don't have your gemstones, then you must be running dangerously low on some artificial energy you managed to suck a little light out of." He licked his lips in a manner that disturbed her to her very core, then grabbed a pair of shears from Graciela's workstation and lunged at her to test his theory.

Celeste held her hand up, hoping he was wrong about the authenticity of the crystals. A shaft of blinding light illuminated from the heart of her palm, hitting him square between the eyes. The Skulk shriveled under the glare, turning his back to her. "Wrong choice," she said, and while he was still flash-blinded, she ran with Sebastian in her arms and her fingers aching from the bite of frost.

CHAPTER TWENTY-EIGHT

Best-Laid Schemes of Mice and Wisewomen

"Keep a weather eye," Dorée called.

Anaïs looked up from the railing to see the old woman standing behind the ship's wheel on the quarterdeck. "What is it you're planning on doing?" she asked, wondering why they were still hiding in a fake pirate ship waiting to ambush the Skulk when he'd likely absconded already.

"Getting ready to sail into a storm," Dorée replied, cryptic as ever.

Anaïs shielded her eyes and gazed down the long pavement leading to the main studio building. Gideon had returned. He circled over the front gate, but where was Celeste? She closed her eyes and checked in with Gideon again. In their shared vision she saw the memory of a cloud of smoke on the lot, but one he'd created. An illusion. He was laughing at his work as only a rook could.

Anaïs opened her eyes as Gideon landed on the ship's railing beside her, squawking in excitement. "Where have you been?" she asked. "You realize we had to rescue ourselves."

Gideon ducked his head and nodded, but he also brought conflicting news. Celeste was on the property, but she'd been robbed of her gems. She was powerless, as far as Gideon knew. Anaïs stared down the narrow lane. They never should have let the young woman leave. She wasn't ready. And if she'd been drained of her energy because of their confrontation, she'd be easy prey for a Skulk lurking about with murder on his mind.

"We have to go," Anaïs said, calling up to Dorée. "Celeste is here, but she's been weakened. Her gems are gone."

"Gone? Gone how? They're protected with enchantments. A Fée Gardienne's gems don't just disappear."

"Gideon says someone stole them, and now that Skulk is going to make mincemeat out of her if we don't do something. Now!"

"Oh, well, if you insist." Dorée held out her hand and called to Benoit. She whispered something in the mouse's ear before he scurried away down the gangplank and into the painted sea below. Anaïs lost track of him in the underbrush of weeds growing up around the forgotten ship. She knew the mouse had hidden talents, but she wasn't sure sending him in their place was going to do much to help Celeste.

"I'm going after him," Anaïs said, hoping the murderous look in her eye translated across the ship's stern.

"You'll do nothing of the sort." Dorée put one hand on the ship's wheel while holding her staff in the other and squinted at the horizon. "I need you to stay here and navigate for me."

Navigate what?

Before Anaïs could question her elder's sanity, Dorée raised the wooden staff in the air. A billowy white sail unfurled from the main mast without a single frayed edge or tattered hole to be seen. Then she stirred the air with the staff to call up a robust breeze. The ship creaked and tugged free of its mooring in the weeds. Anaïs gripped the railing as an earthquake-size movement threatened to break the hull of the hastily built ship. The vessel rocked back and forth. Beams, barrels, and fake cannons slid across the decking, coming dangerously close to smashing Anaïs against the railing. Then the wind caught the sail, and the ship floated off its supports.

"Dorée? Why are we moving?" Anaïs looked at the ground below. The ship slid forward several feet, then staggered hard to the left as it rounded the corner of a decrepit pyramid made of wood and plaster. The sails took on more wind. The ship lurched forward again, gliding past a house on a teeter-totter before sidling up against the frame of a decrepit castle.

"Eyes ahead, Anaïs! We don't want to topple."

"Starboard, pull starboard," she yelled, remembering right from left from some deep recess of her mind. The ship righted itself just as a woman darted out of the main building at the far end of the lot. Anaïs connected with Gideon and squinted through his vision. "It's her!" She bent forward over the side of the railing to see Celeste running at full speed. And no wonder. She had a pointy-toothed Skulk chasing after her with one hand covering his eyes as if the sunlight burned.

"They're coming this way," Dorée called.

"I can see that. Now what?" Anaïs gripped the railing of the ship and pulled herself forward, hand over hand, until she made it onto the bow. One hundred yards away Celeste frantically rattled the handles of every door she passed before giving up and scrambling for cover in a side alley.

"Ready the cannons," Dorée commanded as she sailed the ship forward. The vessel hovered mere inches above the pavement, floating ahead on a wave of Fée Gardienne magic.

"Naturally," Anaïs muttered to herself. "Time to ready the cannons." She clambered back to the center of the ship, but when she got there, the three prop cannons had been transformed into klieg lights. Benoit sat atop one of them, swishing his tail with excitement, the power cord firm in his teeth. The galleon rocked as though plowing headfirst into deep ocean swells while passing between the outbuildings on the back lot. Benoit jumped to the deck and plugged the lights into the generator he'd enchanted onto the ship.

Anaïs positioned herself behind the first spotlight, braced her high heel against the base, and gripped her hand on something that looked like a handle. She had no idea what Dorée was up to, but she'd be ready when the order came. Gideon landed on the light next to her, steadying his wings as the ship picked up speed. His presence was calming, so she took a deep breath and awaited her orders as her silk shawl fluttered off her shoulders from the breeze.

CHAPTER TWENTY-NINE

The Glare of the Spotlight

Desperate to hide, Celeste shook the handle on every door she passed but found them all locked. Had the Skulk sabotaged the entire lot? Or was everything fake and escape an illusion? Not knowing how long her crystal-powered magic would last, she didn't dare spend an ounce of energy on false doors that might lead to nowhere. She'd zapped the Skulk good and hoped he'd be seeing white spots for at least a few more minutes, but there wasn't much time.

There had to be a million places to hide on the back lot, but everywhere she turned, she felt vulnerable. Exposed. Sitting prey. She shrank down behind a water barrel to catch her breath and check on Sebastian. His breathing appeared regular, but he'd barely opened his eyes. She stroked his fur again, only this time she added a little sun-kissed warmth to her touch to counter the Skulk's influence before tucking him away inside her purse. "Come on, Sebastian, you'll be all right. You have to be. I can't do this without you." She couldn't bear to think what might happen if he didn't wake. When he didn't move, she covered him back up and tried to figure out her next move alone.

Aside from temporarily blinding the Skulk with her inner light, Celeste wasn't sure what else she could do to him. She was within her rights to defend herself, but could she kill him? If she did, would the entire Infortunii come for her with their sunken eyes and gray teeth? But what if he killed her first? Celeste stood in a panic. She had to *do* something now, or this trembling feeling was going to end in tears. If she could just find Anaïs and Dorée.

"Come out, Celeste," the Skulk called. "We haven't finished our conversation."

He'd caught up.

Celeste risked edging up to the corner of the building and peering in the direction of his voice. He was still in his misshapen form, searching across the walkway behind some bushes with his ears flexed. She bit her blue thumbnail, thinking. She couldn't disguise herself. Her glamour didn't work on him, though his seemed to work on her. And she couldn't run or he'd hear her footsteps. What she needed was a distraction.

Up the road, where a crew had been putting a fresh coat of paint on the old dressing room bungalows, Celeste spotted a rickety scaffolding. She held her pendant, and with a lift of her brow, she gave the scaffold a shake until one of the two-by-fours clattered to the ground. The Skulk—she couldn't call him Charlie anymore—scrambled toward the crash with the gleam of victory in his sunken eyes. Celeste didn't know the back lot that well from her tour with Nick, but she remembered the set of a Western they were filming somewhere to her right, so she slipped off as quietly as she could to find better cover while the Skulk crept away in the opposite direction.

Two minutes later Celeste thought she was hallucinating when the tall mast and sail of a ship moved toward her. She squinted hard, recognizing the gliding movement as something only magic could conjure on dry land. And then she saw the figure of a woman standing behind the ship's wheel brandishing a wooden staff and knew beyond a doubt.

"Dorée!" Risking exposure, she made a run for it, breaking away from the Old West saloon she'd been hiding in as a phantom wind filled the sails and the pirate ship picked up speed.

The Skulk sprinted from the corral on the other side of the stage set. Celeste hadn't realized he was so close. All she had to do was make it to the ship and she'd be safe. The Skulk knew it too. He snarled and made a bet he could get to her before she reached the ship. For a heartbeat she was convinced she could outrun him, but then a tiny white mouse with the scent of gardenias on his fur perched on her shoulder mid-sprint. He stood on his hind legs and out of his mouth came Dorée's voice. "The ship isn't here to rescue you, it's here for him."

Celeste had to recalibrate her momentum in a split second after hearing Benoit's message. She'd been sent to America on a mission, and though the true reason why had been kept from her through deceit, she recognized in that moment she must fulfill that expectation. There was no need to run anymore. It was time to stand her ground. Let the Skulk get a little closer. Be the bait.

Celeste stopped running. Still panting from the exertion, she turned around and stared down the Skulk. He lowered his head and ran harder. She planted her feet, trusting the Fées Gardiennes on the ship. Did the Infortunii understand the predicament he was in? Had he seen the ship bank sharply to the left as he bore down on her? Had he seen Anaïs poised behind a row of spotlights, ready to flip the switch? Did he know how bright, how hot, those lights burned?

The possibility he'd made an error flickered in the Skulk's eyes at the last minute. With arms windmilling, he came to a vaudevillian stop, nearly tripping over his own feet as he slid on the pavement. He rebalanced a mere ten feet in front of Celeste. Near enough to lunge at her with his cold magic—freeze her heart, chill her bones, and make frost crunch in her veins. But she'd already pivoted. She called up a lasso hanging by the saloon with the flick of her brow. It sailed over the Skulk's head and locked around his arms. There was nothing enchanted about the rope, but he writhed as if it burned just the same.

"I'll tear you all apart with my bare teeth!" The Skulk spit the threat out as he tried to freeze the rope and shake off the binding. When the rope held, he attempted to backtrack toward a shady cover, until something bit him in the ankle and he had to hop on one foot to keep from toppling over. The Skulk winced, then stomped his foot as a fierce brown stoat scurried out of the way.

"Sebastian!"

The stoat leaped into her arms just as Dorée shouted the command, "Fire!" Anaïs let loose with the lights, concentrating all three beams on the Skulk.

A volley of white-hot spotlights converged on the creature. For a moment he appeared like an escape artist attempting a trick with a rope under the spotlight, writhing and twisting to get free, but then the heat and brightness got under his skin. The Skulk sank to his knees, recoiling from the light as his body shrank under the intensity. He vacillated between his natural form and that of the janitor while he shrank before their eyes.

The Skulk writhed on the ground and pleaded with Celeste in his Charlie guise. "Celeste! Help me! I was always good to you. We're alike, you and me. Have mercy."

His sobs were in such stark contrast to the Skulk who'd boasted moments ago about the beauty and silence of death. Still, it wrenched Celeste's heart to witness such suffering. If they kept it up, he'd surely die. The thought of being responsible for another creature's death made her stomach queasy. It was the same tumbling feeling she'd had when she'd thought Anaïs had cursed a child to death. Decency dictated she rise to the bait of injustice, just as he'd said.

Celeste put her body between the Skulk and the spotlight, hailing Anaïs to get her attention. "Enough!" she shouted. Anaïs checked with Dorée first, then shut the lights off after getting a curt nod of agreement. A cool shadow displaced what had been a white-hot space so bright it threatened to burn the corneas out of Celeste's eyes. Even as a creature of light, she had to blink several times until her eyes adjusted to normal daytime brightness again.

"Is he dead?" Anaïs called from the ship's deck with a slight tremor of excitement in her voice.

Celeste didn't think so, but the Skulk had been dreadfully altered. His body had shrunk to a quarter of its size with truncated arms and legs too small for his rotund middle, and his skin had taken on the mottled gray tone of a sea lion's. His facial features had morphed, too, so that he resembled some new form of amphibian with long ears and sunken eyes. "He's still breathing," she said as Sebastian sniffed at the creature from a foot away. One of the Skulk's stubby legs twitched, and the stoat jumped away before hissing and showing his teeth. Celeste allowed Sebastian his outburst, then called him to her, not knowing the Skulk's true condition. Did he still have his magic? His anger? His twisted mind?

"Well, isn't that curious," Dorée said from the upper deck. With a wave of her staff, the pirate ship settled to the pavement and a wooden ladder was extended over the side. She didn't climb down so much as she floated to the ground. Anaïs followed with equal grace despite her tight silk dress and high-heeled T-strap shoes.

Anaïs recoiled when she got close enough to evaluate the Skulk for herself. "What the hell happened to him?" she asked.

"Language, Anaïs." Dorée held on to her staff and winced slightly as she knelt beside the pitiful creature. "It appears the intensity of the light has affected his body's vitality. They're shape-shifters by nature. Cave dwellers by preference. The darker and damper the better. But this transformation wasn't his choice. The light has altered his form," she said, casting a wary eye on the misshapen Infortunii.

The Skulk blinked several times, then wiggled free of the clothes he'd been wearing. Bald and shapeless, he squatted on the pavement, seemingly as bewildered by what had happened as the Fées Gardiennes were. He'd become an oblong blob resembling an oversize football.

Celeste thought he looked like a fat salamander with long ears instead of a tail and tiny cat's claws at the end of his fingers.

The Skulk spit and hissed at them when they stared, so Dorée set up a perimeter of candlelight with a wave of her staff to keep him contained.

"What is he now?" Celeste asked.

"Oh, he's still very much one of the Infortunii," someone said.

The three Fées Gardiennes spun around. Standing behind them was a dapper man in a gray suit. His skin had a sallow cast, and his eyes were slitted like a reptile's. He tipped his fedora at them in greeting.

"Barnaby, why am I not surprised to see you here." Dorée stood and acknowledged the leader of the Infortunii pleasantly enough, though the knuckles on the hand that gripped her staff flexed white from how tight she held on to her power. "You didn't mention you were making the trip to America. Did you worry we'd fail in our mission?"

The Skulk made no attempt to hide the sly angle in the corner of his smile. "Just being thorough. We have much at stake in the outcome, as you well know. A rogue agent in the mix is bad for our survival. By the way, I commend you on your choice of action for our misguided friend."

"Truly?" Dorée likewise didn't bother to mask her doubt and distrust. "I thought perhaps we'd done him the kind of irreparable harm you might have a problem with."

"Oh, on the contrary." Barnaby folded his arms and examined the blob breathing open-mouthed on the ground. "Liam will not be in much pain. Malleability is part of our constitution. The light was understandably uncomfortable and has temporarily robbed him of his power, but this was likely the best solution you could have hit upon, considering his crimes."

"What do you mean by 'temporarily'?" Dorée refocused her attention on the Skulk, prodding him with the end of her staff. He hissed and recoiled. "Are you saying he's still a threat?"

Barnaby tilted his head in a maybe yes, maybe no sort of way that made Celeste hug Sebastian a little closer. "It's possible, given his diminutive size, that his powers have merely been"—he pursed his lips—"concentrated. It's also possible there's no longer a Liam in there to control the direction of the energy. His magic might simply pool within him. Untapped. Unpredictable." Barnaby slipped past the Fées Gardiennes to get nearer to the shrunken Skulk. "I am curious, though. I've never seen any of our kind take this shape before." He bent forward and rested his hands on his knees, taking a closer look. "It's almost as if his skin has been melted by the heat given off by the lights." Barnaby glanced up at the spotlights still pointed at the ground from the ship. There was little regret, repulsion, or even remorse in his statement, as though he were merely making a factual observation. Someone with a seemingly dispassionate interest. The way one might remark on a circus sideshow performer's oddity before moving on to the next exhibition.

"What about the bond?" Anaïs asked. "Will that still be a problem?"

The Infortunii replied with raised brows to effect ignorance. "The bond?"

"Don't play dumb. You know what I mean. Your rogue Skulk went after a prospective protégé. Her first," she said, nudging her chin toward Celeste.

"Anaïs, is it?" Barnaby flashed a nasty fang at her, perhaps recalling it was she who'd had the ill-fated run-in with the Infortunii in Bruges. "What makes you think Liam has bonded with this young initiate of yours?"

"He murdered a woman and tried to frame the protégé *before* she had a chance to make it onto her star path," Anaïs said, practically flashing a fang of her own.

"If so, there's nothing to be done," Barnaby said with a shrug. "I agree it was inappropriate for him to interfere with an initiate's work, but what's done is done. They will always be attached in one form or another."

"That's where you're wrong." Anaïs gave a quick nod to Dorée. "It still has a mouth. What do you think?"

Dorée faced Celeste. "May I see your hands?"

Celeste knew what Dorée was looking for, and it terrified her. What if there really was something wrong with her?

Dorée examined the blue fingernails. She took a deep breath, considering. Barnaby made a small protest, not understanding what they were up to, but she overrode his concerns. "You've been bonded with the Skulk," she explained. "Because you're still reliant on gemstones for your magic, it's much easier for them to attach themselves to an initiate. Once he found out who you are, he invaded your body with his chill. It means that every protégé you choose will be tainted with misfortune from the start. Not a very auspicious beginning."

"But what can I do?" Celeste wiped her hand against her dress as though that might rid her of the affliction.

"We have to remove it." Dorée held out a hand to Anaïs. "Pass me the elixir."

Barnaby grew more animated. "Elixir? What elixir?"

"What about the second one?" Anaïs asked.

Dorée waved off whatever concerns she had. "Don't worry about that. Just give me the vial."

Anaïs did as she was told and retrieved a small brown bottle from the sash around her dress. She removed the cork and took a whiff. She squinted and turned her face away before handing off the vial.

"You first," Dorée said to Celeste.

"Me?" She took a step backward.

"Yes, you. You need to drink half the bottle before your condition deteriorates any further. The rest is for him." The creature hissed and tried to cross the circle of candlelight without luck. "We must dissolve the bond between you. This will flush out the taint of misfortune he's embedded in your skin." Dorée was in no mood for dithering. "Or would you rather have this Skulk attached to you and your protégés for the rest of your life?"

Celeste took a sniff. "It smells like turpentine. What's in it?"

"A little of this, a little of that," Anaïs said, vaguely. Celeste noticed she kept her fingers crossed at her side. "More importantly, it's the cure for what ails, so drink up. But only half. More than that and I'm not sure what will happen."

An involuntary whimper escaped Celeste's throat as she raised the vial to her lips. She closed her eyes and drank the contents. Her mouth filled with a greasy foam that fizzed against her teeth. She covered her mouth with her hand, afraid she might not be able to keep it down, but then it suddenly smoothed out and sank into her stomach like a sweet cordial. She wouldn't have minded another sip after that, but she handed the half-filled bottle back to Dorée.

"How do you feel?" Anaïs asked.

Celeste hiccuped and covered her mouth. "All right, I think. Kind of warm inside."

Barnaby withdrew his protest as the senior Fée Gardienne approached the blob. The shrunken Skulk retreated until its back got singed by a candle flame. It gnashed its teeth and spit at her. Celeste didn't know how Dorée would get the elixir down its gullet to complete the dissolution until Anaïs reached in and grabbed the Skulk by its ears from behind. She pulled back, fighting against him as he thrashed and hissed and tried to swipe at her with his tiny cat claws. Dorée took firm hold of what little chin the creature had and poured the contents into its mouth. It tried to spew the elixir out, so Celeste stunned the blob with a little flash from her palm again. Temporarily dazed, the Skulk swallowed the fizzy potion while Dorée held its mouth shut. When it was done, Celeste felt the slightest relief in her chest, as though a lung had finally cleared of an infection.

Dorée checked Celeste's fingernails again. "The blue tinge has receded," she said with some relief. "Your eyes are clear, your skin is warm." She turned to Anaïs. "I think Edward was true with the first vial. No need to experiment with the second."

"What will happen to him now?" Celeste asked.

Anaïs stepped out of the ring of flames and wiped her hands off on the Skulk's discarded clothes. "Good question. We can't just leave him to wander the streets."

"Well, Barnaby?" Dorée raised a brow to suggest the responsibility for the Skulk's caretaking was now on his shoulders. "We've done our part as agreed."

Barnaby tapped his chest with splayed fingers. "I cannot take him. It's out of the question. What even is he? A man, a toad, or a fish to toss into the sea?"

Anaïs put a hand on her hip. "You said he was still Infortunii. That makes him yours."

"No, no, no, not like this. He cannot come back with me in this state."

Anaïs smirked and hooked her thumb at Barnaby. "He means he'll be thrown out as leader of the Infortunii if he shows up with one of his own looking like this at the hands of a trio of Gardiennes."

It appeared they were at an impasse. Dorée leaned on her staff, thinking. The deep lines around her eyes tensed as she searched for a solution on the back lot of the movie studio. She rubbed her lip, chewed on a few ideas, and finally nodded. She took a deep breath, the kind that cleanses the body of any further unease over a difficult decision, then faced the others. "Is this Liam sensitive to anything that might restrain his inclination to wander?" she asked the leader of the Infortunii. "Temperature? Moisture? Allergies of any kind? Or perhaps something he's especially fond of. Something he's attracted to might work."

"I don't know what you mean." Barnaby wasn't being coy this time, merely confused. "He is like all Infortunii. He prefers cold, dark places. Out in the sun is no place for our kind," he said, snugging down the front of his fedora. "Liam, like all of us, is drawn to caves with pools of dark water in them. Mud is even better, but this would not be enough to contain him, even with your enchantments. Only strong light could do that, as you so efficiently demonstrated."

"We can't just throw him in some canyon in the desert?" Anaïs asked. "Maybe forget about him until he shrinks up like a salted slug?" She was being facetious, but Celeste thought depositing the Skulk far away, where he couldn't do any harm, was a sensible solution. She was also glad Anaïs hadn't really been out to get revenge against her. She'd hate to see what the woman might have dreamed up for her if she had.

Dorée ignored Anaïs's quip. "We need a place that's dark and damp, somewhere he'll be naturally drawn to, so he'll stay put. But ideally someplace that also gets exposed to the natural sunlight."

"To attract and repel at the same time," Barnaby said, nodding at the logic.

"I might know a place," Celeste said. She'd startled herself by blurting it out, but the location popped into her head so quickly, she knew it had to mean something. "The tar pits," she said.

Dorée was intrigued. "Tar pits?"

"Asphalt bubbles up from the ground there into a small pond. It's not far," Celeste said, recalling the route back to the bungalow. "I passed by it just today. Didn't you smell the petroleum in the air when you first arrived here?"

"Yes! It's the strangest concoction of petrol and oranges," Anaïs said.

"Petrol?" Barnaby perked up. "It is a delicacy for us. If there is such a place nearby, he may have already been relying on it."

That got Dorée's attention. "Is this pit out in the open?"

Celeste nodded. "There are some trees and a building of some kind, but the pond is in full sun."

Anaïs hooked arms with Celeste. "Well, I think this calls for an excursion."

After the pirate ship was returned to the back lot and the Skulk was scooped up into a burlap sack stolen off the Old West set, Dorée fashioned a four-seater Duesenberg with whitewall tires and red leather interior out of one of the generators. The group hopped in together and drove off the lot under the powerful guise of the eldest Fée Gardienne's glamour.

Across town, the pool of asphalt made itself known before they stepped out of the automobile. The acrid fumes stung the noses of the Fées Gardiennes as they approached, but Barnaby couldn't get enough. He stuck his nose in the air as though following the scent of his favorite bakery as he hefted the burlap sack on his shoulder. "I'm beginning to understand what Liam saw in this city," he said. "Such a tantalizing mix of glitter and glop."

Still under cover of their powerful glamour, the women ventured near the edge of the natural pool. Black, stinking tar gurgled beneath the water, oily and shimmering. Dorée gathered up her hem and knelt pondside to stick a finger in the water. A glob of tar stuck to her skin. "This will do," she said. Satisfied, the Gardienne asked for the Skulk.

Barnaby reluctantly agreed it was an ideal spot, if incarceration was their objective. "Liam will be drawn to the murky, oily water," he said, then dared a brief glance at the hot sun overhead. "But this sun will prevent him from venturing out of the pit. After sitting in this sludge, his skin will grow much too sensitive to withstand the bright light for more than a few minutes at a time."

Barnaby dropped the bag on the muddy bank next to the eldest Gardienne. The Skulk rumbled inside the burlap, but at least he'd stopped hissing. Dorée held her staff at the ready while Celeste untied the top of the sack. She pointed the opening toward the edge of the pond, making sure to splash a little of the tarry water just outside the bag. The creature, slightly wobbly from his ordeal, sniffed the air before waddling out on legs that ought to be too small to support his round, blubbery body. His toes touched the water, testing, and then he slithered under the surface as if he'd been born in the dark pool and was returning home.

Celeste felt a lump in her stomach seeing him go. He wasn't Charlie, he never had been, but she still grieved for the man she'd come to know by that name.

"In all my days, I've never lost a member of the Infortunii so prematurely," Barnaby said. "I'll have to call up one of the junior initiates now."

"I am sorry it had to end this way. The turbulence of the times has tested us all." Dorée nodded in sympathy, but she, like the rest of them, was drained from being around the influence of so much embodied misfortune.

Barnaby on the other hand, perhaps being a creature that thrived on calamity, took events in stride. "There are no misunderstandings. You dance in the air and light, we loom in the muck and shadow." He held his palms out, moving them up and down like two sides of a scale in flux. "It was ever thus," he said and tipped his hat at them before taking his leave and walking down the shady side of the boulevard. "Until we meet again."

"How can we be certain the Skulk won't cause any more trouble?" Celeste asked when Barnaby had gone.

Dorée shrugged as she watched the traffic on Wilshire go by mere feet from the dark water. "We don't, but the world has ways of evening out too much misfortune in one place." The Gardienne then turned her attention to Celeste as they returned to the car. "Now, what's this about some missing gems?"

CHAPTER THIRTY

Blame It on the Sangria

Anaïs drove her Bentley up the winding canyon road, taking the curves with care while the sun set in the rearview mirror. She was in no hurry. The ship wasn't due to sail for another four hours, which meant Edward, ever the procrastinator, wouldn't have finished packing yet. Still, there was some urgency, as she did wish to catch that sunset from the deck.

Just as she expected, Edward's car was still in the driveway as she approached. Out of extreme caution, she parked down the hill beneath a sycamore tree, where Gideon had already perched himself on a thick branch. He stared at the house on the hill beady-eyed, shifting his weight from foot to foot.

"I'll give him your regards," Anaïs said to the rook before walking up a set of stone steps behind the house that led to Edward's back door. She spotted him through the glass, his hair still wet from a shower and his face cleanly shaved. He moved from room to room in a rush, collecting his bottles and potions and wrapping them in paper so he could pack them safely into a pair of large trunks. Anaïs knew those trunks. They had multiple small compartments inside to hold the guts of his occult business on a long voyage. They'd hold his guts by the time she was through with him.

Anaïs undid the latch on the door with a flick of her brow and went inside. "Well, what have we here?"

Edward froze for a split second before recovering his cool and plastering that damn gorgeous smile on his face. "Anaïs. What a pleasant surprise." His eyes darted to the apothecary bottles half-wrapped in old newspaper.

"Going somewhere?"

"Oh . . ." He looked around at his obvious effort to pack and run. "No, no, just doing some overdue organizing. The workroom gets to be a jumble after a while. Perhaps now isn't the best time for us to catch up. I'm very busy, as you can see. Maybe tomorrow? I'll pick you up at eight. We'll do dinner and a movie."

Anaïs peeked inside one of the trunks. There was a set of pajamas, a shaving kit, and a pair of slippers tucked in beside a revolver and a map of Buenos Aires. "I have a feeling tomorrow might be too late."

The pair locked eyes. The artifice fell away. Edward dived over the coffee table, reaching for the gun. Anaïs's magic couldn't stop bullets, so she kicked the lid of the truck closed, slamming his hand inside. Edward screamed and fought to lift the lid, but she applied more pressure, pressing her full weight against it. "Oh, no you don't." She clasped her ruby pendant and turned the trunk into a wooden pillory, trapping his head and hands in it so that he was forced to lean forward on his knees. "Let's get one thing straight, Edward. I'm going to make demands, and you're going to oblige my every request. Understood?"

"Why are you doing this? I've done nothing to you. I helped you, remember?" He seemed to forget that he'd botched that part of their last agreement.

Before he could start prattling off more lies, she pulled the nasty vial of stinging nettle out of her purse. "Do you mean this?" She uncorked the bottle and held it under his nose, making him inhale the reeking stuff while it was impossible for him to turn his head away.

"All right, all right!" he said, rattling the pillory again in the hope of getting loose. "I was angry, okay. You just show up here and make demands, thinking I'll do whatever you want because . . . because . . ."

Anaïs sat on the sofa and crossed her legs. "Because why? You're afraid of me?"

Edward twisted his head around to look her in the eye. "Because I was in love with you, and you thought nothing of throwing that away. Then you show up here after I've moved on, thinking you can just ask for this or that. I relocated to another continent to get away from the memory of you."

The words struck true as a dagger. She'd known he was in love, which was why she had left him. The part of her ruled by air couldn't be tied to a permanent perch. "Is that why you told the Skulk about me? About Fées Gardiennes and our one weakness?"

Edward looked away. The tense muscles in his neck didn't so much relax as they simply gave up trying to fight gravity anymore. "How did you know it was me?"

Anaïs extended her leg to lift his head up with her foot. "You were the only one I ever confessed that to."

"You were drunk on sangria that night." There was a hint of a smile in his voice when he said it.

He confessed everything then, admitting to picking up on the Skulk's murky energy while visiting an underground gambling den on the strip not far from West Coast Studios. He'd heard about the creatures from Anaïs's descriptions but never had reason to believe he'd ever encountered one. He claimed the energy around the Skulk swirled like a storm cloud, cold and threatening. "Just the mood I was in."

"Auras always were your thing," Anaïs said.

Curious, Edward had struck up a conversation with this unassuming janitor over several games of five-card draw. "We built a sort of rapport between us, once I mentioned I'd been with a Fée Gardienne. Turned out we had similar goals in life."

"You mean to get even with me."

"No, my love, that desire reared its head only after you arrived." Edward paused, stretching his neck to find a more comfortable position. "He just wanted to burn everything down. He was angry. Felt disrespected by your kind, by his kind. Not a real happy guy, you know? But I was feeling much the same after our breakup, so I told him if ever he needed anything, he should look me up and we'd burn it down together."

"Let me guess. He called on you the same time I did."

"The very next day. He was looking for a powder he could give to Nick West, the studio producer."

"What kind of powder?"

"The addictive sort. He wanted to get him hooked and watch him lose everything. We were discussing terms here when he picked up on your energy still floating around the living room. That's when he suspected you were here."

Anaïs was tempted to loosen the locks on the pillory as a reward for him talking when Gideon flew in through the open back door. The rook perched on the wooden frame of the pillory as a warning to her to keep her head screwed on straight in the company of her charismatic former beau.

Edward rattled the contraption with his wrists. "Send your filthy bird away. Isn't it bad enough I have to go through this humiliation on my knees without him shitting on my back?"

"So did you give him the powder?"

Edward sighed. "No. Once he knew Fées Gardiennes were involved, he was done playing his little games. The stakes had been raised, and he was going to do something to really make a statement."

"Murdering Dolores Diaz." Anaïs considered his tale and thought it plausible. "So, what did the Skulk pay you for your information about me? About what you knew about a Gardienne's powers?"

"Nothing. No, no, we never agreed to terms for the information." Edward shook his head as best he could within the trap.

"Are you sure? There wasn't a payment of, say, a jar of gems?"

The muscles in the occultist's neck tensed tighter than she knew was possible. "Gems? No, no payment of gems. What gems?"

"The ones you think are going to pay for your new life in Buenos Aires." Anaïs leaned forward to look in his eyes with a curse ripe on her tongue if he made one false move. "Where are they?"

He said nothing, so Gideon gave him a peck on the head with his daggerlike beak.

"It's your fault they're gone," he said, still defiant. "If you'd have paid me for my potions, I wouldn't have left the movie theater in anger."

"I did pay you. I left you a gorgeous peridot inside the box of candy. Why the hell do you think I would give you a box of Jujyfruits otherwise?"

"What? Who hands someone a box of candy as payment?" He expressed his disgust by shooing her away with his hands. "Besides, I lost those when your girl nearly ran me over in the rain."

"Who? Celeste?"

"Her aura isn't as strong as yours, but I knew what she was when I saw her through the windshield. I also knew she came with jewels, just like you all do. You really can't hold your sangria, my love."

Anaïs began to worry about what other secrets she might have spilled that night. Edward let his head hang down as though he couldn't believe how low he'd sunk. "I went back to the gaming den that night. The Skulk showed up a few hours later. I dangled the information in front of him should he choose to use it, and he rewarded me by telling me which fancy hotel your colleague was staying at. *And* that she wouldn't be in the rest of the night because she was at the studio doing her do-gooder work, should I like to seize the opportunity."

"So you stole her gems. The one thing she had to rely on for her magic." Anaïs didn't know why, but it shocked her. This man she'd nearly fallen head over heels in love with at one time was nothing more than a common thief. Though she supposed she'd always known he was one to skirt the common cloth of morality most people clung to. "Where are they?"

Before Gideon could peck him on the head again, Edward nudged his chin toward the second trunk. Anaïs rummaged through his packed belongings until she lifted his size 10 dress shoe. A small velvet sack spilled out that rattled with the sound of stolen jewels. The discovery drove the final inch of the blade of betrayal through her heart. Because there was nothing left to do but leave. "I'm sorry, darling. You must understand. Blame it on the sangria if you like, but I can't have my secrets floating freely on a man's lips ever again."

Anaïs scooped up Celeste's gemstones, gave Gideon an encouraging pet under his sharp beak, then cast a veil of silence over the house as she stepped outside to leave the two alone. The sunset from the back deck was just as glorious as she imagined it would be, steeped in shades of fiery reds and deep oranges that spoke to her soul. A view she could get used to now that the house would be vacant again.

CHAPTER THIRTY-ONE

A Foot in the Door

Rose had been released from jail the day before, but her mind might as well have still been trapped behind bars. The young woman sat in front of her house aimlessly rocking back and forth on the porch swing while staring at the ground. Celeste knew what she must be thinking: Her career was over. The police hadn't caught the real killer, and never would, so even though she'd been cleared of the charges, doubt would always follow her around. She couldn't show her face at the studio again. And after the scandal of a murder accusation, she'd be lucky to find another job, let alone one in the field she loved. Just when she'd had her first real break, everything fell apart. Of course, she had to also be devastated by the death of Dolores Diaz. Everyone involved was. She'd been a beacon for the people forced to dance outside the spotlight most of their careers. But life could still be full of surprises, even in the aftermath of a tragic death. Celeste was counting on it.

Celeste sat in the driver's seat of the restored Pierce-Arrow convertible as she watched Rose's house. Anaïs sat beside her reading a newspaper article about a man found stabbed to death inside his Hollywood Hills home, while Dorée lounged in the rumble seat with her arms outstretched and her chin pointing up at the sky as she absorbed the brilliant rays of sunshine. The old woman hadn't quite fully recovered from the freezing conditions in the Stage Two warehouse, but the California sun made the perfect balm for what ailed. All three Fées Gardiennes were cloaked in their strongest glamour so as not to be seen by Rose or any curious neighbors. Their companions were hidden, too, as Sebastian and Benoit curled up together on the dashboard munching on sunflower seeds, and Gideon preened his feathers on the roof overlooking Rose's front yard.

"How long do you expect us to wait?" Dorée didn't bother to open her eyes.

Celeste tried not to take the Fée Gardienne's impatience personally. She understood the toll the overseas trip had taken on Dorée, not to mention the encounter with the Skulk and the near-deadly freezing conditions she'd had to suffer through. "Just a little longer," Celeste answered, though she really couldn't say. She'd brought the two Fées Gardiennes to Rose's house on a hunch, believing that something was about to manifest after a noticeable change in the direction of the wind had brought the scent of orange blossoms instead of the reek of oil wells. When she'd begun to doubt that the sign was as strong as she'd hoped, Anaïs had encouraged her to trust the feeling, and so they sat outside the woman's house waiting for something of significance to happen that they couldn't quite describe.

"I say we wait as long as it takes," Anaïs said, catching the old woman peeking at her with one eye through the rearview mirror. "It's what we do, after all."

Celeste clutched her pendant, not willing to accept that maybe her protégé's chances weren't as promising as she'd first hoped. She closed her eyes and took a reading on Rose, sensing the young woman's sadness and disappointment, just as she expected. At first, she thought Rose's emotions were volatile enough to override all her hopes and desires, like storm clouds occluding the bright future she could have if she didn't give up. She worried the Skulk's influence had left a permanent mark on

Rose's future. After all, did she really know for certain that the taint of misfortune had left her blood? But then something else emerged in the woman's aura. The ambition and determination that had first attracted Celeste to Rose's aspirations bubbled up through the muck of self-pity. The young woman still recognized her worth, and she wasn't willing to let anything stop her, despite her current setbacks. She just didn't know how to move forward alone.

Celeste opened her eyes. "Maybe I should go speak to her. See if I can reassure her and let her know it will be all right."

"And what will you say, Celeste?" Dorée asked. "Because you don't exist in this person's world anymore. You've erased the memory of the woman she once knew you as. And if you approach as you are, any help you offer her must be given. Unfulfilled promises are not a currency Gardiennes trade in. If you tell her everything will be all right, then you must be prepared to make it so. Are you able to do that?"

"Those are the rules," Anaïs said with a sympathizing shrug.

Celeste had her hand on the door, deciding if she should get out, when a car approached from the opposite direction. The driver slowed before stopping in front of Rose's house. Celeste leaned forward over the steering wheel to get a better look. "Wait, I know that man," she said, recognizing the driver. "What's he doing here?"

Dorée peered across the street. "Anyone of significance? One of these Hollywood princes, perhaps?"

"I don't know his name. He was at the party we went to two nights ago. The night before Dolores Diaz was murdered. The two of them were talking about Rose when we went over to say hello."

"Ah, so we do have a connection." Dorée reached her hand out to Benoit and had him take his place inside her hair. "Perhaps your hunch was right, and things are moving in the right direction for an advantageous love match after all."

"Not exactly." Celeste avoided going into detail to correct the eldest Gardienne about the future she'd charted for Rose. She caught the approving smirk on Anaïs's face as she leaned forward to get a better look at the man. He was dressed in a smart gray suit with a crisp white shirt and striking art deco–design tie in black and turquoise. The man had dressed to impress, but not in the roguish manner his appearance at the party had suggested. This was a serious man who'd come to discuss serious business. Celeste recalled how uncharacteristically rude Dolores had been that night, speaking to the man about Rose in such derogatory terms. There'd been a moment when she had thought she might have to blister the actress's tongue to get her to shut up. Later it had been confirmed how atypical her behavior had been, according to those who knew her best. A familiar chill brushed Celeste's skin, thinking of how insidious the Skulk's treachery had become, all to prevent one young woman's dreams from manifesting.

Anaïs lifted her ruby pendant and tugged on her ear. The voices across the street were amplified so the women could eavesdrop on the conversation.

"What are *you* doing here?" Rose asked without smiling at her visitor.

"Hello, Rose," the man said. "I'd like to speak with you a moment, if that's all right."

Rose stopped pushing the swing. "What about?"

The man moved closer and leaned against the porch railing. "Well, first I wanted to assure you how sorry Dolores was after she said those terrible things at the party. She didn't know what had come over her. She was mortified, truly. She absolutely adored that dress you made. Before you arrived, she was beaming. Dancing around and showing it off to anyone who would listen. I've vowed to remember her the way I saw her that night in that mood."

"She'd always been very kind to me at work," Rose said before looking away.

"That's who she was." The man stuck his hand out. "We didn't get a chance to be properly introduced," he said. "I'm Adrian, the new head costume designer at MGM."

"I know who you are, but why are you *here?*" Rose looked around at her humble surroundings, as though wondering what madness had brought this man to her door.

"Honestly, I was quite taken with that dress you made for Dolores at the party. It showed a real mastery of design. Cutting-edge stuff. Any chance you have a portfolio I could look at?"

The question took Rose by surprise, but she nodded and went inside the house. When she returned, she handed him her scrapbook of drawings, the same one Celeste had found in her back bedroom. Adrian turned the pages, slowly studying each of the drawings, offering neither praise nor disapproval. He closed the book at last and returned it to Rose, slightly puckering his lips like a man assessing the value of a painting or vase. "Any formal training?"

"I went to art school for a year, and I've been a seamstress at West Coast Studios for a year, but other than that, no." Rose dipped her head as though expecting criticism.

"Well, I'm even more impressed," Adrian said. "What would you say to coming to work at MGM with me as my assistant. I'll be starting over there soon. I think you've got the kind of innovative talent I'm looking for to fill out my team."

Rose looked up at the man with her mouth agape. "Me? Are you sure?" She hugged the scrapbook in one arm, tracing a finger nervously around the edge. "But you must know they accused me of Dolores's murder."

"I know they released you without pressing charges." Adrian leaned in, smiling conspiratorially. "Besides, a hint of scandal will make for the most divine dinner conversation among the celebrities you'll design for. Rose, you are going to meet some of the biggest stars working in the industry. You'll get to dress them and then share in the credit for making them shine on-screen. Big changes are coming to the industry, you know. Sound is inevitable. Talkies are going to change the way they tell stories. They'll get bigger and brighter than anyone ever imagined. Don't you want to be a part of something like that?"

Rose pressed her palm against her cheek as though she couldn't believe what she was hearing. Celeste could hardly believe it either. She closed her eyes and willed the young woman to put away her doubt and accept the offer. When she exhaled and opened her eyes again, Rose was shaking the man's hand, giddy with excitement.

"So, let's meet at my studio Monday morning at eight o'clock sharp."

"I'll be there," Rose said.

It was only a small offer, a job as an assistant designer, but Celeste knew the door had been kicked open and Rose's foot had been firmly planted on the other side of the threshold, and without a hint of a marriage proposal in the offing.

CHAPTER THIRTY-TWO

Land of Enchantment

Celeste nearly collapsed with relief. Sebastian, too, chittered away, jumping up and down on the dashboard until Benoit poked his head out of Dorée's hair to complain.

"But is the young woman's path secured?" Anaïs asked over her shoulder.

Celeste wondered too, because she hadn't felt anything change internally. Nothing to indicate she'd graduated from an initiate to a full-fledged Fée Gardienne. But maybe the change came on more gradually. For all her training, there was still so much she didn't know.

Dorée took a deep breath and gazed at the clear blue sky. "As you know, the universe needs time to reflect on events. In the meantime, could you take me to the place shown in the postcard? I wish to see that enchanting view for myself while we wait to learn about the young woman's star path."

So, it wasn't instantaneous.

Celeste checked with Anaïs on the sly to make sure it was a good idea to go for a drive, then put the car in gear. The journey was slow and twisty as the road snaked through the hillside, but the women enjoyed the ride as they climbed to the spot where the word "Hollywoodland" was spelled out in huge white letters. They'd never seen Dorée behave so carefree, as if she were a girl again, laughing and admiring the smallest hints of beauty along the roadside. She even sang a tune about blue skies smiling at her that made Celeste and Anaïs giggle in the front seat.

At the top, the three Fées Gardiennes got out of the car to admire the view. The entire valley was laid out before them. The sky was clear blue, the sun was warm, and little yellow wildflowers bobbed their heads in a slight breeze at their feet. Below, they could see the road they'd climbed up on, and to the west the broad boulevards where movie studios popped up like dandelions through the cracks.

Celeste hated to break the glorious spell they were under, but she was desperate to know if she'd successfully ushered Rose onto her star path. "Is there a sign we should look for?" she asked.

The women knew what she meant. Anaïs lost her smile and suddenly studied the tops of her shoes, but Dorée kept her face tipped to the sun as she leaned on her staff. "Yes, of course," she said, as though loath to give up the splendor of the moment. "We should see the business settled."

The eldest Gardienne used her carved staff to swirl the air in front of them. The same sort of whirlwind that had encircled them inside Stage Two returned, lit up with a moving collage of images. Celeste covered her mouth with her hand when she saw Rose walking in a circle around a blond woman in a stunning white gown. She was studying the flow, cut, and fit of the gown, making suggestions that might enhance the glamour of the character the woman was playing, and the actress eagerly agreed. Rose was in charge, full of confidence, an assistant by her side. A moment later the Gardiennes saw Rose slightly older as she walked onto a stage in front of hundreds of people. She was handed a golden statue of a male figure, and then another. Accolades showered over Celeste's protégé as she aged, though later the shadow of the Infortunii could be seen awaiting its turn in the wings. And then the screen came down again with the swirl of Dorée's staff. "Best not to see too much."

A marvelous, almost hypnotic pride overtook Celeste knowing she'd changed someone's life. She'd helped them fulfill their deepest desire despite all the obstacles. Yet she felt little changed otherwise. She'd been told to expect an effervescence when she made the leap from initiate to graduate. Her body would fill with the power of the gemstones, all spangled light and buzzy energy swirling inside. But she didn't. There was no fizz, no flicker, and no sparkly aura awakening within. Something was wrong.

"So, she becomes a success in a few years. That means she's on her way, right?" Celeste checked with her fellow Gardiennes for confirmation when the doubt overtook her.

"Yes." Anaïs nodded and wiped her cheek, avoiding Celeste's eyes.

"Dorée?"

"Rest assured you've done it, my dear. Your protégé has found her true pathway."

Celeste thanked her for the congratulations, but it was clear something still wasn't right. Nothing had changed. "I'm pleased to see Rose on her way, but I thought . . ." She stifled the rest of her question, afraid she might sound ungrateful or too preoccupied with herself.

"You expected to feel the surge of transformation and haven't." The eldest Gardienne leaned on her staff and tipped her cheeks to the sun. "But what have you always been told since coming into our fold?" Dorée lowered her head and stared at Celeste with the brilliant blue sparkle that emanated from her eyes. "There can only be thirteen Fées Gardiennes."

Celeste was confused by the reply. No one had ever warned her she'd have to wait a little longer, once her first protégé was set on their way. She'd always been told that was the moment she would feel the transition. Disappointment sank inside Celeste like a hunk of lead anchored to her heart. To negotiate all those troubled waters to clear the way, not just for Rose but for herself too, only to have the rug pulled out from under her at the last minute felt unfair. She opened her mouth to protest, but a harsh stare and shake of the head from Anaïs made her reconsider. Of course she understood. She was still the youngest of the Gardiennes. It wasn't her time yet, and when it was, she'd be ready.

"The sisterhood endures because there have always been thirteen Fées Gardiennes, and always will be," Dorée reiterated. She called to Benoit, who climbed out of her hair and sat on her shoulder. "Those are the rules we all must abide by. Including myself. With that said . . . Anaïs, if you please." Dorée handed off her staff, which Anaïs accepted with a reverent bow of her head that set off alarm bells in Celeste.

"Wait, what's happening?"

Dorée took Celeste's hands in hers. "It has been the greatest honor of my life to serve as a Fée Gardienne, and I wish the same for you," she said. "You'll influence the paths of some of the greatest talents in the world. You'll meet dancers and painters. Scientists and inventors. You'll raise up remarkable minds that will benefit humankind with their ingenious thinking, and you'll discover others ready to fill the world with beauty when ugliness would smother hope. I've done all that and more in my long life. I'm so glad I got to see it all."

The old woman let go and took a step back. Dorée gave her mouse companion a small kiss on the head and said, "It's time to go, Benoit." She clutched her pendant and closed her eyes as a flash of golden light spread out in a halo around the pair. "Good luck and good tidings," she said as their bodies shimmered and faded before fragmenting and transforming into a million sparkling gold spangles. The specks of light hovered, shimmering in the air briefly before drifting out over the Hollywoodland sign and beyond into the valley below.

Celeste nearly hyperventilated. She didn't understand. She'd never experienced what had just happened. She'd never been warned Dorée would dissolve before her eyes. "What happened? Where did she go?" But her mind knew the answer even before she got the words out.

There can only be thirteen Fées Gardiennes.

Celeste lunged toward where Dorée's energy had gone over the hillside and nearly fell herself, until some invisible energy pulled her back. She stood in the power of that force as the pendant around her neck grew heavy and warm against her breastbone. She lifted it away by the chain, not understanding, but Anaïs told her to leave it alone.

"The energy is still finding you," Anaïs said. "Infusing itself into your body. Just let it be."

As she said it, Celeste felt a strange vigor invade her blood as though her veins overflowed with champagne. Bubbles of effervescence tickled the back of her neck, the insides of her ears, and the top of her head. Her eyes flooded with light, and everything appeared brighter in her vision. Colors and shapes were more defined. Auras radiated off living things. Then smells came to her in visible ribbons of scent that wafted under her nose. Her skin prickled with heightened sensation as the air brushed against the hairs on her arms. She stared at her hands, mesmerized by the change in her body.

Anaïs looked her over. "There, I think it's settled."

"But is Dorée really gone?"

"It was her time."

"Why didn't anyone tell me? Had I known—"

"And how do you prepare someone for this experience? How do you tell a starry-eyed young woman that for her to rise, another whom she admires must fall?"

"I could have waited."

Anaïs shook her head. "That's why they don't tell us when we're initiates, because our job then is to keep striving," she said, still drying her eyes. "And the sisters make it seem like the math will work out naturally, but, of course, it doesn't. Not when I got my powers, and not when Dorée got hers. It's just our way, and there's nothing to feel bad about."

Celeste stared out over the valley, where the shimmering gold dust continued to disperse. "What will happen to her energy?"

"It will settle and absorb into the land, though I'm told it will continue to influence everything in the vicinity," Anaïs said, cradling the staff in her arms like a babe. "Where a Gardienne ends her days will always be an auspicious location. Dorée knew when we embarked on the journey here that this would likely be her final resting place. I think she also knew her continued influence would be needed to act as a counterbalance to the energy of that Skulk we dropped in the cesspool. That was her final sacrifice. It's why she was determined to travel all the way here from five thousand miles away."

Celeste glanced at the staff. "And is that yours now?"

"This? No. It goes to the eldest."

Celeste thought of Gertrude, the eldest now, in her salon surrounded by all her artists and writers. Then she thought of herself years from now, having influenced the trajectories of dozens of talented and creative people who just needed a nudge in the right direction to make their light known to the world. She smiled at the continuity of something so magical enduring in the bodies of the Fées Gardiennes for centuries. To think she was a part of that tradition made the effervescence already stirring in her blood fizz even more.

Celeste swept her arm out, and a scattering of golden light trailed in its wake.

"Ah, you're already getting the hang of it," Anaïs said. "The golden light is only one expression of the energy. For when you really need to draw up your power."

Celeste was amazed. She'd thought she'd understood the full spectrum of her magic after charging with the gemstones, but that was like crumbs from the table compared to what her body feasted on now.

While Anaïs cradled the staff in her arms, her rook settled on her shoulder. In his mouth was a black velvet bag. "I nearly forgot," she said, taking the bag from Gideon's beak and handing it to Celeste. "Your gemstones."

"Where did you find them?" Celeste opened the bag in disbelief. "I thought they were gone forever."

"That would have been a problem," Anaïs said. "Those work like currency for you now. To make your way in the world. Use them wisely."

Celeste closed the bag and tightened the string. "I will." Sebastian climbed into her arms, took the velvet bag in his teeth, and chittered as though daring anyone to get near them again.

Behind them, a car rumbled up the road and stopped. A group of day-trippers jumped out to admire the view.

The two Fées Gardiennes exchanged a glance, knowing it was time to go. Anaïs quickly transformed the staff into a normal-looking walking stick and rested it in the back seat of the Pierce-Arrow, where their mentor had sat only recently enjoying her last rays of sunlight. "I can't believe she's gone," Celeste said, full of wistful reflection.

Anaïs shaded her eyes and looked over the valley. "Oh, I don't know if any of us are truly gone, do you?"

Celeste supposed Anaïs was right. Their unique sensitivity to the energy of mothers who had passed but were still watching over their children was proof enough of that.

With a final glance over her shoulder, Celeste couldn't help but wonder what effect all that glittering energy of Dorée's floating over the valley would have on a town already steeped in its own movie magic. Would she watch over the burgeoning city? If so, there was pure magic waiting on the horizon. An influence as vibrant as Dorée's might just usher in a whole new Golden Age.

Acknowledgments

As always, there are several people to thank for *The Golden Age of Magic* making its way through the publishing process. And by "process," I mean the diligent effort made at each stage by people with only one goal in mind: to create a book worthy of its readers. Thanks, of course, go to my agent, Marlene Stringer, for allowing me to keep writing my brand of historical fantasy stories. Thanks also go to my former acquisitions editor, Adrienne Procaccini, who brought this one on board knowing only a hint of what was to come. So much gratitude also goes to my new editor, Elizabeth Agyemang, who picked up the project in its infancy and guided it through production with nothing but optimism. To my longtime developmental editor, a brilliant writer in his own right, Clarence Haynes: thank you for your dedication to getting the story right. And to the ever-patient copyeditors Jon and Kellie, whom I've worked with so many times, though I keep making the same mistakes for them to fix: much thanks and appreciation for what you do so that my words don't go out in public dressed like *that*.

Thanks also to the entire team at 47North. This is our eighth book together, and I've been fortunate to work with many of the same people in that time. Thank you all!

About the Author

Photo © 2018 Bob Carmichael

Luanne G. Smith is the Amazon Charts and *Washington Post* bestselling author of *The Vine Witch*, *The Glamourist*, and *The Conjurer* in the Vine Witch series; *The Raven Spell* and *The Raven Song* in the Conspiracy of Magic series; and *The Witch's Lens* and *The Wolf's Eye* in the Order of the Seven Stars series. Luanne lives in Colorado at the base of the beautiful Rocky Mountains, where she enjoys hiking, gardening, and a glass of wine at the end of the day. For more information, visit www.luannegsmith.com.